Diary of a Confessions Queen

KATHY CARMICHAEL

Medallion Press, Inc.
Printed in USA

Diary of a Confessions Queen

KATHY CARMICHAEL

DEDICATION

This book is lovingly dedicated to my other mother, Pauline Golden.

Published 2010 by Medallion Press, Inc.

The MEDALLION PRESS LOGO
is a registered trademark of Medallion Press, Inc.

Copyright © 2010 by Kathy Carmichael
Cover design by Arturo Delgado

APR 1 6 2010

Typeset in Adobe Garamond Pro
Printed in the United States of America

ISBN: 978-160542095-0

10 9 8 7 6 5 4 3 2 1
First Edition

ACKNOWLEDGMENTS

Many thanks to the Dan Thompson family for putting me up and putting up with me during my research trip to Kansas.

Writing a book set in a real location presents a number of challenges to an author who doesn't want to get details wrong. However, if I did, the mistakes were my own.

A number of people from Independence, Kansas, were particularly helpful. My thanks and gratitude go out to Tammy Freeman of the Independence Police Department; Dick Wilkens, an Independence native; Julie Julians and the helpful staff of the *Independence Daily Reporter*; Bradley Blake and the research staff of the Independence Public Library; and Gwen Wilburn, president of the Independence Chamber of Commerce.

I'm greatly indebted to two talented authors who dropped everything to come to my assistance, Alfie Thompson and Tara Randel. And here's a shout-out to author Kimberly Llewellyn.

Writing books can be extremely lonely and one of the things that keeps me at the keyboard is the response I receive from readers. Thank you all!

CHAPTER ONE

My Husband Took out the Garbage and Never Came Back

Karma is as karma does. It's what Nana, my grandmother who raised me, always said. Her intentions were kindly. They always were. She strove to find ways to help me feel good about myself, so my basic inner confusion isn't her fault.

I should have kept karma in mind that morning.

Everything was going well. Too well.

As I stepped out my front door and headed for my mailbox on the street, dew twinkled in the April morning sunlight like faux diamonds on the Neelah queen's tiara. I looked up the curving road and a shocking silence reverberated. All was still on my small street, and my elderly neighbor Mrs. Mitchell's lace curtains didn't twitch as they usually did when she's home, watching for something to talk about.

I earned my living by writing short stories for *True Lies,* a confessions magazine. Sue Ann, my best friend, insists I have enough Catholic guilt I'll confess to almost anything, and I suspect she's right. My *True Lies* editor was about to go on maternity leave and my source of income would at least temporarily dry up. Imagine my excitement when I checked my mailbox to learn she'd bought eight confessions from me in advance. What a relief.

I desperately needed the money.

My house was about to go into foreclosure. The house Dan bought for me—for us—when we got married. I had sixty days to pay, or I would risk hell and brimstone in the hereafter. I simply could not lose our home. It had been seven years since Dan simply disappeared and I had no other choice than to put the wheels in motion to have him declared *permanently out of print*. That morning Sue Ann's attorney husband, Ron, assured me I would have the insurance proceeds in time to save my home.

Now most people probably aren't as worried about facing the hereafter as I am, but they don't share my past. My parents were devout Catholics. Two days before my confirmation, when I was thirteen and it was the main focus of my life, my parents were involved in a fatal auto accident. I was distraught. Not only had I lost my folks, but I never was confirmed.

Instead I went to live with Nana, who didn't believe in such nonsense. Instead, she was a spiritualist and believed in a totally different set of nonsense. Or not.

As a result, I'm basically totally confused about the hereafter and have one leg firmly planted in each realm. The good news that day was I no longer had to worry about burning in hell for losing Dan's house. The bad news was that neither my parents nor Nana had visited from the Eternal Divide to let me know one way or the other. I expected better from Nana.

Since the people I loved had a way of going to their spiritual reward or just plain disappearing, like Dan, I recently decided it had something to do with the Law of Attraction. By concentrating on my losses, I attracted more loss. It had taken me awhile, but I came up with a new affirmation: *I attract people into my life who stay.*

As I picked my barefooted way back up the graveled drive toward my front door, I glanced at the redbud tree I planted when Dan and I moved in. Its bare limbs were a tangled puzzle and I willed it to hurry up and bloom.

The next good thing to happen that morning was that when I went to get dressed, I found a twenty-dollar bill stuffed into my ill-fitting Wonderbra. I vaguely remembered wondering where the money had gone to a year ago, so now I knew. Another new affirmation: *I attract money into my life to stay.*

Feeling as if I was on a roll, I tried on my too-tight jeans and they fit perfectly. I could even bend and sit without causing my fallopian tubes to screech in protest.

There was edible food in my refrigerator.

And to top it off, I wasn't out of toilet paper after all.

Incredible, exceptionally good karma.

So when I saw the corner of a crisp, white envelope peeking out from a stack of books on the coffee table, I pulled it out. There was my name, Amanda Crosby, written in block print. It bore no address or postmark, so it hadn't come in the mail.

When I turned in my story "Diary of a Teenage Psychic"—which was retitled by my editor (I don't know what it is about my titles, but she changes all of them) to "I Can Read My Best Friend's Mind, and She's Messing Around with My Boyfriend"—I honestly believed I was now somewhat clairvoyant. Or at least warning bells and whistles would go off before something dire was about to happen.

Boy, was I wrong.

As I opened the envelope, I can't tell you my hair stood on end or chills chased down my spine. What I can state without any hesitation is that I was merely curious.

Who expects to receive a blackmail note?

But that's what it was.

I collapsed onto my sofa.

The note said:

Insurance fraud is a felony criminal offense. Before contemplating cashing in your

missing husband's life insurance policy, you might try to discover where he is

living or, at the very least, ask his mother. Should you wish the fact he's still alive

to remain confidential, place $2,000 in unmarked bills in the waste bin on the

corner of Main and Knox on Friday at 6:00 a.m. **Or else**.

Or else *what*? Unanswered questions pelted me like a hailstorm. What kind of insane person would write a blackmail note like this? Who would want to blackmail *me*? *Why* would someone blackmail me?

And most of all, was there a chance Dan was alive? And if he were, why would I want to keep it confidential?

Were the Law of Attraction and my new affirmation working?

I scanned the note again.

Obviously, I'd be thrilled to welcome my husband back into my life. I hadn't wanted to start the legal proceedings, because of the off chance Dan might return someday. I knew it wasn't likely after this long, but I missed him and dreamed of the day he would come home. Now it felt as if the legal proceedings had done the trick that years of praying and tears hadn't. Was Dan alive?

The blackmail note didn't make sense. The logic of blackmailing me at all seemed senseless, and with such a small amount, it was peculiar. Plus, why put the money into the trash? One segment of my brain analyzed the physical attributes of the note—it was a computer printout similar to those of most city, school, or library-owned printers as well as my own, and there were no identifying marks—while the emotional part of my brain short-circuited.

I suppose I need to digress. Technically I was still married in the sense that I hadn't been divorced or that my husband hadn't officially corked off.

It wasn't as if I hadn't waited long enough or grieved enough.

It wasn't as though I'd be unhappy if Dan turned up alive, either.

I saw an image in my mind—in black and white like an old movie. It was my favorite fantasy in the early months when Dan first disappeared. I was in my kitchen, cooking something. Okay, okay—I don't know how to cook, but it's my fantasy, and I reserve the right to fantasize I'm the next Rachael Ray. So there I am, pans steaming, vegetables bubbling, and I'm chopping something green, and I'm not even afraid of my knife. Hmm. Maybe instead, I'm *ladling* something, when the sound of the front door being thrown open startles me. The next thing I know, I see Dan, tanned, brimming with health, stride into my kitchen. I drop my ladle, in thrilled shock. Then Dan swoops me into his arms and, in a Fred-Astaire-like-dip, leans me over. His lips press against mine.

Nope. The fantasy no longer worked for me. All I could think was *Where the hell has he been for seven years and why does he look so tan and fit?*

Nothing less than his being kidnapped by those sex slavers his mother was always ranting about would satisfy me. Unless they allowed him to use a tanning bed?

Or maybe he'd been recruited by the CIA and they needed him to invent some top secret thing and it's now invented. He's finally allowed to come home and return to me, his devoted wife.

Nah. The CIA would have let him bring me along—or at least he should have found some sly way of letting me know he hadn't kicked the bucket.

No matter how many scenarios I played in my head, none truly satisfied me, because I'd long since concluded that if Dan were alive, he would have found some way of clueing me in. The only other option was he would never be coming home again, and the very idea made me more than sad, worse than devastated, lower than the bottom.

It also left me truly pissed off at the jerk who willingly reopened this emotional can of worms for me. Who could have done this to me? I wanted to lash out at whoever it was.

And there was the problem with losing Dan's and my home. If I wanted to save it, maybe I should pay the blackmail? Putting off having Dan declared legally *non compus life-os* would mean my house would definitely go into foreclosure. But what if he came back and I'd done that to him? Would he be able to forgive me? Would he understand I'd done it to save our home? Would I be able to forgive myself?

Before I had a chance to make sense of it all, my friend Sue Ann chose that moment to come barging into my house.

"You didn't knock," I said with a sort of surly tone.

She ignored my statement, of course, as she always does, because she doesn't think knocking is necessary. Instead she stopped in her tracks and asked, "What's wrong, Amy?"

I hadn't realized I'd given myself away other than a slight trembling of my hand fisting the blackmail note. Then I realized tears silently streaked down my face.

It was amazing how a little detail like that could slip past me.

This was *not* how my life was supposed to pan out. I wasn't quite sure yet how it was supposed to go, but this wasn't it. "My louse of a husband has apparently been alive all this time."

"What?" screamed Sue Ann, making a dive for the letter. Snatching it from my shaking hand wasn't a problem for her and she quickly scanned it. "Do you think it's likely?"

"I hadn't really considered that. I'm still reacting to the very notion Dan's alive and chose to skedaddle out of town." Was it really possible he'd done this to me? My breath left me and, with a *whoosh,* I deflated back onto the sofa. "I told you I didn't want to start the legal proceedings to have him declared officially sleeping with the fishes."

"This letter doesn't change anything."

"You're wrong. It changes everything."

"Let's not jump to any conclusions just yet. Scooch over," said Sue Ann, parking herself beside me. "That's the weirdest blackmail note I've ever heard of. I thought they usually threaten someone missing, not threaten to prove someone's alive."

I wiped my tears away with the back of my hand. "It is strange."

"We'll get to the bottom of this," she said reassuringly. "I just know it."

The two of us are not much alike. Sue Ann's blond hair is cut in one of those pixielike bobs and her blue eyes flash with life. She's an extrovert, sure of herself and her place in the world, certain everyone will like her, and she likes them all back. She jumps into life with her limbs spread akimbo and with all the effervescence of sparkling champagne.

Me? I'm not so much like that. I have long, dark brown hair, boring grey eyes, and the only flashy thing about me is the thumb drive on my computer. I'm more the hide-in-my-office-and-hopefully-no one-will-want-to-talk-to-me sort. With very good reason, my favorite animal is the turtle.

Sue Ann glanced over the note again. "The way I see it is, either Dan's alive or he's not."

Since she'd stated the obvious, I ignored her comment. "So why blackmail me? It's not as though I'm rich or anything. Between the confessions and the monthly check I get from Dan's inventions, my ends are far from meeting." When he'd first turned up missing, the money from his inventions had been sufficient. But it had been years since any new devices had been invented, and accordingly my monthly income flatlined.

One look at my house and anyone could see it desperately needed repairs—things Dan would have taken care of if he weren't MIA. Not only did the house need updating; it needed repaired gutters, a new roof to stop the leaks, and the shutters tacked back into place. Surely any blackmailer could see that if I had a spare two thousand lying around, I would have paid for a fresh coat of paint. A pale canary yellow might be nice.

"Why only two thousand dollars? Why not twenty thousand or two hundred thousand?" asked Sue Ann.

"If it's over twenty dollars, it might as well be two million, considering my budget."

"So maybe the point isn't blackmail." Sue Ann yanked her bangs, which were always about an inch too long, over her forehead. "Maybe someone's trying to let you know, in a sneaky way, that Dan's still around."

I sighed, sending my sunshiny paint fantasies skittering away. "That doesn't make sense. Why not just write an anonymous letter saying, 'Dan's alive and well and living the good life in Tahiti'?"

The more I thought about why the note had been sent, the more it worried me. I'd been caught up in thinking Dan was alive rather than considering the motive of the person who delivered the note.

Sue Ann leaned over to pick up the envelope. "This doesn't have a postmark. Did someone slide it under the door or what?"

My forehead furrowed, but I quickly smoothed it out. I had enough wrinkles already, even though I hadn't yet crossed into thirty-something territory. "That's another weird thing. It was here, stuffed between a couple of books on my coffee table."

"How'd it get there?"

"I have no clue."

"When did you find it?"

"This morning."

"Was it there last night?"

I slowly shook my head. I couldn't recall seeing it there, but I didn't remember actually looking in any more than the usual cursory way. It could have been there since the last time Sue Ann cleaned the room out of desperation because I'm such a hit-and-miss housekeeper.

Since then I'd barely left the house because I'd been busy writing. "I don't know when or how it arrived, but it couldn't have been here long, since you cleaned a couple days ago."

"So all we know for sure is this anonymous person knows you well enough to come in your house and put it here. The blackmailer wants you to believe that your husband is alive and that your mother-in-law is fully aware of this and is keeping it a secret from you."

Hearing it put like that, I felt even shakier than when I'd first read the note.

"So, someone I know wants me to talk with Dan's mother about whether he's alive? There's no way. Even if she knew he was alive, if he'd asked her to keep it quiet, the secret would go with her to the grave. She's already one olive short of a pizza. If it's not true, even a hint he's still around might send her to the loony bin or putting together a séance."

"Maybe there's another way to find out," said Sue Ann. There was no mistaking the devilish gleam in her eye.

"What did you have in mind?"

"She asked me to clean her place. I said I'd work her in this week."

I didn't know whether to roll my eyes or lock myself in the bathroom. I knew where she was going with this and it made me nervous. "Tell me you don't have a key to her house."

"I have a key." She grinned malevolently. "Now before you get started, I know you don't clean. But you *do* know how to search."

"No, no, no." Searching was a skill I acquired when I wrote a confession about being a private detective. But it wasn't a skill I was eager to use. "You know anytime I try to do anything remotely wrong, I always get caught."

"It's either we snoop to find out if she knows anything or you tackle her directly. Your choice."

"There's got to be something else I can do. How about I go to the bank and ask for a discreet loan of two thousand bucks in unmarked bills?"

"Don't be ridiculous. Have you called Brad yet?"

We'd known Brad Tyler, now a detective with the Independence police, since the days when he'd been a troublemaker himself. He'd been assigned to handle Dan's missing persons case. "Wouldn't calling the police be overreacting?"

Sue Ann pushed back her bangs again. "You received a *blackmail note*. Calling Brad should be the first item on your agenda, I'd think. Besides . . ."

"Yeah, yeah. I know." How many times had she told me this? Trying to mimic her voice, I said, "Besides, he's always had a soft spot for you."

"Well, he does. I think if Jerome wasn't hinting that he's about to pop the big one, Brad would ask you out."

"Why is it everyone knows my business long before I do?" Jerome and I didn't have that kind of relationship yet. We were close and I knew he wanted more, but I wasn't ready.

He was a really good guy and assured me he was willing to wait for when the time was right. The idea he was about to ask me to marry him rocked me because it would change what I felt was a very comfortable and comforting friendship. A friendship that involved kissing, but not much more in the way of physical contact. His kisses were nice, and I had missed being touched, but I always felt as if I was cheating on my missing husband.

Possibly for good reason, if Dan had merely done a disappearing act. "Jerome hasn't proposed and I think Brad's only interested in me as a murder suspect. If he'd found Dan's body, I'd probably be in the clinker right now."

"No one ever mentioned anything about murder."

"No one had to. Dan's gone, as if he evaporated in thin air. Law enforcement always looks at the spouse in any suspicious circumstances. I'm sure Brad thinks I did something."

"Brad doesn't think anything of the sort. You're so clueless about men. Look at you and Dan."

I growled. "I don't want to talk about it."

"It's about time you did. You've been running in place all these years. And why? The two of you never had a close relationship. When he didn't come home, it didn't much affect your life one way or the other except you no longer had anyone to do all the household repairs or take out the trash."

I opened my mouth to argue with her, then shut it firmly. Unfortunately, she was right in some ways. Don't get me wrong—I loved Dan. But time had given me the chance to see that he was more like a father figure to me rather than a typical lover. I missed the closeness, having someone to hold me, care about me. What I didn't miss were the bits and pieces, nuts and screws—Dan's spare parts for his inventions always cluttering up our living room. Or the inventions he'd created that didn't quite work, like the combination coffeemaker-slash-band saw.

I recently began tossing his invention stuff into our spare room, unsure what to do with it but unwilling to part with it entirely. Over the course of the past month, I'd gradually moved his belongings from our bedroom into there as well. It felt so . . . final.

Perhaps in addition to the foreclosure issue, the action had been what spurred me to ask Sue Ann's husband to petition the court to declare Dan officially mortality challenged. Right now I needed to clear the air about Dan and me. "We *were* close. So what if our relationship wasn't like your marriage? Dan was a wonderful man, and I miss him."

Sue Ann gave me a quick hug. "I know you do. But I still think you should call Brad. If he finds out you didn't call him about the letter, it'll make him suspicious—like you've got something to hide."

Her comment surprised me. "You don't think I had anything to do with Dan's disappearance, do you?"

"Of course not. He *always* went to the Independence Tavern on Friday night to play chess. He *always* walked home when the bar closed at two in the morning. Everyone in town knew it, and if anyone had wanted to harm him it would have been the best time."

"Yeah, but who would want to hurt Dan?" The question had haunted me for years. Had Dan been in an accident, or had someone set out to harm him? Other than during the Neewollah Festival—a ten-day festival aptly named with the reverse spelling of the word *Halloween* because it celebrates, what else, All Ghouls Day, when the city population rises from 10,000 to around 80,000—Independence, Kansas, isn't exactly a crime hotbed.

"It's not like Dan was rich or cruel or anything," I added. "He was just a real sweet, harmless guy who liked to invent things. It's no wonder Brad suspects I had something to do with it. In his shoes, I would, too, even though I don't have a motive."

"I'm certain he doesn't think you had anything to do with it. But you do need to call him." Sue Ann placed the cordless phone between my stiff fingers. "Maybe this blackmail note will make him reopen the case and find out exactly what *did* happen to Dan."

I dialed 9-1-1 and Peggy picked up on the first ring. Things rarely hopped this time of year at the Independence Police Department. Although they received plenty of calls, most were minor incidents, such as dog bites, rather than true emergencies.

"Hi, it's Amy Crosby. Is Brad available?"

"No, hon. He's over at the diner. But if it's an emergency . . ." Her voice trailed off and I could tell she was hoping I'd say it was.

Sue Ann piped in, "Tell Peggy it's an emergency."

When I heard the excitement in Peggy's indrawn breath, I did what I could to dispel it—I laughed. "Peggy, this is *not* an emergency. Don't listen to Sue Ann. Just have Brad call me when he gets a chance."

After disconnecting the call, I threw the phone at Sue Ann, who deftly caught it with one hand.

"You know better than to tell Peggy it's an emergency," I grumbled. "It's like broadcasting it over the radio. She'll blab everything to Maureen down at the Clip 'n Curl."

Sue Ann smirked. "You think this won't get out? Better we have the law on our side than the other way around."

"I suppose you're right," I said grudgingly. "And you'd better tell your husband to withdraw that petition. No use having Dan declared awake to life immortal if he simply walked away."

Just then the phone rang, and my new psychic ability told me Peggy hadn't listened when I'd told her to wait. I grabbed the phone from Sue Ann's lap and answered it.

"What's the emergency?" Brad sounded annoyed, as if he thought I was the sort of woman who overreacted—just as I'd told Sue Ann he would.

"I gave Peggy explicit instructions not to tell you it's an emergency."

"Now that you've interrupted my lunch," he teased, "you might as well tell me what you called about."

"I thought we'd established I didn't interrupt you. Peggy did."

He gave a long-suffering sigh. "Amy, will you get to the point, please?"

"All right already." How would I go about telling the law, even if he was an old friend, that I was being blackmailed? Should I build up to it or blurt it out? "I received a letter today."

"A letter?"

"Well, an anonymous note, actually."

"And you want to report receiving an unsigned note?"

"Not exactly."

Again, he sighed. "Is it a death threat?"

"No. It's more like, eh, blackmail." I didn't relish the way my voice squeaked. Sue Ann grabbed my hand and gave it a little squeeze, providing me with the courage to go on. "Or at least that's what it says. Sue Ann and I aren't sure that's the intent."

"You guys are getting your fingerprints all over it, aren't you?" he snapped.

Dropping Sue Ann's hand, I tossed my head. "Generally you pick up a letter in order to read it. It's not like I wear gloves when going through my daily mail."

"Just put the letter in a plastic bag. If there's an envelope, toss it in as well. It'll take me five minutes to finish up here and then I'll head over to your place. You *are* at your place?"

"Duh. You just called me here."

"Stay there. Don't let anyone else in and don't handle the letter more than you have to. Got it?"

The man was far too bossy for my taste. "Got it."

After disconnecting the call, I said to Sue Ann, "He should be here in about fifteen minutes and I need to grab a quick shower first."

"What did he say?"

"Bag it."

"Fingerprints." Sue Ann hightailed it to the kitchen. After a few seconds of sounds of drawers and cabinets being opened, she yelled, "Where's your plastic bags?"

"Like I buy any?"

More rumbling noises, then she returned with a plastic Wonder Bread bag and my bacon tongs. Using the tongs, she gingerly slid both letter and envelope into the wrapper. "There. I need to head over to Mrs. Henderson's, so I'll leave you to your shower. Want me to make you some tea first?"

My gaze shot to the shelves in my living room. The ones Dan designed to hold my teacups when we first got married. I shook my head. "That's okay."

She grabbed her handbag. "When I get done cleaning Mrs. Henderson's, you can go with me to your mother-in-law's and tell me what Brad has to say."

Bowing to the inevitable, I agreed to go with her to Dolores'. Somehow I had to find out if Dan was still alive. Besides, this gave me an idea for another confession: *I Was a Professional Snoop until I Found My Cheatin' Husband with Another Woman.*

CHAPTER TWO

i Was Blackmailed by My Husband's Mistress

If you've ever lost anyone, you're familiar with how some small circumstance will trigger memories. In my case, almost tripping on my frilly pink bathroom rug brought to mind a similar incident.

This time I saved myself from falling by grabbing the porcelain sink. The last time, Dan was shaving at the sink and he caught my arm. Whenever I was about to come to harm, he always seemed to be there, like my own personal safety net.

I glanced at myself in the mirror, but all I saw was the ghost of Dan catching my lips with his and reminding me to be more careful. It's odd seeing yourself in third person, as if you were on a movie screen. But there I was, a young woman eager to love and be loved, and defining herself by the shining light in her husband's kind eyes.

Losing Dan hadn't been easy to cope with and I still wasn't sure I'd quite managed it. But what had become of that young woman? Was I an improved version of her, or in my expenditure of innocence had I forever lost something more important?

Sue Ann said I'd been running in place. Maybe she was right, but I didn't know how to do anything else. With Dan, I always felt I belonged and had a place in the world. That I was loved. I'd had so much loss and turmoil in my life before I'd met him, I couldn't help but believe a feeling of fitting in and belonging was highly underrated.

After showering, I dressed in shorts and a T-shirt and wondered what criteria I now used to define myself. Had I been running in place simply because I no longer knew who I was?

My hair was still dripping when I heard thunderous knocking at the front door. To have reached here this quickly, Brad must have left the diner with his lights flashing.

Unless it was the person Brad had warned me not to let in the house.

If it wasn't Brad and I peeked through the curtains, whoever it was would know I wasn't letting them in—deliberately. I really hated this.

I wiped my hands on the towel wrapped around my neck, straightened my T-shirt, then leaned forward and tried to squint through the crack between drape and window. I wasn't able to see who was at the door, but I relaxed instantly when I made out Brad's Chevy Tahoe parked at the curb.

I marched over and slung open the door.

"Took you long enough," he groused.

Even though Brad was incredibly attractive, especially in his dark navy police uniform, there was something about him that really set my teeth on edge, and it wasn't the fact he considered me a suspect in my own husband's disappearance.

"Nice to see you, too," I said as I led him to the den. It actually was nice to see him. What woman doesn't enjoy eye candy? Except for his nose, broken multiple times and set at an odd angle, he perfectly fit the description of tall, dark, and handsome. His wide shoulders provided a physical expression of his personality. Brad always made me feel safe when he was around—which was probably a good thing in a law enforcement officer.

He didn't take a seat on the sofa next to me, instead choosing a worn armchair halfway across the room. Maybe because he and Jerome were good friends, sofa-sitting with me was off-limits—but it was just one more annoyance. In fact, he was simply annoying—in a protective, good-looking kind of way. I tossed my head, which had worked so well earlier at conveying my feelings and was now a mistake—because the effect was something like a wet dog giving himself a shake.

Wiping away the water droplet tickling the end of my nose, I said, "I didn't have time to dry my hair."

"And here I was about to compliment you on your new style."

Then something happened to his face. It seemed to become all angles and planes and his pearly whites flashed. Did he have indigestion from snarfing his lunch too quickly?

I egged him on. "Is that supposed to be a smile? Does it scare small children?"

He was smart enough not to take my bait. His eyes narrowed and his face returned to normal. "Where's this blackmail note?"

He obviously intended our visit to be strictly business. I indicated the plastic bag on the coffee table, wondering if he expected me to bring it to him since he'd chosen to sit so far away. He surprised me, though, by rising from his chair and bending over the table to observe the letter. One of his eyebrows rose up wryly when he noticed the tongs lying beside the bag.

"They were Sue Ann's idea." I shrugged. "I figured we'd both handled it already so it wouldn't make a difference." Why was I feeling so defensive? It wasn't as if I had done anything remotely wrong—except for maybe checking out his posterior when he'd walked past me.

Then his other brow joined the first when he noticed the Wonder Bread logo.

"I'm out of Baggies, so sue me."

That was when our gazes met and I really hated it when that happened. In movies and romance novels, when a man's and a woman's eyes meet, you just know it means they're attracted to each other. They'd experience some delightful electric-like shock to their system, telling them they were meant for each other.

When Brad's gaze met mine, I, too, experienced an electric-like shock. But rather than it feeling delightful, it just convinced me he thought I'd offed my husband. Being the guilt-laden person I am, I piped in, "I didn't kill my husband."

Brad seemed to be fighting amusement. "No one said you did."

"Yeah, but it's there in your eyes."

"You think?"

I didn't want to think about his eyes. They were a delicious Hershey-syrup brown, and his lids lazily covered the top of his irises. Now, to my list of sins, I had to add guilt about thinking of Brad in a biblical way when I was sorta kinda dating his friend Jerome. While I knew

Jerome wanted something more from me I wasn't quite sure I had that much more to give him. But Brad was definitely the hands-off-my-friend's-girl type of guy, and I had to admire him for it. So, yeah, I felt a little shamefaced about checking him out.

"I may make my living confessing, " I said. "And heaven knows I have a guilty enough conscience for any three people, but I've tried to keep a firm rein on reality as opposed to fantasy. I make it a rule not to confess to crimes I didn't commit."

Brad's teeth bared again. At least now I knew he meant it as a friendly gesture and I didn't need to look around for a means to protect myself.

As Brad scanned the note through the plastic, he asked, "How'd you get this?"

"I found it here, on this table, this morning."

"How'd it get here?"

"Sue Ann and I were trying to figure that out. I'm not exactly a careful housekeeper—" I waited for the usual snicker I get when making a comment about my domestic skills, but Brad surprised me by keeping his lips zipped. I liked that about him.

"Two days ago the readers' club met here and I had about twenty people in the house. The only people I can think of who've been here since then, that I know of, are my in-laws and Sue Ann."

"This doesn't make my job any easier."

"Tell me about it. I can't figure out why someone would want to blackmail me, especially with the information that my missing husband is alive. Why would I want to keep it a secret?"

"It's downright peculiar." He gave me a look that was difficult to read, but I suspected he assumed I was pulling some stunt.

Picking up the bag containing the note, he went back to his chair, obviously keeping his distance between himself and a suspect—namely *moi*. "Have you talked with your mother-in-law?"

"Are you kidding? If Dolores hasn't said anything before, do you think she would now?" I cringed. Dan was too responsible to simply disappear, wasn't he? Dolores clung to the hope he'd return someday, and while I did, too, deep inside I'd accepted that he had probably joined my mother and grandmother at the pearly gates. "After Dolores' alien kidnapping and sex slavery theories, I do *not* want to consider what she'd come up with if she had a hint he might still be alive."

"If you don't do anything, then day after tomorrow whoever wrote this thing will reveal the information about your husband's whereabouts or possibly make another attempt at blackmail."

"If they know where Dan is, maybe they'll blackmail him instead of me. He probably has deeper pockets anyway. If he sneaked off like that, he'd want to keep it a secret, wouldn't he?"

"Or they might hit up Dolores."

"I can't imagine any reason why she would want to keep it quiet if he's alive."

"She might pay someone to tell her where he is, even if it's a scam."

I hadn't thought of the possibility. While Dolores and I couldn't be said to be intimate, I was genuinely fond of her and didn't want anything to upset her, no matter how many bodacious bats she had in her belfry. Maybe Sue Ann's plan to snoop wasn't such a bad idea after all.

Brad pocketed the letter and stood. "You and Sue Ann need to stop by my office later to provide your prints. If there are any others, it'll give us something to go on."

"Okay, I'll tell Sue Ann." She'd been right about telling me to call Brad. He was dependable. Putting the blackmail note into his hands reassured me.

Brad hesitated, like he wanted to say something more, so I shot him an encouraging look. He cleared his throat, then slanted his too-craggy face into a frown. Man, compared to his smile, if it weren't for the warmth in his eyes, his frown could terrify a whole flock of buzzards. I wondered how many people had confessed to him simply based on the strength of it.

"You will be careful," he said.

His statement surprised me. It wasn't as though there was any physical threat in the note. In fact, as far as blackmail notes go, it appeared to be a friendly little number. But since I couldn't figure out why anyone thought they could blackmail me about Dan in the first place, maybe he had a point. "I'm always careful."

"Don't take any unnecessary chances." He reached out and brushed a damp lock of hair out of my eyes.

Trying to dismiss the rush of warmth I felt when his fingertips brushed my face, I nodded. I'd only take necessary chances.

My nod seemed to appease him, though, because he strode to my door. When he turned back, his expression was pensive.

"I don't like it," he said. "Independence doesn't have much crime. It's one of the things I like best about it. The idea it's someone we know, a respected member of the readers' club doing this, disturbs me. Watch your back."

With that reassuring thought, he exited, leaving me to confront my fears by myself. I didn't realize how not safe I'd feel when he left. The least I expected was that a dependable person like Brad could be relied upon to leave me feeling secure. Not that he wasn't reliable. He was. I knew he'd do his best to track down the blackmailer. But until he did, I felt anything but safe.

I hadn't been afraid earlier. I'd been angry at the thought that Dan may have chosen to desert me, I'd been confused by the idea of being blackmailed, and I'd seen this as an intellectual game.

Brad's comment changed everything.

It became too intimate. Someone I knew, someone I trusted, apparently wanted to hurt me. Whether physically, financially, or emotionally I wasn't sure. But the intent was there.

So there I stood two hours later in Dolores' bedroom, clutching a small bottle of brilliant blue glass cleaner in one hand and a ratty cloth in the other, wondering exactly what it was Sue Ann wanted me to do with the things. Sure, when I was a teen, my nana periodically, under threats of death or tuna à la king dinners, coerced me into using what she referred to as elbow grease to wipe down the bathroom mirror. But quite frankly, I never was any good at it back then.

Equally frankly, I wasn't sure exactly where I was supposed to spray the stuff now, considering there wasn't a mirror in sight. Behind the dark and thick curtains I was sure there would be some glass, but did Sue Ann expect me to go back there?

Her instruction to "look busy" didn't make much sense. We were alone in the nineteenth-century house, and my mother-in-law's bedroom was already clean as far as I observed. Thankfully, Sue Ann didn't demand I also search my sister-in-law, Liz's, bedroom as well.

Shrugging, I stuffed the glass cleaner in my large back pocket and the rag down my shirt front and concentrated on what I was there to do: snoop.

Glancing around the bedroom, I noted the bed, the antique oak bureau, and matching dresser along with an old-fashioned chaise lounge. Otherwise, there wasn't much in the room. I pulled open the closet doors, then let out a sigh. Dolores had kept every shoe box for each pair of shoes she'd ever owned. Box upon box was stacked on the shelves. Three-quarters of the hanging space was also taken up with shoe boxes. There wasn't much room for clothing at all.

I knew the woman had a lot of shoes, but I'd never expected her to have an entire shoe museum.

I firmly shut the closet door and looked guiltily over my shoulder. I heard Sue Ann vacuuming in the living room. Hopefully, she wouldn't remember all those boxes in the closet because, otherwise, she'd insist I search them all.

I turned my attention to the ten drawers in the room, four in the bureau and six in the dresser. Should be a piece of cake. That was before I opened the top bureau drawer and realized my mother-in-law had saved all her correspondence—ever.

In the drawer beneath, I saw even more letters. They hadn't been organized; simply tossed into the drawer. Mixed in with condolence cards for the death of her husband twenty years ago were recent birthday cards. There was no rhyme or reason to how they'd been put away.

I dumped the contents of both drawers on the bed, an action which raised a huge cloud of dust, making me sneeze. I then made a quick search for recent correspondence from Dan.

After I pulled out a Mother's Day card signed by Dan, my heart almost stopped. When I realized the postmark on the envelope was dated ten years earlier, I breathed easier. My sigh skittered across her bedroom, like an echo in a canyon. I ran my finger over Dan's signature, recalling how Dolores had been genuinely touched that first Mother's Day after my marriage, when I'd timidly told her how pleased I was to have a mother again. She vowed to always treat me as one of her own and she'd never swayed from that promise. It was one of many reasons why I felt uncomfortable searching her home.

I took a seat on her bed, letters and envelopes sliding against my hip—the detritus accumulated through sixty years of living. Why hadn't I known she was the sentimental sort, hoarding notes and letters? Did she sit on this bed, like me, rereading them?

Breathing became more difficult, as if I'd stirred up sixty years of dust. Yet part of being a good daughter-in-law meant protecting her from hurting all over again. It was why I was here, wishing I could be somewhere—anywhere—else.

I shuffled through the papers, and it didn't take long to see there weren't any *new* letters from Dan, although for Dolores' sake, I'd nearly wished there were.

After stuffing the cards and letters back in the drawers, I went to check on Sue Ann while tamping down the guilt eating at me for going through Dolores' personal belongings.

While I hadn't believed it likely that she was an accomplice in her son's disappearance, eliminating the possibility was for her own good. She'd never accepted the probability that Dan was no longer among the living, and even I found the idea challenging. After discussing it with her daughter, Liz, I'd made a point of protecting her by not informing her I planned to have him declared living impaired. Once the deed was done, there would be time enough to tell her, and even then it would have to be as gently as possible—with smelling salts and an oxygen tank standing ready.

If he'd made the choice to leave not only me but also his mother without a trace, that knowledge would send Dolores over the edge. Encouraging her to believe he was alive wasn't a very good idea either— that is, if he had kissed the dust. But I had no way of knowing whether he was alive unless I could find some clue pointing to his having run out on me, his family, and the entire town.

Some of his inventions were still in use for the Neewollah parades— particularly the Doo Dah floats. Surely he would have come back to town when his volcano failed to erupt during the queen's coronation year before last—if he'd been physically able to come back, that is. He'd been particularly proud of that darn volcano and held some sort of a patent on it, making up a big chunk of my dwindling monthly income.

No matter what the blackmail note contended, I couldn't accept he had willingly disappeared, which made our search of Dolores' home unlikely to turn up any clues. I had to be certain, one way or the other.

As I entered the den, I saw Sue Ann sliding the center drawer closed on an old wooden desk. "Find anything?"

"Bills. Nothing helpful other than a great recipe for chocolate pie." Sue Ann puffed at her bangs. "How about you?"

"I found where she stores her correspondence, but no luck." I very deliberately didn't mention all those shoe boxes. If I honestly believed Dolores might be hiding something in one of them it would be worth the effort, but I didn't, so it wasn't.

"I haven't searched the hall closet," Sue Ann said as she rose from the chair in front of the desk. "Why don't you check the bathroom cabinets?"

I nodded my agreement and headed first to the guest bath. As expected, considering how much time I'd spent in there over the years, there wasn't much besides a spare toothbrush, three rolls of toilet paper, a neat stack of soap bars, and an ancient Tootsie Roll that I found wedged under the counter. I decided not to eat it.

Next I headed to the bathroom shared by Dolores and my sister-in-law, Liz. It was one of those Jack and Jill baths, with a dressing table on each side and, separated by doors, a sink, counter, toilet, and bath combination in the middle.

I'd never had cause to use that bathroom before. The room seriously needed to be updated, although I rather liked the late-sixties brilliant yellow and green flowered wallpaper. If coffee didn't wake you in the morning, this certainly would.

I quickly checked through the cabinets and drawers and didn't see much of interest—until my gaze settled on the toilet.

It was one of Dan's best inventions. During his phase when he was hoping I'd learn to clean house if I was provided with the right tools and incentives, he designed something for me—the self-cleaning toilet. Just inside the rim was a track, and on the track ran two sets of brushes. When the toilet flushed, the brushes spun around, looking a bit like a bristly cat chasing a spastic mouse. Until now I'd only seen Dan's prototype—in our bathroom at home.

But this one was cool because it wasn't plain white porcelain like mine. Instead, it was beige and had black rubber gaskets covering the tracks. The machinery making it work had been disguised within the tank. I flushed and watched as it quickly did its thing. I flushed it again. (What can I say? I'm easily entertained.)

Just then I heard Liz's voice. She must have come home early, which meant I needed to speed things up.

My sister-in-law was one of the side benefits of my marriage. While her personality was a lot like Sergeant Friday's on *Dragnet* repeats ("Just the facts, ma'am"), she was also an exceedingly kind and patient woman. Proof of this was evidenced by the fact that she still lived with her mother, my mother-in-law.

Dolores could be trying.

Don't get me wrong. I adore her. But I'd do almost anything to avoid living in the same house. She's a bad-o-chondriac. Not only does she imagine she has every illness under the sun, but anything awful that's happened to anyone else in the world is minor compared to her trials.

She's been kidnapped by aliens, widowed because of a government conspiracy to cover up corn chip addiction, her phone and house are bugged, and AAA refuses to return any of her calls. She's the target of a Mafia hit squad, singled out by every scam artist, and if it weren't for her *pills*, she'd have been an alcoholic. We won't go into her *pills*.

Liz was practically a saint. And, judging by the clip clop of her footsteps, she was heading my way.

Panic set in.

Given our history, I really didn't want her to discover me snooping in her home. I also didn't want to tell her about the blackmail note and exactly why I was snooping. She might say something to Dolores.

I yanked the bottle of glass cleaner from my back pocket and began spritzing it liberally on the mirror, on the bathroom counter, and in the air. By the time she reached the doorway, I was literally asphyxiating on the fumes.

She had a startled look on her face—as if she hadn't expected to find me in her bathroom. I had to hand it to her. It was mighty strange.

She asked, "What are you doing in here?"

Nana once told me that some women are blessed with beauty but even fewer are blessed with something better—sass. She added that like her, I had been blessed with the latter.

Now, that woman was so full of sass, you never knew if she was dead serious or full of beans.

Sass certainly helped pay my bills via my confessions, although I could have stood a bit more in the beauty department. The problem was that I knew back then what I'm even more sure of now: sass doesn't come naturally to me.

I have to work hard at it.

Being ever the optimist, I took this to mean I was blessed with unnatural sass.

And here I was, expecting my unnatural sass to pull this off. Not a good sign.

"Considering my financial situation," I quickly said, "I figured I'd better learn some wage-earning skills. Sue Ann gave me an offer I couldn't turn down—learning on the job."

For a moment, Liz looked at me without any expression on her face, then seemed to do some sort of internal shrug before eyeing me curiously. "Is there any reason why you're wearing an old diaper in your cleavage?"

I wasn't sure what she meant until I looked down and realized I hadn't removed the cleaning rag. Yanking it from my shirtfront, I said, "Storage."

It was time for me to get out of there and let Liz into her own bathroom, so I headed to the doorway. Liz stopped me and pointed toward the mirror. "You missed a spot."

CHAPTER THREE

i Bribed a Cop with a Kiss

My mother-in-law is a generous woman. She's also bonkers, but that's not polite to say. An example of her generosity is that a while back, she gave me her car, an early model Gremlin. Independence is a small town, and between walking or cadging rides from family and friends, I'd been able to make do without a vehicle.

Dan's car remained parked beneath a tarp in our garage, undriven since the day of his disappearance. That contraption had a ton of knobs, gauges, and buttons, and he'd souped it up with every imaginable device possible (and for an inventor, there's lots to imagine). Just thinking about trying to start it up gave me the heebie-jeebies because he once warned me not to let anyone drive it. If they didn't know what they were doing, the resulting explosion might depopulate the entire Independence business district. I had no reason to doubt him on the subject.

A-hmm.

So it was very thoughtful of Dolores to give me a car.

Now before you get all excited about such a lush gift, there's a story attached to it.

Over the past number of years, the state had been building a new road between our town and one down in Oklahoma. The new road would cut off about thirty minutes of driving time to the Will Rogers Airport in Oklahoma City. Unfortunately, the construction had been slow—something to do with the two states having to agree about who pays for what.

Now Dolores had been planning a trip to Hawaii for a long time, but she's notoriously pokey. So when the morning of her departure came, she ran behind as usual. Dolores felt frustrated that the road-work was progressing at a snail's pace, and the vision of the beautiful stretch of fresh blacktop proved too much of a temptation for her that morning. The road looked completed, with only its stripes missing, so she swerved around the orange cones blocking traffic from it and high-tailed it out of town.

At first, flush with success, she had the pedal to the metal. She'd gone about twenty miles, into the middle of nowhere, when suddenly she ran out of blacktop and dropped down an embankment about three feet to freshly graded soil. The Gremlin seemed to be running fine, so rather than turn back and take the long way, she figured the ground was really smooth, and she continued on.

After she'd kicked up dust for another fifteen miles, the road dead-ended into another embankment, again about three feet above ground level. Faced with the choice of missing her flight to Hawaii or turning around, she decided there was no choice but to back up and floor it. Surely, the Gremlin would make it up that embankment.

It didn't.

After catching her flight (the noise she created attempting to drive up the embankment drew a crowd, and she was able to hitch a ride into town), she phoned me from Honolulu and gave me the car.

Now my new Gremlin was being looked after by one of Independence's automotive experts, Ecclesiastes of Ecclesiastes Service Station. Ol' Eck was the best man for bodywork for at least a three-county span.

Unfortunately, welding an axle back onto a car body isn't for the faint of heart, and Eck was taking his time to do it right.

So when Sue Ann and I left Dolores' home, she automatically turned her car in the direction of the service station in order to check on the evolution of pasting my Gremlin back together again.

I have to admit, I was really excited about the prospect of owning my own wheels, and for the past four months, Eck had given me visitation rights. I'd come and stroke the car hood, ask if it would be ready soon, then get inside and toot the horn. Hey, I take my amusement where I can find it.

When we pulled up, Lam came out to meet us. Lam is Eck's younger brother, thoughtfully named Lamentations by their Bible salesman father. Considering the number of boys in their family (thirteen), I honestly believe the man had simply run out of names.

Their service station is right out of the 1940s, with those old floating ball pumps. The colors have faded a bit, but those balls still pop around like young'uns. Eck and Lam have a firm rule about hiring help to operate the pumps. They only hire honor students from the high school, figuring they're the only ones capable of handling the math calculations since the pumps have only two-digit gas prices.

"Here to check on your car?" asked Lam.

"How's she doing?" I asked him as Sue Ann and I got out of her Lincoln Navigator. Sue Ann's husband had insisted she needed a status vehicle since he was a prosperous up-and-coming attorney with designs on a county judgeship. Sue Ann insisted she needed something that could hold all her cleaning supplies. They'd compromised.

"Eck just went around back. He's starting work on her now."

Wild redbud trees bloomed in the empty lot next door to the station, and I wondered if there was something wrong with my tree. The purple buds danced on ebony branches, making me think of fuchsia icing flowers on a dark chocolate birthday cake. Redbud blossoms are the first sign of spring. I chewed my lip, wondering if I needed to contact a tree specialist. I'd had more than my fair share of death.

As Sue Ann and I rounded the side of the gas station, I turned my thoughts to what we'd learned, or more like what we hadn't learned, from our investigations so far. "I can't believe detective work is so tedious."

"Just because we didn't find any clues at Dolores' doesn't mean we won't succeed," said Sue Ann. "We just have to decide what our next step should be."

And there was the problem. How could we proceed when we had so little to go on? Rounding the corner of the redbrick building, I caught sight of Eck leaning over my new baby. He was polishing the car body, which was propped up on concrete blocks over a semi-grassy area. The front axle rested on the ground beside it. Not a good sign.

"Hey, Eck," I called.

He started at the sound of my voice and turned to greet me with a sheepish smile on his face. After pulling a pink, oil-stained cloth from his back pocket, he wiped his hands on it as he walked to join us. "She sure is a pretty little thing."

He was right. She was. "You courting her?"

His smile was shy. "Guess you could say that."

While it may have seemed as if Eck didn't know what he was doing, in actuality, he's an artist—a genius with chunks of metal and motors. He can turn the worst lemon into a purring pussycat of a vehicle. But the problem with many artists is they can't create until the muse strikes them. The same can be said of Eck.

"I guess the time's not right yet," I ventured.

He shook his head. "Gotta look for the woman in her first."

"You're brilliant, Eck." It was my turn to give him a broad grin because inspiration had struck in the form of Eck's muse. *Look for the woman. Cherchez la femme.* Our readers' club was boning up on Sherlock Holmes, and the phrase had been the key to solving the crime in one of the stories we'd read. Now it provided the answer to how to proceed in our investigations. We, too, would look for the woman.

I was struck with a thought. I never thought of my husband, Dan, as a womanizer. Had he led a secret life? If he was still alive, then it was possible I'd been mistaken in never considering this possibility. I never thought he'd one day disappear, either.

Even if he hadn't led a secret two-timing life, I still had greater than a fifty-fifty chance that *some* woman *somewhere* would know *something* about what happened to him, especially considering the blackmail note that indicated his mom knew more than she'd previously told me. Even though I didn't want to ask her. But if she knew something, I'd find a way to discover the information without sending her off the deep end or to a Ouija board to consult the spirit world.

As I opened the Gremlin's door, preparing to climb inside to give it my customary horn toot, feeling all generous because Eck had inspired the direction of our investigation, I said, "Take your time working on her."

As I leaned into the car, I froze. Lying curled up on the passenger seat was a large, scary, staring-at-me-with-his-fangs-showing rattlesnake.

I don't *do* snakes. I might even be able to make a case that I'm allergic to them.

I couldn't move. I couldn't scream. I couldn't do anything but stare at the snake as he began shaking his rattle at me.

I was relieved I hadn't actually taken a seat yet, but I was at an uncomfortable angle, halfway bent to lumber into the car while my backside teetered outside it. I managed to croak out, "Help."

Sue Ann, who hadn't been paying attention until then, glanced into the car and yelled, "Snake!"

Her scream, or maybe it was the weird arm-flailing-hopping contortions she was doing, sent the rattler into a frenzy.

I had to move.

I closed my eyes. Eck threw out an arm and pulled me back from the car while slamming the door closed.

"You okay?" he asked.

I nodded, throwing open my eyes and hoping I'd get my voice back soon. My throat felt so cottony dry I couldn't swallow, and my hands quaked. I eyed the irate snake inside my Gremlin. The snake lunged and struck at the door.

I screamed, and so did Sue Ann. Even Eck jumped back a little.

Beads of venom marked the car window.

The fear-induced paralysis passed, and I spent several moments simply taking deep breaths. "Thanks for saving me."

Eck shrugged. "I just closed the door."

He'd done more than that, but he was being modest, just as he was modest about his auto repair skills. "How'd the snake get in there?"

"Beats me." Eck looked at the snake, whose rattle was still waving, then frowned. "It doesn't seem likely it could get in there on its own."

"The question is, now that he's in there, how do we get him out?" Sue Ann, with the danger over, wasn't above taunting the snake. She tapped the window.

The snake lunged again.

"Don't do that!" I pulled her back from the car. "Eck, what can we do about the snake?"

"I'll get Cory to take care of him and make sure there aren't any other critters hiding inside. I'll try to find out how he got in there."

His brother Corinthians worked at animal control. "Thanks."

We turned to leave and go back to my house. About the time the hair on the back of my neck had calmed down, Sue Ann's cell phone rang. She dug it out of her bag as we reached her car.

While she answered the call, I carefully checked her car for reptiles, then climbed inside. Sue Ann opened her car door. "That was Peggy from the police department on the phone. She says there's been an intruder reported at your house."

"What? First my car, and now my home is violated? It's not enough the bank is threatening to take it away, but now someone's broken in?"

"It'll be okay." Sue Ann quickly pulled out of the gas station and headed toward my home. I'd never had a break-in before, and the very thought of it gave me the creeps. Questions and worries bombarded me. Home was supposed to be secure and safe—not rampant with blackmailers and burglars. "Did she say who it is? Is my house okay?"

"She said not to worry, that everything's okay at your place. But I'm not sure about everything being okay with you." She shot me a concerned glance.

"I'll be fine as soon as we get there and I see everything's all right."

"That's not what I meant. I'm seriously concerned about your *mental* health. Do you realize you told Eck to take his time on your car?"

"Oops. I probably shouldn't have done that."

"Not if you want to get your car back in the current century."

I shrugged my shoulders, glad for her transparent attempt at distraction. I didn't want to think about snakes or intruders. I didn't much want to think about Dan's disappearance, either, but I didn't have much choice. Right then, talking about my car seemed a much safer subject—as long as we weren't discussing snakes. "Eck said he had to look for the woman. That's what we need to do. It's our next step to finding out what happened to Dan."

"What are you raving about?" Sue Ann crinkled her nose and looked at me.

"If you'll keep your eyes on the road, I'll tell you."

"Fine." She redirected her gaze straight ahead. "Spill."

"The readers' club has been totally into Sherlock Holmes. He solved the mystery using the phrase *Cherchez la femme*. That's what we've got to do. Look for the woman."

"O-kay." Sue Ann turned a corner. Then she thought about it a moment. "Actually, that's a great idea. If Dan just left—if something bad didn't happen to him—there would have to be a woman in the picture. It's the only theory that makes sense."

"Do you think Dan was involved with another woman?" Somehow, my encounter with the rattlesnake gave me the courage to voice my fears. The idea didn't resonate. Dan hadn't seemed the cheating type, but they always say the wife is the last to know.

"I never heard any rumors."

"Rumors? I know who we need to talk with."

"Maureen at the Clip 'n Curl!" we said in unison. Mo knew every morsel of gossip within a one hundred-mile radius of Independence. No matter how secretive anyone tried to be, Mo always knew the scoop. Her nose was like a hound dog's when it came to sniffing out dirt, rumor, and innuendo.

At last we reached my house. When Sue Ann slammed on the brakes, her tires squealed. Brad's Chevy Tahoe was parked in my driveway, and my front door was open. I didn't see Brad, so he had to be inside.

I jumped out of the car before Sue Ann had time to cut the engine, then darted to my door. I stepped inside, and there was Brad, walking toward me. I ignored the relieved expression on his face, and my voice only shook a little as I said, "I heard there was an intruder, but I didn't expect it to be you. What are you doing in my house? Are you the intruder?"

As I watched, his expression was replaced by pique. "Why don't you lock your doors?"

"You don't lock your doors?" asked Sue Ann as she came up behind me.

I looked at her. I looked at him. I threw up my arms. "I really don't need this. Sue Ann, please go home. I'll call you later. Brad, don't intrude in my house anymore."

"Ignore her, Brad. She just had a shock."

Brad leaned around me to talk with Sue Ann, as if I weren't there. "That's okay. Everything is under control here, Sue Ann. I checked, and it doesn't look like the intruder took anything."

Obviously he thought my shock was at finding a law enforcement official in my house. I'd had enough and didn't much want to tell him about my tryst with an entirely different kind of snake. All I wanted was to be left alone so I could go hide in my bathroom and have the nervous breakdown I'd been delaying. A little privacy wasn't too much to ask. My annoyance grew as Brad and Sue Ann continued talking about me as if they were alone.

"*Peo*-ple," I said. "I'm here. This is *my* house. You can talk directly to me instead of over my head."

Sue Ann pushed passed me. "You need a drink. Brad, you want something, too?"

"Thanks, but I'm on duty."

That left me alone in the living room with Brad. Under other circumstances, it might have been a good thing. But I was out of patience. Did Brad truly think I had something to do with Dan's disappearance? Why else would he be in my house? "You still haven't said what you're doing in here. Don't you need a search warrant if you're searching my house?"

The frown that made me want to duck for cover enveloped his face again. "Your neighbor Mrs. Mitchell reported an intruder. I arrived, the front door was unlocked, and you didn't answer. What did you expect me to do—sit outside while some intruder harmed you?"

"Oh. Sorry." I smoothed my T-shirt, more embarrassed by my hotheaded mistake than fully comprehending there had been an actual break-in. "Thanks. Did you catch him?"

"Apparently he left before I arrived. I did a thorough walk-through and didn't notice anything missing. Want to check before I leave?"

"Uh, yeah. Someone broke in." A sense of urgency had me reaching out to grab his arm. Of course I needed to check things out, and I wanted a big, strong detective nearby. What if the intruder was still in my house? What if he'd been hiding and Brad hadn't found him? "Let's go check together."

I headed toward the kitchen, one arm still clutching Brad, who rushed to keep up. Sue Ann met me with a glass tumbler.

"Drink up."

I did. I hadn't expected her to give me straight bourbon. I'm not much of a drinker, but a few bottles of alcohol had been left behind after some long-ago gathering at my house. They had collected dust in my pantry for years.

After spluttering and making a fool of myself and wondering why I always managed to look my worst in front of Brad, the bourbon seemed to go directly into my bloodstream and I soon realized I'd stopped shaking, which I'd evidently been doing since my run-in with the rattler.

Go figure.

"I'm better now, thanks." I inhaled deeply, then turned to Brad. "Do you think the intruder left because you got here so quickly?"

"It's possible. Your back door wasn't locked, either."

The glare he slanted in my direction was enough to fell a lesser woman. Good thing I'd had the bourbon. I didn't want to admit I'd lost my key. I could lock my house while I was inside but couldn't do a damn thing about it when I was outside. It was just one of those little life details that sometimes slip away from me when I'm busy writing. Like buying toilet paper.

"She lost her key," blurted Sue Ann.

I resisted the urge to harm her for ratting me out and, instead, settled on glowering at her.

Brad faced me. "You don't have a key?"

What could I say? "There's a dead bolt."

"But you can't lock up when you leave?"

Again, what could I say in my defense? "Even if someone considers breaking in, I can't imagine them thinking there's anything of value to be found here. There isn't much to be made on combination toaster oven–vacuum cleaners."

Brad ran a palm over his mouth, as if he was trying to keep himself from saying something he shouldn't.

"Are you sure you want me to leave?" Sue Ann glanced at her watch. "I hate to go, but I still have one other job today. If you're okay, I'll call you later."

"I'm fine." I gave her a quick hug, then whispered so that Brad couldn't overhear, "We'll talk later about the Clip 'n Curl."

Sue Ann gave me a knowing look and headed out the door. "Talk to you later."

"If you'll make sure nothing is missing, I'll be out of your hair, too." Brad pointed toward the bedroom that functioned as my office.

I first checked to make sure my computer was okay. Once reassured that it hadn't been disturbed, I turned my eye to the rest of the office. Nothing appeared to have been touched. Next, I walked room to room, but nothing was amiss. "It looks like he left empty-handed."

"Perhaps Mrs. Mitchell scared him away." Brad made some notes on a pad. "I'll head out, then. Let me know if something turns up missing later."

"Fine."

We walked back through the den, where something on the coffee table caught my eye. It couldn't be, could it?

"Wait, Brad." I pointed at the envelope stuffed between the stack of books on my table, in the same location the blackmail note had been earlier.

His expression became grim. "Don't touch it. I'll be right back."

He went out to his cruiser, then came back wearing latex gloves. Gingerly picking the envelope up off my table, he pulled out the note. If possible, his expression became even grimmer.

"What does it say?" I crowded beside Brad's elbow, trying to get a good look.

It was another note like the other. The first line jumped out at me like a snake:

Did you like my s-s-surprise?

CHAPTER FOUR

Everything i Know about Sex i Learned at the Clip 'n Curl

"I told you the snake was the surprise." If I thought I'd been creeped out before, I was completely wrong. Nothing could touch the amount of creepiness I now felt.

"Shut up and eat," Brad ordered.

After he'd called for backup and my house had been turned inside out—only to find no other surprises, three hours later Brad and I were alone at last. We were seated at my kitchen table where he miraculously produced Chinese food.

"Where'd you get this?"

"It's takeout. Afraid I cooked it?"

"No. Wondering why you bothered since I've got plenty of food in the refrigerator."

"If you like rabbit food."

"What's that supposed to mean?"

"Look, Amy." He gave a low sigh. "I was hungry. I didn't want to cook. Eat!"

"I'm not sure I can." I toyed with the peanut chicken.

"You look pitiful. Eat the egg drop soup. You need to keep your strength up."

"Yeah. I need to be ready for the next surprise." I did as he asked and took a sip. It was a little too salty for my taste—but I took another sip.

He scooted back his chair, and it made a scraping noise on the linoleum. "I'm finished. Do you want me to stay the night?"

My soup spewed.

"I didn't mean it that way. I can sleep on your couch."

Of course he didn't mean it that way. Using my napkin to blot up the mess I'd made, I hoped Brad wouldn't notice the scarlet hue my face had to be. He wanted to become intimate with my sofa, not me.

"Do you think I'm not safe?" I asked.

"You're as safe as any one person can be."

"Then I'll be fine." In an attempt to get the image of being intimate with Brad out of my head, I began gathering the takeout boxes, preparing to put them away. But the distraction didn't work very well. Especially when he reached out a fingertip and traced my cheek.

"Are you scared?"

I nodded. I might have had many things to be fearful about, but what scared me most was the look of caring on his face and what it did to my insides. Imagining there might be a future between us was pure fantasy, a product of my overactive imagination. He was just being a nice guy, looking after me, doing his job. "Don't get me wrong. I'm not scared about sleeping alone in my house, especially after every law enforcement official in town has gone over it with a fine-toothed comb. I'm scared about what's going to happen next."

"Whatever happens, we'll take care of it." He stood, grabbed the boxes, and stuffed them in my fridge. "I'll make sure you're safe. You lock your doors. Keep your phone handy and dial 9-1-1 if anything at all suspicious happens. Got it?"

"Yes, Detective." I felt protected and safe enough. The dead bolt worked fine and I could lock myself in.

Besides, if he spent the night, I wouldn't be able to sleep. God knows, it would take me all night to clean Dan's stuff off the bed in the guest room. Brad was too big for my sofa and wouldn't be at all comfortable—and I wouldn't be at all comfortable knowing he was in my living room.

I followed him to the front door.

"I checked all your doors and windows, and they're locked. Lock this one behind me. Use your dead bolt."

"Will do."

He closed the door behind himself, and I stood there for a second, feeling bereft.

"I said to lock the door." His thundering demand boomed from the other side.

Bossy, bossy, bossy. I turned the dead bolt, then leaned my forehead on the door. "Night, Brad."

"Sweet dreams, Amy."

The next morning, after I told Sue Ann all about the officers searching my house, we agreed I should go see Maureen on my own, then report back to Sue Ann whatever I learned.

The walk to the salon didn't take long, and before I knew it, Mo had draped me in several layers of plastic. I felt like a choice drumstick on display at Marvin's meat counter.

I hadn't planned on getting a perm, but Mo insisted it would slightly lighten my dark hair and complement the gold flecks in my grey eyes. Assuming it was the best way to set her on gossip mode, I bowed to the inevitable. Besides, I hadn't even known I had gold flecks.

The Clip 'n Curl is Independence's rumor central. Anything worth knowing could be discovered here. Mo, the owner and operator, redecorated the salon during the seventies, and it still sported disco décor, including one of those mirrored balls over each beautician's station. An immense motor-powered disco ball rotated on the ceiling in the center of the main room.

It had long been my theory that the ball hypnotized the customers and encouraged them not only to dish the latest but to agree to whatever beautification horrors Mo came up with in her desire to be trendsetting. It certainly worked that way with me, I thought, as Mo prepared perm rods for use in my hair.

While her mind was busy calculating how much perm solution would be needed for my too-thick head of hair, I decided to spring my main question on her. "I've been thinking, Mo . . ."

"Hmm."

The bell over the door chimed, cutting off my question, as one of the future contenders for Neelah queen entered the salon. The girl, a high school junior, seemed jittery. She stood stiffly, but her hands trembled a little and she kept glancing over her shoulder at the salon's large front windows.

"What can I help you with, hon?" called out Mo.

"I'm here for a piercing."

"What, did your ear holes grow back together?" Mo dropped her instruments of torture and rushed toward the girl.

"Not my ears. I'd like a belly ring. Mary Stanza has one, and it's so hot."

Mo turned back to me and winked, but she continued talking to the girl. "Sure thing, hon. Take a seat. I'll do you when I'm finished with Amy's new look. I'm giving her a makeover."

The girl's stiff posture relaxed, and her pretty features softened as she settled onto a chair at the waiting area while I contemplated Mo's concept of a makeover. My posture went rigid, and my features seemed to have pulled back into a snarl. I was after gossip, not a new look and, considering the outdated décor, I seriously feared I'd end up looking like an actor from *The Mod Squad*.

As Mo reached me, she didn't pay any attention to my expression. She again addressed the girl. "While I work on Amy, why don't you pull out that permission slip from your mama?"

The girl stood. "Permission slip?"

"Yeah. You know the one I require from minors."

"Oh. *That* permission slip. I forgot it."

"Run along and get it, then come back. I can fit you in around four o'clock."

The girl groaned and couldn't seem to leave quickly enough as she dashed for the door.

Maureen laughed as she wrapped my hair onto the curling rods. "Those girls think I fell off the pickle truck. Why, you wouldn't believe it, but Nancy Halpern's youngest came in for a piercing last week."

Nancy was the president of the Temperance League. She was personally responsible for a number of Kansas counties remaining dry, although she hadn't made headway in Montgomery County—yet. Nancy had several daughters. I asked, "Is that April Halpern?"

"No. June. And you know what she wanted me to pierce? Her unmentionables. I told her I wasn't ready for her mama to come gunning for me."

As Mo squirted perm solution on my hair, I squirmed—and it wasn't just from the chemicals permeating my scalp. I got up the nerve again to ask my question. "You might think it's borrowing trouble, Mo, but I was wondering. Do you think Dan was ever involved with another woman?"

She stiffened for a long second. "What makes you ask that?"

"Well, he's been gone seven years, and if he hasn't checked into Chateau Eternity, there has to be a good reason why he hasn't come back."

She patted my arm reassuringly. "I know you want to believe he'll come home someday, hon. I always believed Dan met with foul play. But I'll be honest with you. At the time of his disappearance, there was some talk . . ."

"Why didn't you say something?" If there had been talk, I deserved to know. It might have saved me from years of grief and unanswered questions.

"You had enough worries, hon. I couldn't add to them. But Gayla Mullen abruptly left town the day after Dan disappeared. You know *that* set the tongues wagging, but I didn't buy it for a minute. Dan wasn't the cheating type."

"I never thought he was." Gayla had been a teacher at the high school and, certainly, I'd been so upset about Dan's disappearance that I'd never made any connection between the two of them. I searched my memory for any sign or indication he might have been a wayward husband, but I came up empty-handed. Yet some people must have believed all these years that he'd left me for another woman and never turned back. The idea made my stomach clench.

By the time Mo finished creating my new look, I resembled a toy poodle more than a human being, but I had leeched every morsel of rumor and innuendo from her until her well had run dry. I glanced at myself in the mirror and deemed my sacrifice worthwhile.

However, if anyone asked if I was housebroken, they'd so live to regret it.

CHAPTER FIVE

Coffee. Tea. or Murder?

Thursday afternoon found Sue Ann and me at the basement-level Independence Police Station, having our fingerprints taken. Sue Ann went first. Then it was my turn. The Independence Police Department was outfitted with all the latest and most up-to-date equipment, including a digital fingerprint machine. It worked kind of like a flat-bed scanner. The officer on duty had me place each palm on a glass pane while it scanned for my fingerprints.

Turning to Sue Ann, I grumbled, "I feel like a criminal."

She had managed to find an old ink pad, probably once used in the bygone days of inked fingerprints. She wiggled her ink-stained fingers at me and made a move toward my face.

After watching the two of us dashing around the room for several minutes, each of us giggling like schoolkids, the officer said, "Don't you girls have something better to do?"

We absolutely did. We had a missing husband to find. The next morning the blackmail payment was due and I had no intention of paying it. Couldn't afford to even if I wanted to pay it. Which I didn't.

I just wasn't sure what to expect come Friday morning. Would the blackmailer reveal Dan's whereabouts?

"Maybe we should leave a note for Brad," suggested Sue Ann.

I glanced at her and my jaw dropped. A flash of inspiration came to me. A simply wonderful and shiny new thought. I'd be more than willing to pay the blackmailer for information on Dan's location. However, there had been no means of two-way communication between us.

I now knew exactly how to reach the blackmailer.

Although I started to tell Sue Ann about my newly conceived plan, I kept my lips shut. There was no point in telling her about my idea. There was no guarantee it would work and, besides, she'd either try to talk me out of it or come up with a crazy twist.

So as she drove me home I remained silent on the subject, letting her chatter about her day and the problems with being a housekeeper.

Once she dropped me off, I immediately put my plan into action. I rushed to my office, without bothering to discard my shoes and bra, both of which I usually toss off as soon as I returned home. My handbag was still strapped to my shoulder when I took a seat in my office chair. The arm of the chair snagged my bag, almost yanking me to the floor.

I quickly shoved it aside and settled in front of my computer. It was "asleep," and I awoke it with a firm joggle of my mouse.

I clicked on my word-processing program, tapping my shoe-clad feet as I waited for it to load. Once the screen appeared, I began typing and didn't stop until I hit the *print* button.

There was one way to reach the blackmailer. It merely required a little effort on my part *vis-à-vis* early rising.

The blackmailer had demanded that I place money into the trash receptacle at five o'clock the next morning.

Instead of money, I'd leave the following note I removed from my printer:

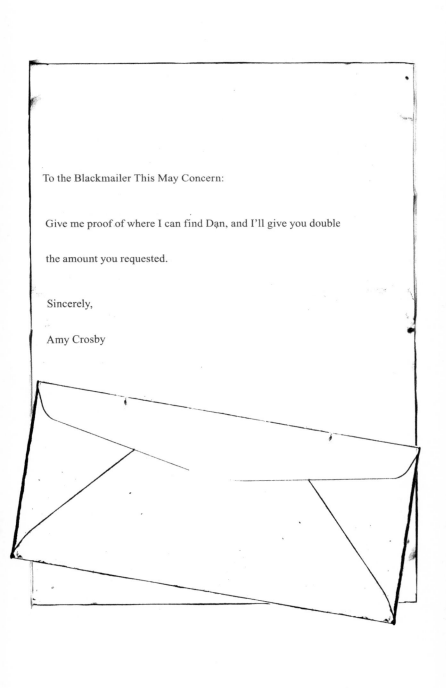

To the Blackmailer This May Concern:

Give me proof of where I can find Dạn, and I'll give you double

the amount you requested.

Sincerely,

Amy Crosby

I had to make the gesture, even though it was unlikely the black-mailer would receive the note. The police would probably stake out the trash bin, but the blackmailer might be staking me out, too.

I had to at least try.

While there are pluses and minuses about working at home, the best benefit is that I can wear anything I like. There's no need to put on makeup or even do my hair. That day I wore my usual comfy writing attire: one of Dan's old T-shirts and a pair of baggy pink pajama bottoms depicting numerous cows with the word "moo" plastered all over it. My tangled hair was pulled back in a scrunchie and I had morning breath. I'd awoken late after having stayed up to deliver the blackmail note, which I'd sealed in a manila envelope. Around three in the morning, I'd dressed all in black and, feeling like a thief, sprinted the short distance to the trash can, deposited the note, then hightailed it back home to bed, hoping Brad would never learn I'd been there.

When I awoke late the next morning, I only felt a little groggy from lack of sleep as I got to work. Comfy clothes are a must when you're tied to a computer. An Internet search for Gayla Mullen turned up nothing, but Sue Ann had sent me an e-mail, promising to do what she could to locate her. The muse was calling, so I went right to work, deliberately trying to ignore the fact that I might hear something from the blackmailer before too much longer.

I tried to practice patience, not my strongest attribute. I've chatted with other writers I met on the Internet about this patience "karma," and they all agree that we must have become writers because patience is a lesson we need to learn. There's not much that can make me happier than a speedy response from an editor on a story I've submitted to her.

I was deeply in the creative zone, writing my next confession about shoplifting, which was what I'd need to resort to if some money didn't come in soon, when I heard pounding on the front door. Although I hated leaving my keyboard, I rushed to the door, hoping for word on the blackmailer. I threw open the front door. "Jerome? What are you doing here?"

Jerome Keller, the man I had been kinda sorta dating, stood with one hand in a half-knock position and the other hand glued to his fancy cell phone. *Kinda sorta* because I wasn't sure of my status: abandoned wife or widow? We'd all known each other forever. He and Dan had been close throughout high school, and he'd been the first to console me when Dan disappeared. Jerome had insinuated himself into my life to the extent he wanted to make our friendship more official. He wanted me to acknowledge our relationship, and I found that almost impossible given the circumstances.

His fastidiously combed blond hair camouflaged the beginning of a receding hairline. Dressed in his customary dark pin-striped suit, he appeared every inch the "successful accountant." Behind him were two men I didn't recognize, clad in basic workman attire: tool belts, jeans, and brown work shirts with the phrase "You Lock It" embroidered over the pocket. One of the men was tall and lean. The other was not so tall but, considering the wide smile that apparently never left his face, was good-natured and jovial.

A small, red truck was parked in my driveway, with the same slogan as on the workmen's pockets, as well as a Wichita address. Jerome's pristine Lexus was parked at the curb near my mailbox.

"I'm here to look after you," he said.

My eyes narrowed. "What's going on?"

"That's my question for you," he replied, then addressed the work-men. "Can you give us a minute?"

They nodded and stepped back while Jerome pulled me into a hug. After a quick smooch (with me worrying about my morning breath), he gave me a gentle squeeze and brushed a lock of hair from my face. "Amy, I just don't know what I'm going to do with you."

I bit my tongue to keep myself from saying something I shouldn't along the lines of *No one asked you to do anything with me to begin with.* Instead I asked, "Why are you here?"

"Because you need me. I know how upset you must be, but I'm here for you. I've always been here for you."

My only excuse for not immediately putting two and two together was writing-brain. The fog hadn't totally dissipated. There stood Jerome, and behind him were locksmiths. It wouldn't have taken a genius to guess what was going on, but I wasn't thinking clearly. "Jerome, I—"

"Don't worry, Amy. I'm going to take care of it. I'm going to take care of you. Let's go get you dressed." He came in the door.

Before I headed to my bedroom, I stopped and turned back to him. "Jerome, what are you talking about?"

A momentary expression of irritation crossed his brow via a slight crease, but it only lasted a second before he said, very calmly, as if I were a child, "Brad called me."

"Oh. He told you about the break-in?" I had no clue Brad was such a blabbermouth, and I resented it.

"The break-in and the snake—" Now he sounded truly whiny. "Amy, why didn't you call me right away?"

"I'm sorry. It slipped my mind." I never thought about calling him—which was probably symptomatic in terms of our relationship. He'd been such a good friend for so many years that I didn't want to hurt his feelings. However, I noted he didn't mention the blackmail note. Brad probably was keeping information about it close to his chest while the investigation continued. "With so much happening at once . . ."

"I'm here now, and we'll get you all straightened out." He reached out and patted my shoulder, and I took a quick step toward the bedroom to change. He turned back to the doorway and motioned for the two men to come inside. "You guys can get started now."

They nodded and turned to examine the front door.

"What are they doing?"

"Brad said you don't have a key, so they're here to change out the locks. We want to make you safe."

It would have been nice if he'd asked me first, but I felt guilty for being so unappreciative of his efforts to protect me. He meant well, even though he treated me like a schoolgirl. I needed to start taking care of myself, but I didn't want to start an argument with him, especially not with an audience.

After quickly changing my clothes and brushing my teeth, I emerged from the bedroom to find Jerome overseeing the locksmiths' efforts. "I'm going to make some tea. I don't suppose you want some?"

"Instant coffee will be fine."

"Would either of you men like something to drink?" I asked politely, but they just shook their heads and continued dismantling my front door lock. Even though it was hard work, the not-so-tall man's smile remained intact.

I headed to the kitchen and Jerome followed. He shrugged out of his suit jacket and wrapped it around one of the kitchen chair backs, then took a seat and waited for his coffee.

So much for taking care of me, I thought, wondering how hard it would have been for him to have offered to boil the water. But I was being mean. He meant well, and in the past I'd always made his coffee. I filled the kettle at the sink, then set it on the burner. I returned to the living room to get teacups from the shelf.

The telescoping shelving was one of Dan's greatest inventions. I'd inherited my grandmother's beloved teacup collection. But we were cramped on space, and there wasn't a good place to display it. So Dan built a shelf around the entire room and invented a method for lowering the shelf so I could easily reach it. The Shelf-a-lator worked on the same principle as a casement window. Because of counterweights, it moved effortlessly and weightlessly. When I grasped the handle and slid it toward me, the motion lowered the shelf so that the cups were easily within my reach.

The tall locksmith saw what I had done and said, "Cool."

"It is, isn't it?"

"My wife would love one of those shelves. Where'd you get it?"

Chewing my lower lip, I considered how to answer. I always felt uncomfortable whenever I wanted to mention Dan to people who didn't know my situation. Jerome had made himself totally at home in my kitchen, and it was apparent we were closer than just friends, so how could I mention my inventor husband? It would sound like he was still around. I couldn't call him my ex, because he wasn't. And I couldn't refer to him as "late," because who knew? I merely replied, "Someone made it for me, but I think you can buy it at the hardware store."

"Thanks. It'll make a great anniversary gift for Sheila. We'll be married nine years in June."

"That's great." Dan and I would have celebrated our ninth anniversary this year, too. If he were around. Years of not having any word of or from him had worn at me, and my heart was bruised and sore. Small things, like a couple celebrating their own anniversary, or two people holding hands, would often open the unhealed wounds. I'd given some thought to this, why such small things could hurt so keenly. I came to the conclusion that it was the very unexpectedness of those moments, the inability to figuratively gird my emotional loins that made them especially painful.

Biting back the bitter taste at the back of my mouth, I chose two delicate teacups and saucers, each with a lovely yellow rose pattern, then raised the shelf. One of the locksmiths went outside to get more tools or something, while the other busied himself pulling hardware out of boxes.

I reentered the kitchen to the whir of the locksmith's electric drill just as the kettle whistled. It took me only a minute to fill the cups with water, spoon in Jerome's coffee, and dunk my tea bag in my cup. As I spun to carry the cups to the table, Jerome glanced up from his cell phone.

It was the type of cell phone that had a slide-out keyboard. His index fingers dashed across the tiny keyboard, probably writing one of his clients a text message. Not only was he a popular accountant in Independence; he also had clients throughout the state. I could only imagine what message was so important that he had to text a client. Considering how the locksmiths kept coming and going, each time bringing more hardware into my house, Jerome was probably suggesting his clients invest in lock companies.

He punched a button on his phone and looked up. "Hey, you."

I didn't immediately reply because, knowing Jerome and his phone fetish, I couldn't be sure whether he was talking to someone on his headset or to me. Considering his expectant expression, I decided he really was talking to me. "Hey."

Dipping my tea bag in and out of my cup, I wondered how to broach the subject of paying for all the new locks with Jerome. For financial reasons, I hadn't replaced them or called out a locksmith to make me a new key. However, if I admitted this to Jerome, he'd want to pay all my bills. He'd make a big deal about collecting all of my outstanding debts, then insist on paying them all off.

I owed him enough already.

Since Dan's disappearance, Jerome encouraged me to think of him as a rock I could lean on. Not that he was controlling. He wasn't. For some reason, I seemed to bring out his strong paternal instincts. He could have had a pet. Instead, he had me.

My financial situation was a touchy subject and, while I genuinely cared about Jerome, I wasn't interested in our relationship progressing further. At least not yet.

But he was determined to look out for me. I'd sworn Sue Ann to secrecy about my fiscal situation. Now I found myself in a pickle. With all those locks, and two men hard at work, it was going to cost some serious cash, and that was the one thing I was incredibly short on.

"Jerome, I wish you'd told me before you called the locksmiths. I can't afford—"

He cut me off. "I'm paying for them. I can't sleep at night thinking someone could so easily enter your house. It's an invitation to mayhem."

When he said "mayhem," I smiled. I loved the way he spoke in an old-fashioned manner, as if he were from a century ago rather than our current age. Even when we disagreed with each other, I was extremely fond of him. "I'm paying for my own locks. But I can't afford all this"—I waved my hand toward the living room—"right now. I'll pay you back."

He leaned forward and gave me a quick kiss, then raised his eyebrows in a semi-leer. On another man it might have been a full-out leer, but on Jerome, it looked more like a Boy Scout eyeing cookies. "We'll talk about payback later."

I sat up straight in my kitchen chair. "No, we won't. I'm not going into debt with you. I will pay you back. It'll just have to be a little at a time, okay?"

"Whatever you want." He looked amused, as if I were a clever child showing off some newfound skill, and it annoyed me. I took a sip of my Acaí Mango Zinger tea, trying to rationalize my feelings. Jerome's reaction was exactly what I'd expected, so why was I so put off? Maybe I just felt particularly sensitive about the money because of the blackmail note and needing to delay having Dan declared legally absent without leave. Or maybe having everyone trying to take care of me had begun to cloy.

I never thought I'd be in a situation of near-desperation when it came to money, but I couldn't lose Dan's and my home. I had to solve the matter of his disappearance so I'd know how to proceed.

"I still don't understand why you didn't tell me about someone breaking in," Jerome said.

He was like a compass. No matter how I misdirected the subject, he kept turning back north. I mistakenly believed I had sidestepped this line of questioning. I deliberately shrugged, as if it weren't important. "I called Brad, so I guess I figured it was in his hands."

"But after the break-in, I would have thought you would call me immediately." He sounded disappointed, as if I'd let him down. It was the same tone my father had used when I'd broken a house rule. My Catholic guilt ate at me.

"I guess I sort of freaked out about it."

He placed his palm over my hand. "I want you to think of me whenever you're in trouble, Amy. You need to know I'm always here for you."

I consciously left my hand beneath his, even though it meant fighting an urge to drag it away because somehow I felt buried beneath the weight of his concern. "I know that. I appreciate it and you."

"Tell me what happened. What did Brad say? Is anything missing?"

I took a few minutes to fill him in on the details, omitting anything to do with my mortgage situation or the blackmail note. No need to go into it with him now. I'd get around to telling him eventually, when the timing was better. "I think the break-in had something to do with Dan's disappearance. It's long past time for me to find out what happened to him."

"That's quite a stretch in logic. What does a break-in have to do with Dan?"

"Call it my latent psychic abilities, but I'm sure they're connected." I wouldn't lie to Jerome, but if I thought he was being overprotective now, I didn't want to think about how he'd react to the knowledge I'd received a blackmail note.

"What are you planning?"

"Right now, Sue Ann is asking around to see if anyone knows the address for Gayla Mullen. I tried finding it on the Internet, but nothing turned up."

"What does Gayla have to do with Dan?"

"She left town around the same time as he disappeared, so we're hoping she might know something about his disappearance."

Jerome's forehead wrinkled. "Once you have Gayla's address, what are you planning to do?"

"Go visit her and ask if she knows anything about Dan."

"That's a very bad idea." He pulled his hand off mine and I felt less trapped.

"You and Sue Ann don't know what you're up against," he continued. "Give the information to Brad and then leave it alone. If this does have something to do with Dan's disappearance, and I'm not convinced it does, there's no reason to deliberately put yourself in further jeopardy."

When I haven't sought advice, I don't much care for the unsolicited sort, and my latent crabbiness began to rise. It didn't matter that he was right. What he couldn't comprehend was how much I had at stake and how that changed things. "Don't you think I'm already in jeopardy? The rattler wasn't in your car."

He raised his hands. "You've made my point."

He didn't get it.

"The authorities don't seem to have any leads on whoever did it. Considering how well they investigated Dan's disappearance, if I want to know what happened to him, I'm going to have to find out myself." The sudden feeling of taking control of my own life gave me an unexpected courage and I found myself liking it.

"The last thing you want to do is draw more attention to yourself."

"I'll try to be subtle."

"We can be certain of one thing. Sticking your nose where it doesn't belong will bring you nothing but grief. What's the rush? Give the information to Brad, and see if he turns up anything."

When I didn't reply, he added, "The break-in and the snake can't be taken as if they're a lark. Brad thinks someone planted that rattler in your car. Someone who knows you well enough to be aware you have car visitation rights. And I don't want them coming after you again."

"What makes you think they won't, even if I don't do anything?"

"Why take unnecessary chances?"

That was the second time in two days a man had told me that. Depression settled on my shoulders. If the blackmailer didn't reveal where Dan could be found, he might go after someone else. I just hoped it wouldn't be Dolores, but my latent psychic abilities warned me otherwise, a totally depressing thought. "I'd just like to know what happened to Dan. I told Sue Ann's husband to hold up on filing the paperwork to have Dan declared . . ." I couldn't finish my sentence.

"Dead." Jerome supplied the word I couldn't utter. "Amy, in all likelihood the man is dead. I loved him, you loved him, but you have to learn to say the word. Dead."

It was a word I'd formed in my head a thousand times. I simply couldn't, wouldn't, use it in reference to Dan. Tears welled in my eyes, but I blinked them away. I would not cry. I had a houseful of workmen, and I would not embarrass myself in front of them or Jerome.

"There's no reason to hold up on the court procedure," Jerome began, but a cat's wail interrupted our conversation.

"Miz Crosby?" called the jovial workman.

The interruption came at a good time, since I didn't know how to explain to Jerome without telling him about the blackmail note. I dashed to the front room, where I saw there truly had been a cat wailing, or rather, a kitten.

The tall locksmith held a brown and white tabby ball of fur, which was screeching up a storm. While he wasn't a tiny kitten, he was far from a grown-up cat. The workman said, "Your cat's hurt."

"What's wrong with him?" I asked.

Jerome, who had come up behind me said, "It's not her cat."

The injured kitten looked up at me with his buttercup eyes, and my heart went out to him. His eyes crinkled shut as he let out another cry, and the workman held him out to me. I gently took the injured animal in my arms, careful to avoid touching his bloodstained and swollen rear leg. "Poor lamb."

"Are you sure he's not your cat? I can hear him purring from here."

He was right. The animal purred and seemed to relax in my arms. When I looked down at him, his silky soft fur, his warm trusting body, I knew I was a total goner. He was too sweet for someone not to be out looking for him. Whoever he belonged to was probably devastated he'd gone missing. "I need to find his owner."

Jerome shot the kitten a glare. "Aren't you allergic to cats?"

"No." I shook my head. I'd always wanted a pet, but Dan was allergic to both cats and dogs. Somehow a goldfish never appealed, so I'd done without. "That was Dan."

"Oh, that's right." He bussed my cheek. "I've got a meeting and need to head out."

"Okay. I'll see you later."

"At least now if you go out, you can lock up." He then handed his business card to one of the workmen. "When you're finished here, just send me your bill."

"Thanks, Jerome," I called as I waved good-bye from the front porch. Still cradling the kitten, I wandered into my kitchen and cleaned up his leg as much as I could without hurting him. I poured some milk into a saucer. He quickly lapped it up, so he must have been hungry. I opened a can of tuna and flaked it onto a paper plate. He purred as he ate, then curled up on the towel I placed on the floor for him and promptly went to sleep.

I'd have to find out whose he was. From the look of his leg, he needed to see a vet. Perhaps the vet would know who the owner was. In the meantime, with any luck, my next-door neighbor Mrs. Mitchell would recognize the kitten so I could return him to his owner.

It didn't take much longer for the locksmiths to finish up. The tall one called me over to explain the new lock system while Mr. Smiley gathered up their debris.

"There's no key?"

He shook his head. "When you're outside and want in, you just punch in a number. You need to think up a pass code—a set of numbers you'll remember." He indicated the keypad, which had two vertical columns of numbers plus a few letters. "I'll turn my head, and you punch it in."

How cool was it that I wouldn't have a key to lose? "How long should it be?"

"A minimum of four numbers, and a maximum of seven."

"Okay." I knew exactly the numbers I would use. It went back to childhood and playing with calculators. Other kids and I discovered we could make words by typing certain numbers and then turning the calculator upside down. I punched in 0-7-7-3-4. Upside down it spells *hello*. "All done."

He turned back and hit a couple of buttons, then nodded. We repeated the process on my back door as well. After taking me through opening and closing the doors and trying the locks a few times, the locksmiths headed out.

The house was truly quiet with everyone gone. I knew I should go back to work on my short story, but all I could do was stare at the new lock on my front door. What I experienced next was probably similar to claustrophobia. There was no sense to it since I'd always been able to lock my doors when I was inside. But I guess emotion isn't always logical.

I glanced at the new lock and chains, and all I could think of was being locked up. I did want to feel safe, but now I felt entombed—buried alive. My heart pounded and beads of perspiration formed on my forehead. Everyone making decisions for me, telling me what to do. And a blackmailer bullying me. There were too many dead ends and closed doors in my life.

I had to escape.

I wanted out.

I needed out.

CHAPTER SIX

A Captive in My Own Home

I had a friend from junior college who I lost track of long ago. Nancy suffered panic attacks. If the door wasn't open in the classroom, she'd feel the walls closing in. If the walkways between buildings got too crowded, she'd break out in a sweat and her eyes would dart back and forth as she looked for a place to hide.

While I sympathized with her, I never empathized. Until now.

Panic kept me rooted to the mat inside my front door for I don't know how long. I needed to leave, but I couldn't get my body to obey my thoughts. *Just open the door.*

Perspiration trickled along my hairline. The walls in my house closed in on me. And I couldn't take my eyes off the new lock and chains.

The kitten thankfully emerged from the kitchen and hobbled toward me beside the front door. He *meowed* his cute little squeak of a sound and looked at the door as if he, too, wanted to be free. His presence thawed the ice in my veins.

"You're my lucky charm," I said as I gently lifted him into my arms and stroked his silky coat. "Let's go outside."

I slid back the chains, twisted the lock, and opened the door. When I stepped onto my front porch, my panic instantly abated and I inhaled the clean outdoor air. Turning to my right, I walked the short distance to Mrs. Mitchell's house. A quick flutter of her draperies let me know she'd watched my approach.

"Maybe she'll know who your owner is," I whispered to the kitten as I climbed the two steps leading to her front door. I didn't immediately knock.

You know how when some women age, they just get sweeter? They turn into that nice little stereotypical granny? Their hair is white, their sight isn't so good, but they welcome you into their home because they just baked the most wonderful cookies and want you to try some?

Mrs. Mitchell is nothing like that.

She's nosy, grouchy, and just a bit scary, but she keeps an eagle eye on the neighborhood.

She opened the door before I had a chance to knock and while her hair was white as snow, her vision was twenty-twenty or better. She narrowed that eagle-eyed gaze on me and I felt the need to confess something.

"If you're here to give me your new key, the answer is no."

"No key," I quickly responded. "I—"

"Whadduyouwant?" she interrupted. "Make it fast because you're interrupting my *muay thai* lesson."

From my prior research into fighting methods, I recognized *muay thai* as being a particularly brutal form of kickboxing. I couldn't rid myself of the image of a nice, sweet little granny kickboxing an opponent into submission. Not that I was shocked in this case, mind you, because Mrs. Mitchell is nothing like her benign appearance.

The kitten mewed, and I jiggled him gently in my arms. "I was wondering if you know who owns him?"

"Why, he's just one of them chapel cats." She looked at me impatiently, as if I was being dense.

"Chapel cats?" I had no clue what she meant.

"You know, Amy." She gestured back behind our houses. "There was a brood of them over at the church. I heard the new pastor ran them off."

"Are you sure he's one of them?"

"They're accidental Maine coons. Started with the Persian the old pastor had. She mated with strays, and after a few years they all had that Maine coon look."

I saw what she meant. With his long fur and tabby markings, the kitten did resemble a Maine coon.

"You should just turn him loose."

How could anyone be so heartless? "I can't do that. He's hurt."

She shrugged. "Just a stray."

"Not anymore." I glanced down at the cute little chap. "You're my cat now, aren't you, Chappy?"

He purred.

"Better take him to the vet. Make sure he's not rabid."

Rabies? Glancing down at him, I didn't see any signs of rabies, not that I'm fully aware of them. But he wasn't frothing at the mouth, and his temperament was friendly rather than ferocious. "I will."

I turned to leave, but she called me back, saying, "What did the detective find out about the robber? Did he catch him?"

"Brad didn't really find out anything. And whoever broke in was long gone. But if you see anyone trying to break in again, please call the police. I appreciate that you called them the other day. I meant to thank you."

"Probably just one of them damn teenagers. Emos."

Emo is short for *emotive*. At first it referred to a type of music, but it's filtered down into a type of style. Emos dress kind of like goths but sadder.

I asked, "Why do you say that?"

She sniffed the air. "Dressed all in black. Had to be one of them emos."

Sounded like the basic cat burglar to me, but what did I know? "Well, thanks." I turned again to leave.

"'Bout time you let me get back to my kickboxing. With break-ins in the neighborhood, a woman can't be too careful or too prepared."

It took all of my willpower not to shake my head. I could only imagine what would happen to the poor guy who tried to break into her home. He'd end up like a human pretzel.

Perhaps I should consider taking *muay thai* lessons, too. *Kee-ah.*

"Have you heard anything?" Sue Ann brushed her bangs from her face as I climbed into her SUV. She'd agreed to take Chappy and me to the vet since she had to run several errands in town.

"Heard anything about what?" I carefully positioned Chappy in my lap, then buckled my seat belt, hoping she wouldn't see I was holding out on her. Since I hadn't heard a peep from the blackmailer (probably too soon), there was no point in mentioning it.

Sue Ann screwed up her mouth in thought. "I guess I was hoping since you didn't pay the blackmail . . ." Her voice trailed off as she pulled out of my driveway, but I knew what she meant.

"Nothing's happened that I'm aware of." It would have made my life much more pleasant and easy if the blackmailer had coughed up Dan's forwarding address. "So much for his whereabouts *not remaining confidential*."

"Maybe the whole thing was just a scam. Someone wanted to get some money out of you."

Chappy evidently didn't enjoy riding in cars, because he started caterwauling up a storm. He dug his little claws into my hand, trying to escape, but I held on as tightly as I could without hurting him. Once he'd settled down and only let out plaintive mews every few seconds, I said, "Everyone knows I live on a shoestring budget. Trying to get money out of me seems rather futile."

If the blackmailer had no plans to give me Dan's location, then he had to have some other motive for sending the note, unless he was just insane. I just wasn't sure what the blackmailer intended and why I was being singled out. Until we learned more, there was no use obsessing over it. "Were you able to find out anything about Gayla?"

"I heard she's living not too far from here now. In Belle Plaine."

Chappy mewed louder as Sue Ann pulled onto Main Street. I stroked his head and he seemed to calm down a little. "Belle Plaine is really close."

"Just over a hundred miles."

"If Dan were with her, I'm sure someone would have spotted him by now. I'm sure I would have heard something, at least some hints." I continued stroking Chappy's head. Between loud meows, he purred, evidently unsure whether to be frightened or thrilled to be in my arms.

"I was thinking the same thing. But Gayla originally went to work at a school down in Oklahoma City. If Dan went with her, it's possible he didn't come back to this area with her."

"True." I shrugged. I just couldn't imagine Dan going with her, no matter what rumors or speculation circulated about their disappearing at the same time. The very concept humiliated me.

Diary of a Confessions Queen

Sue Ann pulled up in front of Dr. Mary Elden's veterinary practice, Paws and Claws. As Sue Ann killed the engine, Chappy stopped crying.

The drab brown building housing the vet clinic had dark tinted windows just below the roofline. They were too high to see into the building, and with the tinting they wouldn't bring in much light. The brown brick and dark-stained wood trim had seen better days. The whole building looked forlorn, as if those who entered might not come out. There were three other vets in the area, and I wondered if I had chosen the right one.

"Quit dawdling," said Sue Ann as she sprang out of the vehicle. I gathered Chappy into my arms and climbed out as well, all the while telling myself that at least I knew Dr. Elden. She was a well-respected vet, and Chappy couldn't be in serious condition considering how he'd squirmed in my arms during the drive over.

After an assistant took my basic information, it didn't take long to get in to see Dr. Elden.

"Oh, is that one of the chapel cats?" Dr. Elden asked as she entered the examination room where Sue Ann, Chappy, and I waited.

"That's what I've been told," I replied.

Dr. Elden approached the stainless steel table I'd placed Chappy on. "How are you doing, Amy? I haven't seen you in a while."

It had been years. Seven years to be exact. I hadn't seen her since the week before Dan's disappearance.

The seven years had been easy on her. There wasn't a wrinkle on her face, and her trim figure hadn't changed. She had been Dan's major competition at chess matches. The two of them were serious rivals, each trying to win or maintain the Independence Cup, the Independence Tavern's highest award for chess aficionados.

"It has been a long time."

"So what do we have here?" She tilted her head, and a smooth sheath of blond hair fell forward as she examined Chappy's injured leg.

I hoped she could do something to help him. Something that wouldn't cost too much. "I'm not really sure what happened to him. I was having new locks installed on my house today, and one of the locksmiths found him."

"Nice of you to bring him in. Not everyone would have bothered."

"I've always wanted a cat, and Chappy seems to like my house."

"Lucky cat. I'm sure you'll give him a good home." She straightened, her blond hair falling back in place. "It doesn't look like a bite. More like a cut. I'm going to take him in the other room and get him cleaned up."

"Okay."

She gathered Chappy in her arms, and I started to follow her to the next room.

"You and your friend can wait here," she said as she left the examination room and disappeared into a hallway behind it. Before she closed the door, I caught sight of cupboards below a long shelf holding a small scale and varied medical equipment.

I turned and smiled sheepishly at Sue Ann, who had taken a seat on the lone chair in the small room. There wasn't much to look at in the room except cat and dog anatomy charts hanging on the walls. I wondered if I ought to be snooping. I hadn't previously considered the idea that Dr. Elden might have a reason to want Dan to disappear, but their mutual lust for the Independence Cup might have been motivation. "How seriously do you think chess players take their games?"

"I was wondering the same thing," Sue Ann replied. "Wasn't there something in the news regarding a world chess competitor who did something to his opponent?"

"That was on the world level. Being the undisputed chess champion in a small town like Independence can't count for much, can it?" My forehead creased and again I consciously smoothed my brow. "You don't think Dr. Elden—"

Sue Ann bobbed her head. "Anything is possible. At this stage, can we afford to rule anyone out?"

Just then the vet in question returned with Chappy. "Good news. The cut wasn't deep enough to need stitches. I cleaned him up and gave him his required shots plus an antibiotic. He should be good as new in a few days."

"That's terrific," I said.

"You'll want to keep him inside until he's fully mended."

"Definitely."

"If you plan to keep him—"

"I do."

"Then I recommend he become a house cat. House cats live longer and remain healthier. The other thing is, he should be fixed."

"I hadn't considered that." I sighed. I didn't know if that would be expensive or not, but quite honestly, if it cost more than twenty dollars, I'd have a tough time paying for it.

"Because he's one of the chapel strays, I can give you a special price today, and the neutering won't cost you anything."

"That's great." The smile I beamed at her had to be enormous. My teeth probably sparkled. This was truly good news compared to what I'd been dealing with lately. "But why don't I have to pay?"

"One of the parishioners created a fund to care for the chapel strays if they're adopted. So far, only a few people have adopted one, so there's plenty of money to take care of your kitten's neutering expenses."

"Thanks. How soon do I need to bring him back for that?"

"We want him healthy, so let's give it a month."

I nodded, but then remembered I needed to discover whether it was possible she had something to do with Dan's disappearance—like offing the competition. "So, how's chess going?"

She lifted one shoulder. "It's okay. Not nearly as much fun as when I had some real competition. Playing against your husband taught me so much. Now it's not the same. But I guess that's even truer for you, isn't it?" Her unsmiling gaze met mine.

"It's been hard. But it's nice to think he's missed by others besides me and family."

"Oh, he's missed." She lowered her shoulder and stroked Chappy. "Sometimes, when I'm playing at the Tavern late at night, I almost expect him to come waltzing in the door, demanding a game." Dr. Elden laughed. "God, I miss him."

Dr. Elden was married, but just then I got the impression that perhaps she'd once had a small crush on Dan. He was truly sweet, so it wasn't much of a surprise.

Sue Ann's gaze met mine. While I thought it seemed as if Dr. Elden was truly fond of Dan, the glare in Sue Ann's eyes said the opposite. How could a look convey so much? But the slight nod of her head told me to go on. "Do you play chess with your husband?" I asked the vet.

"He's not the least interested." She laughed. "He's more into contact sports. Football, basketball. That kind of thing. How about you? Do you play chess?"

"I never learned."

"You should come down to the Tavern, and I'll give you a few lessons," she suggested.

"I might take you up on that," I replied, and she didn't seem the least unhappy over the notion.

It didn't take long to settle the bill, and Sue Ann and I were on our way.

Sue Ann headed west out of the town center on Peter Pan Road. The new Wal-Mart Supercenter seemed to be the best place to buy the items I'd need as a proud new cat owner.

Sue Ann stayed in the car with Chappy while I went inside to purchase a litter pan, a heavy bag of litter, and Cat Chow. I wanted to buy a number of toys, but my wallet was mostly bare, so I settled on a soft, stuffed mouse. Once I returned to the car, Sue Ann headed back toward my place but had to make a couple of stops along the way. Less than three hours after we left, she pulled back into my driveway.

"Can you come in? I'll make you some tea," I bribed.

"Sounds good." She grabbed the bag of litter.

We made our way to my front door and my new keypad entry lock. I kept telling myself, *Hello, hello, hello,* as I approached the door. Balancing Chappy, my handbag, and the other items I'd purchased at Wal-Mart, I saw a pink strip of paper fluttering above the new lock.

As I stepped closer, I saw it was a Post-it note with some writing scrawled on it. Two more steps, and I saw it was written in neat block print. I read the note and my heart stopped.

It said, *At least your house isn't being staked out.*

CHAPTER SEVEN

Bandits Drove Me from My House

"I can't believe it." I reached to snatch down the note. Sue Ann grabbed my arm before I made contact.

"Don't. The police will want to take fingerprints." She placed the bag of cat litter on my porch and it crunched as it hit the wooden slats.

My stomach twisted as I realized the blackmailer had returned. However, it didn't seem my message had been received.

"What do you think the note means?" Any hopes I had of finding out what had happened to Dan were dashed when I realized the trash can had been staked out by the police. I should have thought of that before sneaking out and putting my note in the trash bin. The blackmailer would not have received my note, and would have assumed I'd paid the ransom.

"It means the jerk isn't going to leave you alone."

I couldn't decide whether that was a good thing or not. While I wished the blackmailer would go away and leave me alone, I really wanted to find out if he knew anything about Dan's whereabouts. "What now?"

Sue Ann pulled out her cell phone. "We call the police."

"I just want to go inside and hide my head under my covers."

"Someone might be inside your house right now."

That perked me right up. But then I deflated. I wanted to communicate with the blackmailer, but perhaps it wasn't so great of an idea to confront him in person. What if he was armed?

She flipped open her phone and dialed the police. "Hey, Peggy. Looks like someone may have broken in at Amy's again." She nodded as Peggy told her something. "Okay . . . Uh-huh . . . You got it."

Flipping her phone closed, Sue Ann said, "Peggy said for us to wait right here. Not to go inside. Not to leave this porch."

"Maybe the blackmailer only left the note and didn't break in. I think we should go look to see if there's a broken window or something."

"Brad will be here in a few minutes. Just wait."

That was easier said than done since I had a bundle of teeth and claws in my arms. The problem with adopting a stray was that he wanted to be free and kept struggling in my arms. I managed to rid myself of my purse and bags while still clutching the young cat. "Calm down, Chappy."

His unsheathed claws dug into my chest, and he clambered his way up my body to reach my hair.

"Ouch."

Sue Ann helped me remove his claws, but I wasn't going to let him go. Dr. Elden had said to keep him inside. "Would you mind if I put him back in your car? It's definitely cool enough outside."

"As long as we set up the litter first. I don't relish the idea of him using my Lincoln as a sandbox." She grabbed the bag of litter, and we made our way back to her vehicle.

It didn't take long to pour litter into the new litter pan and deposit it on the floor in the back. Getting Chappy to stay in the SUV was another matter, but at last I managed to close the door with him safely inside and the windows partially open.

Brad's Tahoe pulled onto my street, and I waited for him beside Sue Ann's vehicle while she returned to my door.

"We have to stop meeting like this," I said as Brad emerged.

"What happened to you?"

"What do you mean?"

He closed the space between us and ran his fingertips along my clavicle. I shivered at his touch but didn't step away. When Jerome touched me, it never felt like this—as if I'd been dipped in chocolate fondue.

Brad said, "You're bleeding."

Oh. He wasn't making sexual advances. What had I been thinking? Why had I let myself react to his nearness? I was such a tool. Pointing inside the SUV, I said, "I had a run-in with a scaredy-cat."

Brad looked through the window and raised a lone brow.

I shrugged one shoulder. "I have a new cat."

"So I see. So what's going on? Peggy said you had an emergency."

"It's getting to be a habit." I nodded toward my front door where Sue Ann waited for us to join her. "There's a new note."

"You'd think the guy would have moved on to other victims by now."

"You'd think." At least now I wasn't going all girlish, as I had before. No trembling hands or chattering teeth. I walked Brad to my door. "Did you stake out the trash bin this morning for the blackmailer?"

He nodded. "Routine surveillance. The blackmailer was a no-show."

I took a deep breath. The blackmailer definitely hadn't received my message.

Sue Ann pointed at the Post-it. "We stayed out here to wait for you. Do you think someone's inside?"

Brad grunted, and that frightening glare appeared on his face. "Stay here and I'll go find out."

"The door's locked."

He eyed the keypad. "You got some new hardware."

"Yeah. That's another thing." This time I was the one to glare—at him. The blackmailer wasn't the only one who bugged me. "Why'd you go blabbing to Jerome?"

"Seemed like the thing to do. Someone has to look after you."

"I've been doing a pretty good job of it all these years."

Sue Ann kept a straight face, God love her.

But Brad made a noise that sounded an awful lot like he'd bitten back a laugh. "That why you called me for the third time?"

"Who else am I supposed to call when I'm being blackmailed and my house is being broken into? The FBI? CIA? Mounties?"

"I live to serve."

There was no way I could respond to that one without insulting him. If he'd done such a great job of serving seven years ago, I might not be in this fix. But I knew that wasn't fair. Brad had done everything in his power to find Dan. "Shall I punch in the numbers?"

"Need to dust it for fingerprints first." He flipped open his cell phone and began to dial. "Forensics should be here soon. I'll go look for signs of forced entry."

Great. More waiting.

Brad disappeared around the side of the house, all the while muttering into his cell phone.

I turned to Sue Ann. "I'm going to follow him. If someone's broken in, it'll be easier for me to tell."

"Fine." She leaned against the railing. "I'll wait here and keep an eye on Chappy."

I stepped off the porch and went around the side of the house, where I watched Brad looking at some leaves on the ground. He glanced up. "Looks like someone's been walking around here recently."

I noticed a heel mark on the ground, but it wasn't a full footprint. "Is it from a sneaker?"

"Think so. Anyone else have a reason to be around here? Lawn crew?"

I shook my head. The grass hadn't needed mowing yet. A neighborhood boy always took care of it whenever I called him.

"We'll get forensics to make a print." He stood and pointed toward the window to my office. "Looks as if someone may have entered through that window."

I didn't see any broken panes. "How can you tell?"

"Fresh marks on the hinge. You didn't have any open windows, did you?"

"No. Everything was locked up like Fort Knox." I looked more carefully and saw scrape marks and noted the window hadn't been completely closed. I hoped the jerk hadn't stolen my computer. "You know, whoever broke in might have used the sticky pads on my desk. They're pink, too."

"Good to know. It's likely that whoever broke in put up the note as he left. He's long gone now." Brad finished checking out the area. "Let's check out the back."

"We can go in that way, if you want."

He nodded. "You wait here and I'll make sure no one is hiding inside."

It was a tense several minutes while I waited for him to rejoin me. The entire time he was inside, I worried that he'd be attacked by the burglar.

At last he came back out. "All clear."

My shoulders relaxed. "Shouldn't I check to see if anything is missing?"

"We can do that after the others arrive. They'll dust for prints, and the less traffic beforehand, the better."

I leaned against a tree. "I wish you hadn't told Jerome what was happening. Isn't that against the police officer code or something?"

"Honestly, Amy, I didn't think it would be a problem. You two are an item."

I bristled. That sounded like something Jerome would have said. "Is that what he told you? That we're a couple?"

Brad remained silent in thought for a minute. "He certainly gave that impression."

"We aren't an item. It's not like that with us." I struggled to be truthful, not only with Brad, but with myself. "While we're very good friends, we're hardly a couple. It wasn't your place to tell him."

He looked doubtful. "You've been dating."

"Kinda. Sorta. But nothing serious." I couldn't explain what I didn't fully understand myself, and I was making a mess of it. "Like I said, we're very good friends."

"I wasn't clear on your relationship. Jerome and I were talking. I mentioned the break-in before I realized he didn't know anything about it." His gaze met mine. "Was the break-in a secret?"

I shook my head. "Not really. He gets too protective. You saw the new locks."

"Seemed like a great idea to me. Probably slowed down the burglar, too. More likely to have witnesses as a result."

"Mrs. Mitchell might have seen something again." I hadn't noticed her peeping out the window, but I hadn't particularly been watching for her, either.

"I'll check with her later." Brad pulled out a small notebook and jotted a note. "Where were you?"

"Sue Ann and I took Chappy to the vet, then ran some errands."

"She was with you the entire time, right?"

I narrowed my eyes. "Are you checking to see if I have an alibi for breaking into my own home?"

"Standard detective work."

Men. Just when we were sort of getting along, Brad had to go and suspect me of breaking and entering into my own home. Like I didn't have anything better to do? By the calculating look in his eyes, I knew I should take him seriously, but it wasn't easy. I loved poking at him. In my best matter-of-fact voice, I said, "Yes. We were together the entire time. There wasn't a note when we left. You can check with Sue Ann to make sure I'm telling the truth because she came to the door."

Again he made a note.

"Is it against legal protocol for me to ask you a question?"

"Fire away."

"Why do you think the blackmailer is still after me? I mean, I didn't pay. Shouldn't he have gone and done whatever it is he's supposed to do when I didn't pay? He's tortured me enough. Why continue going after me?"

"Are you asking about the psychology? Amy, the why isn't important. The why might never make sense. The fact is, the blackmailer is pissed because you didn't knuckle under, and he's not going to be happy until you're doing what he wants when he wants it. It's a matter of control."

"So what do I have to do to stop him? This is the third time he's broken in, and my house now has the security of a Brinks truck."

"If I knew the answer, I'd tell you. I don't know how to discourage him. This guy has a screw loose. Look at the piddling amount he wanted you to pay. It's not about money."

"So what is it about?" In my experience, people seemed to be driven by basic urges: sex, money, or power. Could this be about having power over me? "Are you saying he's just a loony?"

"I don't think he's dangerous, Amy."

"You don't *think?* What if he is? What if he planted something else venomous in my house?" If I'd felt panicked before, it was nothing compared to now. My skin was clammy. My heart pounded hard enough to rip out of my chest. "Why don't you think he's dangerous?"

"He's broken in before without doing anything more than trying to scare you. I think that's all he's after."

I fully expelled the breath from my lungs. My tone was composed when I asked, "When will he realize I'm already frightened enough?"

Brad didn't answer, because that was the moment forensics arrived.

Sue Ann had to head out, so we said our good-byes and I waited outside my house with my new kitten. When I held him in my arms, he relaxed and promptly fell asleep.

At last, Brad emerged from my house. "We searched and nothing appears to have been stolen. They'll finish up in a few minutes."

"Thanks," I said, grateful that he'd come out to reassure me. I so appreciated that about him.

He nodded, about to say something else, but a member of the forensics team called him back inside. I wondered what he'd been about to say. Would it have been something to comfort me or something to get me riled up? He had that way about him.

A female officer finally allowed me in to look for anything missing. First, I tucked Chappy and his paraphernalia into the laundry room at the back of the house. I closed the door, and then calling on my unnatural sass to keep me from being scared, I began searching for anything out of place. The first place I checked was my coffee table, just in case another extortion note had been delivered. I came up empty-handed.

Both my TV and my computer were where they were supposed to be. I started over again in the kitchen, making a sweep through the living areas.

When I entered the guest bedroom, something seemed off, like a vibe in the air. I looked around and at first didn't notice anything, but I did notice when Brad came up behind me. I deliberately tried to ignore him, and my gaze homed in on the bed. "There's something wrong here."

Then I saw it. A corner of the bed had been cleared of piles. I pointed to the spot. "I didn't leave it like that."

Brad looked at me with a creased brow. "Like what?"

"Neat."

"Amy, there's nothing neat about this room." His gaze wandered from the stacks of clothing on the bed, to the heap of inventor parts on the floor, to the towers of toppling papers and the mounds of other debris Dan had left spread out all over the house and that I had relocated to this bedroom.

"Look at the head of the bed, near the pillow. You couldn't see the pillow when I left the house."

Brad immediately leaned out of the door into the hallway and called in a member of forensics. A short time later, the detective had lifted all the prints he could find or potentially find. "Have you noticed anything missing?"

"I've been wondering about that. It's not like I have exact recall of what all was in here. There's no specific object I know to be missing. It looks like the burglar moved the pile near the headboard so he could sit on the bed. But I can't figure out why just that one spot, unless he was searching through Dan's things."

"Was there anything of value in here?"

"Not that I'm aware of." There was something rather embarrassing about having all these men and women looking through my disorganized and, yeah, totally messy house. Talk about airing dirty laundry. I itched to get out of the room. Hell, I itched to kick the lot of them out of my house. I inched my itchy way toward the hallway. "I'll go check my office now."

I turned and fled.

When I entered my office, it instantly eased my troubled thoughts. The room is tiny, more like a large closet than a third bedroom. But it was cozy and held all of my favorite items: a stuffed penguin Dan gave me when we were dating, the cute apple-shaped paperweight my confessions editor gave me, and photos of my friends and family.

The room was a soothing mint green, with crisp white trim, making me think of a beachside cottage rather than a down-at-the-heels Midwestern tract house. Taking a familiar seat at my desk, I switched on the monitor.

There was a tab for an open Word document. Odd. I always save my files, back them up, and close them before turning off the monitor. I moused over to the tab and clicked it.

A document opened, but it wasn't one of my stories.

Instead, it only contained a few words. *Since you don't want to know where Dan is, I know who does.*

That one person would be Dolores. Could she survive such an ordeal?

I must have let out a blood-curdling shriek, along the lines of "I do, dammit!" because next thing I knew, my tiny office was filled with fuzz—of the police variety. After the chaos died down, and Brad assured himself that I was okay, I said, "Well, I guess that answers my question about the blackmailer's motives. He or she wanted me to do something I haven't done, like beg for Dan's location. But how I'm supposed to do that without knowing how to reach him or her, I don't know."

"It's perplexing. If the blackmailer had wanted you to respond, surely he'd have demanded something other than cash?"

"It looks like my biggest worry is being realized," I said.

Depression weighted my shoulders. The last thing I wanted was this blackmailer to contact Dolores, but who else could he mean?

"What's your biggest fear? More locks?"

"Very funny." I slugged his arm. "No, I'm worried he's going to go after my mother-in-law now."

His lips thinned. "That's not a good idea."

"You said it."

"Do you know how many reports of alien sightings she's registered with my department?" Brad asked.

"Only aliens?"

"There are sex slavers operating out of the convenience store, terrorists planning to drive a tractor into the hardware store. That's not to mention the weekly grilling she gives me about Dan's disappearance and what I'm doing about finding him."

Obviously I wasn't the only one to suffer through Dolores' delusions. "At least you aren't related to her."

"Saving grace."

"I'm really worried about what she'll do."

"Maybe we're borrowing trouble. Even a psychotic blackmailer wouldn't want to get tangled up with Independence's *charge' d'nuts*. Is there anyone else involved he might go to next?"

"His sister, Liz. Or Jerome."

"If I were the blackmailer, I'd consider either of them better choices."

With any luck, he was right, although my luck seemed to be at low tide lately. "Once you guys are done here, I'll go visit Dolores and Liz. I haven't been to visit them in almost a week, so it won't seem odd, like it would if you showed up at their door. And if neither of them is involved, I really don't want to bring them in on it just yet."

"With the way news travels in Independence, I'm surprised Dolores isn't already camping on your doorstep with her broom to fend off burglars."

I shivered at the thought. The last thing I needed—anyone needed—was Dolores trying to look after me. "I guess I'd better tell her before she learns it from someone else."

For the next three hours, Brad and the forensics team dusted every area of my house. They were extremely thorough.

The only thing they missed dusting for prints was me.

CHAPTER EIGHT

Lovin' the Hand That Beats Me

After what seemed like the entire Independence Police Department left, my house looked like the victim of paintballing. I shrugged. It gave the décor a sort of *je ne sais quoi*.

I left to go next door to speak with Mrs. Mitchell. Just as I approached her yard, Liz pulled into the driveway on the far side of the house, with Mrs. Mitchell in her passenger seat. I wondered where they'd been together, but it explained why I hadn't noticed Peeping-Mitchell earlier.

Liz exited the car first. Mrs. Mitchell opened the passenger door, and a baseball bat rolled out. Liz laughed and scooped it up. "My anti-theft device."

She placed the bat in her backseat. Then the two of them walked over to where I stood near the walkway to Mrs. Mitchell's front door.

"What's going on?" asked Liz, giving me a quick hug. "Mrs. Mitchell said you've had a break-in."

"More like break-ins," I replied with a shrug of the shoulders, not wanting to make a huge deal about it in case Liz might say something to Dolores.

Liz is an attractive woman in that tall, athletic way. She's nearly six feet tall and is well proportioned. In high school she played basketball, softball, and volleyball. She attended college in Wichita for two years before being called home when Dolores had a stroke.

At college, Liz had majored in accounting and was very good with numbers. She'd played on the softball team, and at one point there had been talk of her eventually turning pro.

Her mother's illness had ended all that. Liz ultimately began managing Dan's invention business. Their partnership had been a winning combination, and the business had taken off.

But it all had changed once Dan disappeared. While she continued handling the books as a full-time job, there were no new inventions to market and fewer markets in which to license the inventions that already existed.

I felt sorry for her because her career had stymied before it had truly begun. As a result, she still lived at home with her mother—and while I love my mother-in-law, living with her was something I wouldn't wish on my worst enemy.

To say Dolores is excitable is a vast understatement. Even the bats in her belfry had bats in theirs. Dolores had been one of my grandmother's closest friends. They shared an interest in spiritualism and met weekly for séances and meditation. But even she warned me that Dolores, while kindhearted, was an egg short of a dozen.

I now knew what she was missing—an internal editor. It's that dratted thing that helps me write better, keeps me on the straight and narrow, and tells me when to shut my mouth. It was sadly lacking in Dolores.

As a result, there was always some problem for Liz to deal with. She had to be a saint, considering the multitude of ruffled feathers she'd soothed—from waitresses to physicians to choir directors. The list was endless.

Another of her saintly duties, obviously, was picking up her mother's woo-woo customers who were unable to drive. Although in Mrs. Mitchell's case, that's not exactly correct. She's perfectly able to drive, but her license was suspended for too many speeding tickets. The fact was, nearly everyone in town was trying to keep her off the streets.

"There's been more than one break-in?"

I couldn't very well hide the number of break-ins from Liz since Mrs. Mitchell had probably filled her in on each police arrival at my house.

Mrs. Mitchell saved me from having to think up a speedy reply by saying, "Damn emos. In my day, teenagers had better things to do.

You might need an anti-burglary device of your own, Amy."

She pointed at the baseball bat in the back of the car.

"Good thinking. Dan used to have one out in the garage." Located on the opposite side of my house was the detached garage at the end of my driveway, where Dan's vehicle was entombed. It had been months since I'd ventured in there, fearing a nuclear disaster and spiders. It would be easier to visit the Wal-Mart Supercenter and buy a new bat. "What have you two been up to?"

"Dolores gave me a reading," said Mrs. Mitchell, referring to the tarot card readings Dolores does in order to raise bingo money.

Mrs. Mitchell continued, "Said I'm a cougar and a much younger man is coming into my life."

She seemed delighted, rather than offended by the cougar label, and I felt a shudder of empathy for whoever the young man might be.

While I'm still young enough to find the idea of a younger man somewhat grotesque, I could understand where Mrs. Mitchell's enthusiasm stemmed from.

A younger man would appeal to someone like Mrs. Mitchell. In fact, we'd probably both be attracted to a man of the same age.

"Go for it," I encouraged.

"Reminds me, I need to run," commented Liz.

I glanced up into her face. Even she wasn't as young as she once was. Although she was only a few years my senior, the hours she'd spent out in the sun had taken their toll in fine lines.

"Mom said to tell you she's doing a séance tonight. Trying to contact Dan."

Oh, God. A séance? Had the blackmailer already contacted Dolores? What other reason could there be for her to hold a séance? Until now, she hadn't wanted to contact him for fear she would keep his spirit earthbound. "Why Dan? Why now?"

"Said it was to learn what happened to him," piped up Mrs. Mitchell.

"I'd sure like to know," Liz mused. "A séance, however, won't provide anything definitive, at least not legal evidence. Jerome is coming, and Mom's expecting you to attend."

Guilt chomped at me because I hadn't thought of it before, but I wondered whether the business had insured Dan's life. If it had, Liz had a strong financial reason to want to know if he had met his maker.

"Is there key man insurance?"

Liz paused for a long, drawn-out moment before replying, "We always intended to get around to insuring both of us but never did, unless Dan took out some insurance without telling me."

"I think he would have told one of us if he had," I said. While I was reassured that my dawdling on having Dan declared legally checked out hadn't had an ill effect on Liz, I felt for her. Not only had her brother disappeared without a trace, but the way she made her living was slowly drying up. I reached out and patted her arm reassuringly. If the life insurance he took out with me as beneficiary paid off, presuming he was no longer alive, then after paying off the mortgage, there should be a little left I could share with Liz. Considering the situation, that was presuming a lot. Dan could be anywhere or nowhere. "Maybe the séance will give us an idea what happened to Dan."

Liz shook her head. "I don't think we'll learn anything tonight." Liz was a secret unbeliever. She'd never be able to cohabitate with her mother if Dolores knew. In general, Liz kept her skepticism to herself, especially in front of Dolores' paying customers. No one in their right mind would get between Dolores and her bingo money.

My gaze darted to Mrs. Mitchell, then back to Liz. "Any particular reason why you don't think she'll reach Dan tonight?"

She shrugged. "If Dan wanted to contact us, he'd have done so long ago."

Her words hung in the air for an awkward moment. I narrowed my eyes. Did Liz mean from the other side, or was she implying Dan was still alive? Maybe all these years she'd known something the rest of us didn't. After all, they were business partners as well as blood relatives. If she knew something, though, surely she would have said something or given me some hint. I had cried so many tears back then, and she'd sat with me through many late and lonely nights. She couldn't be cruel enough to keep vital information from me. Finally I asked, "You still think Dan's alive?"

"Who knows? I sure don't," Liz said. Her face didn't indicate any emotion, and I couldn't tell what she was thinking.

She was a puzzle; a woman not easily read. If she didn't want to let something slip, she wouldn't. No amount of cajoling on my part could get her to speak further.

Chewing my lip, I wondered if the blackmailer had already contacted her. How could I ask without giving myself away?

My chance to act passed because she turned and walked back to her car.

"When does the séance begin?" I asked.

"Eight o'clock," she answered as she opened the driver's-side door.

"Who else will be there?"

The list she mentioned included everyone I had suspected of possibly knowing something about Dan's disappearance, with the exception of Gayla Mullen. Very interesting. Had it been deliberate on Dolores' part? "That seems like an odd assortment of people."

"Mom's got a new psychic medium who chose the guest list based on tarot card readings."

Her psychic must be good since she'd managed to gather most of the people I suspected might know something about Dan's disappearance. "Please tell Dolores I'll be there, but I'm bringing Sue Ann."

If anyone could get information out of Liz, it was Sue Ann. She was much better at being sneaky.

"Bringing Sue Ann is so not a good idea, Amy. The last time . . ."

She trailed off, and I knew it was because she didn't want to mention the fit Dolores had back then, calling Sue Ann a filthy skeptic and saying her congested aura messed up the etheric vibrations.

"Sue Ann's done a total one-eighty," I insisted. "Believes in everything hocus-pocus now."

"When did this enlightenment come about?" Liz's voice dripped irony as she stood wedged between the car door and the driver's seat.

"It's been recent." It was my turn to give a nonchalant shrug. I needed Sue Ann to attend. Having her there would help me endure one of Dolores' séances, and she would help me watch our suspects.

"Any particular reason she had a change of heart?" Liz settled into her car.

"I'm not sure. But I bet if you ask her tonight she'll tell us all about it." Heh. A small surprise for my best friend in all the world. Merely a small token of my gratitude for ratting me out about not having a house key.

Liz appeared to be unconvinced, but she couldn't very well call me a big fat liar to my face. She'd wait until I was out of sight. She said,

"I'll see you later then."

Mrs. Mitchell and I watched as Liz drove off.

"Better go give myself a facial. My young man might turn up at the séance tonight and I want to look my best." She tilted her head coyly. On some older women, the look might be cute and appealing. On Mrs. Mitchell, it was a nightmare.

"You always look good, Mrs. Mitchell." I crossed my fingers behind my back, but it was true that she never left her house without having her hair neatly arranged or without makeup. "Maybe you could give me some cosmetic tips?"

"What? Aid and abet the competition?" she asked with a cackle, then toddled inside her front door, leaving me alone to contemplate the cracks in the concrete sidewalk.

The sidewalk made a great metaphor for my investigative progress in "The Case of the Missing Husband." There were lots of clues, I was certain, but I couldn't figure out any way to connect them. Each trail I followed led me further and further from the central question of what had happened to my husband.

Since Mrs. Mitchell had been with Dolores and Liz during the last break-in, she wasn't any help in identifying who was behind the blackmail note and break-ins.

With a sigh, I picked my way through the still winter-brown grass in my yard to check my mailbox at the curb. I glanced up at my redbud tree. Tiny knobs had formed on the no longer barren branches, promising flowers to come.

It was with only a small amount of trepidation that I swung open the door on my mailbox. The first item I saw was an envelope from *True Lies*. It was exactly the right thickness for a check. Finally some money.

The bundle of mail danced into my happy palms. The excursion to purchase necessities for Chappy had depleted my budget, and now I wouldn't have to live off the half-empty box of instant rice in my cupboard. A girl needs protein.

I flipped through the envelopes as I sashayed back to my door. A second envelope from *True Lies,* this one thicker, indicated another publication release. Yay.

Electric bill, gas bill, two advertising flyers, a slim catalogue from an office supply company, and—

A letter from my mortgage company. It had to be another foreclosure notice.

Damn.

What was I going to do?

Not only were my options running out. Time was running out, too.

CHAPTER NINE

Seduced by a Ghostly Lover

Since Sue Ann had to finish up a housecleaning job before going to the séance, it meant I had to ride my bike over to Dolores'. When I was ready to pedal over, I heard Mrs. Mitchell's distinct rap at my door.

"Thought we could drive over together," she said.

She'd gotten all dolled up. Not only was her hair done and makeup perfect, but she wore a very cute little sundress revealing the perfect amount of ankle and bosom. "Sorry. Sue Ann's not driving me tonight. She's going directly to Dolores'."

"Works for me to ride with you."

If she thought I was driving the death trap in my garage, she was sadly mistaken. "On my bicycle?"

"In *my* car."

Sometimes I'm a little slow off the mark. "I thought your license was suspended."

She patted the curls on the side of her head. "Yours isn't."

"Oh. Ohhh." Mrs. Mitchell owned a beautiful boatlike Cadillac Eldorado convertible. The claret-colored car was in pristine condition with very little mileage and had to be at least thirty years old. It had lived in her garage its entire life, other than the short hair-raising excursions she'd made in it until her license had been yanked. And she wanted me to drive it.

I couldn't help the huge grin plastered on my face. "I'd love to."

"Splendid. I've already pulled the car into your driveway."

I briefly closed my eyes, wondering if she'd taken out my mailbox or landscaping en route. "Is the top down?"

"Wouldn't go anywhere with it up," she replied.

With that assurance, I braved opening my eyes again and gazed past where she stood on my stoop. A streetlight penetrated the dusk and illuminated my yard. There in my driveway, the ancient Cadillac called to me, sans items large or small sticking out from under or around it. A good sign.

"Okay. Let's go," I said, stepping onto my porch and closing the self-locking door behind me, all the while half-fearing the blackmailer would visit while I was out. If so, he'd find notes plastered all over my house stating that I was willing to pay, and pay big, for Dan's where-abouts. I had nothing to lose, just in case.

Getting into the Caddy to drive sent a thrilling sense of freedom through me. For once, I got to be the driver in control instead of being ushered around. The sense of joy put me in good spirits and gave me a renewed sense of energy. No crazy, scheming blackmailer was going to bully me.

I swung that Caddy out of my driveway and onto my street. Dolores lived only a few blocks away, but her nineteenth-century historical registry home was on the other side of Main, in the block of East Myrtle just before it dead-ended into Burns Street at the Verdigris River.

Mrs. Mitchell growled above the wind noise, "Put the pedal to the metal, Amy."

I happily complied, within reason. I didn't want Brad to have a reason to take away *my* license.

"Wimp," muttered Mrs. Mitchell.

But there was nothing she could say to shatter my good mood. Even though there was a chill in the spring air, Mrs. Mitchell had thoughtfully cranked up the heat, so it felt more like a windy summer day. It took only minutes to reach Dolores' home, and I hated for the drive to end. It had been a very long time since I'd driven a car, and I'd almost forgotten how freeing it is to have a set of wheels beneath you and plenty of gas in the tank.

"That was awesome," I said, turning off the ignition. "Do you think—"

She cut me off. "No way. I'm getting my license back next week."

How'd she know what I was about to ask? "Well, if you ever need a driver, you know who to come to."

A short time later, we found ourselves seated in Dolores' dimly lit dining room. The extra large room was furnished entirely in Victorian antiques, down to the carpet beneath the monstrous table and chairs. The table could comfortably seat twenty, and even more if she extended it. Tonight, however, it had been set up for twelve.

Dolores had greeted each of us as we'd arrived and directed us to our appointed positions at the table. That, too, had evidently been determined by tarot cards.

Although the table wasn't quite circular, if you imagined the face of a clock, Dolores sat at midnight. Based on her peculiar behavior, one would think she'd be wearing some incredible costume for a séance. That wasn't her character. She looked every bit the society woman, wearing a single strand of pearls at her neck and a sleek custom-tailored suit. It wasn't her physical appearance that was odd.

Nope.

Looking at her, one would never expect to find the eccentric that lay beneath her refined exterior. When new people met her, they considered her to be perfectly charming. And she could be. However, once her latent loony surfaced, people couldn't escape quickly enough.

Yet I'm extremely fond of her. In her own wacky manner, she's done her best to look after me in these difficult circumstances and make sure I still felt like a member of the family.

To Dolores' right at the table, in the eleven o'clock position, was Karen Tanke, an attractive woman in her midforties. I'd never met her before, but I immediately warmed up to her when she told me all about the trip she and her mother had just made to the Bahamas.

That was before we took our seats and Mrs. Mitchell whispered that Karen's mother had passed away nearly a decade earlier.

O-kay.

Now I was seated in the nine o'clock position beside Karen, and we were holding hands. To my right, in the eight o'clock position, was an empty chair. At seven o'clock Mrs. Mitchell was seated, and our hands were joined across the empty chair. At six o'clock was the other Independence inventor, Fred Cook.

His wife, Yvonne, the high school administrator, wasn't with him. It wasn't unusual since it was rumored their marriage was on the rocks.

At one time, Fred had worked for the military. He'd invented a number of weapons of not-so-mass destruction, before retiring and spending his time creating inventions for the general market. He and my husband had been competitors, each trying to one-up the other on the most outlandish invention; hence, my band saw-slash-coffeemaker combination. And the lawn mower-slash-washing machine in my garage. It had never quite worked properly, unless you wanted very clean mangled strips of sheet. It was sort of like a laundry shredder.

Sue Ann was seated at five o'clock and was a little pissed about not being seated beside me. To her right was Liz. Dr. Elden was seated at three o'clock, directly across the table from me. Jerome sat between her and Dolores, rounding out our group. The chairs at two, ten, and eight o'clock were empty.

In the center of the table Dolores and Karen had placed a number of items, such as a tambourine, paper and pencils, handbells, and a small glass tumbler filled with water. So far we hadn't heard any movement in the room, nor had any of the items made noise, but Dolores was just getting warmed up.

"We've waited long enough for our other guests to arrive. Shall we get started now? Liz, if you'll turn off the lights."

Liz immediately turned off the switch controlling the lights. It had been dim before, but now the room was draped in shadow.

Dolores' voice dropped an octave as she cried, "I call on the spirits present to make themselves known!"

No response.

"Speak, move one of the items on the table, or knock," she commanded.

Immediately, we heard a loud rap and several people drew in noisy breaths.

Had we been contacted by the spirit world? My heart skipped a beat.

The knocking sounded again, and I sheepishly realized where it was coming from. For a moment there, I thought Dolores had been onto something. "It's the front door."

"Oh," said Dolores with pleasure in her tone. "That must be Bradley."

Liz hadn't mentioned Brad would be attending, and my heart, which had skipped before, now did cartwheels.

We heard Dolores' chair squeeze back from the table on the wooden floor; then instantly the room was flooded with light. My gaze fell on Sue Ann, who mouthed, "Loony bin," to me.

I deliberately turned away, not wanting anyone else to see that rather than the believer I professed her to be, she remained the total skeptic. If she wasn't careful, she was going to get both of us kicked out.

Brad entered the room. How interesting that he had been invited. Perhaps he, too, realized the séance was rife with suspects? He wasn't wearing his usual coat and jacket, but instead wore jeans and a dark T-shirt. Have I mentioned how good he looks in blue jeans?

I turned back to face Jerome, who stood and shook Brad's hand. I thought at first Jerome would take the empty seat beside me because he took a couple of steps my way, but Mrs. Mitchell wasn't having any of that.

She called out to Brad, "Hey, sweetie. Dolores assigned you this chair. Come over and sit by me. I promise not to bite."

She gave him a girlish giggle, and I saw that she'd crossed her fingers behind her back.

Brad did as instructed, totally unaware of the designs she had on his—virtue. It was obvious to me that Mrs. Mitchell had decided he was the younger man mentioned in Dolores' reading.

Whatever.

What I hadn't taken into account was the fact that I would have to hold Brad's hand—in front of Jerome, and in the dark. What I also hadn't taken into account was the warmth of Brad's hand holding mine. Those electric-like zings I'd come to associate with Brad started ping-ponging along my nerve endings, heating up the space between our palms. The last thing I wanted him to think was that he made my palms sweat, but . . . he made my palms sweat.

He gave my hand a little squeeze as Dolores dimmed the lights again and began her schtick. Of course, that set me to wondering whether he'd deliberately squeezed it or if it was an unintentional nudge. Should I squeeze back?

I squeezed, very slightly. Enough to let him know I'd received his squeeze, but not enough to be an all-out "I'll see your squeeze and raise it."

It was hard to concentrate on what Dolores was doing when I was so busy paying attention to Brad and those zings. I had the impression she was calling on the spirits to *come forth, come forth*, but I was busy squirming in my chair. Had I embarrassed myself by squeezing Brad's hand?

My squirming stopped the minute the rapping started. At first I figured someone had knocked against the table. The rapping became louder, moving around the room in a circular pattern. A cold gust of wind came out of nowhere, causing the tablecloth to shudder and the draperies to billow.

Mrs. Mitchell gasped when the tambourine on the center of the table jingled. I didn't blame her. I gasped, too. But mine was more from Brad giving my palm a warning squeeze. I don't know how I knew it was a warning to keep my lips zipped, but I simply knew. Maybe that latent psychic bent of mine.

Dolores called out, "Is that you, Daniel?"

The tambourine again jingled, but what did it mean? Was someone on the other side trying to tell us something?

"Jingle once for yes and twice for no," instructed Dolores, who must have had the same question.

Immediately, the tambourine jingled once. Although the room was dark, there was still enough light filtering in from the streetlight through the draperies for me to see that everyone gathered still held hands around the circle.

I tried a small experiment, lifting my knee and banging it on the underside of the heavy mahogany table. The tambourine remained silent, although Brad caught on to what I was doing and gave my hand an encouraging tiny squeeze.

I didn't need the distraction.

What I needed was to know what was making the tambourine play on command. It couldn't really be Dan, could it?

"Is this my son, Dan?" continued Dolores.

One jingle.

"Did the sex slavers kidnap you?" Dolores asked.

Two jingles.

Brad, a total copycat, tried banging the table with his knee. The water glass wobbled, and the table beneath my hands vibrated, but the tambourine remained silent. Brad cursed under his breath, as flummoxed as I was about what was making the tambourine jingle.

"Aliens take you up in their saucer?" she asked.

Two jingles.

"Nuns get you?"

Two very angry sounding jingles.

Dolores asked, "Are you on the other side?"

The tambourine sounded five times. What did that mean?

Dolores rephrased her question, "Dan, have you passed away?"

One jingle.

I didn't know what to think as Dolores began to quietly cry. I glanced around the table at the shadowy faces of the other participants. I couldn't see their expressions, but I imagined they felt the same disbelief, mixed with fear of the unknown, as I did. Except for Karen.

I could see her more clearly since we were seated so close to each other. She smiled and nodded with approval, as if this was exactly what should be happening. I suppose it should be, if one believed in the ability to contact the otherworld.

If this was truly my husband, surely he would find a way to let me know.

Because Dolores apparently couldn't continue, Karen stepped in. "Dan, if this is you, please feel free to use my body to communicate with us." She abruptly slumped forward, and I wondered if this was some sort of parlor trick, when just as abruptly she raised her head and sat straighter in her chair.

"Am-my," she said in a low timbre. Was this supposed to be Dan?

I bit my lip, not sure what to do, when Brad nudged me with his elbow. "Say something."

"Yes, I'm here," I said. My tone came out much more wobbly than I wished, but there was nothing to do about it. I coughed to clear my throat. "I'm here."

"Get the insurance. The insurance is for you."

How did Karen know about the insurance money? "But we don't know where to find you."

"I'm here. Waiting. For you."

Great. Just what I wanted to hear. Some unearthly creature was on the other side waiting for me. It didn't matter if it was truly Dan or not. It creeped me out.

Karen slumped again, and there was a long moment of silence. I figured the séance had come to an abrupt end. But suddenly, Karen opened her mouth and yelled, "Bastard!"

Was Dan calling me a bastard?

Karen raised her head and pointed at Fred. "Thieving bastard. What's he doing here?"

Fred visibly shook with anger. "Me a thieving bastard? Why, you low SOB. You stole my tomato pickler."

"That was mine. After I'm gone, you go and steal my battery charger. It was worth a fortune."

Fred shook on his seat. "Did not steal it from you. It was my idea. What about my idea for the electronic high chair?"

"Your idea? Why, you horse thief. I'm waiting for you, too. Just wait until I get my hands on you."

A high wind howled through the room and if ever I doubted this was indeed Dan, I did no more. We were being subjected to some kind of otherworldly inventor pissing contest. It had to be my missing husband.

The tambourine jingled and banged against the table. The handbell levitated and rang, then flew through the air and would have struck Fred on the head if he hadn't ducked in time. Guess he'd been expecting it.

At that moment, that exact microsecond, it occurred to me that if Dan was on the other side, he wasn't ever coming home to me. He was—dead.

"Oh my God. Dan's dead," I said, verbalizing a word I hadn't been able to spit out of my mouth for years. Seven years of pent-up worry, of not knowing, of anger and dread surfaced. I began to cry convulsively and couldn't stop, no matter that someone had turned the lights back on and Sue Ann and Liz were leaning over me, trying to comfort me.

At least I think that's what Liz was doing as she banged on my back. Either that or she was trying to knock me senseless. Sue Ann had the forethought to grab my hand and drag me from my chair. "I'm taking her to the ladies' room."

I did what I could to keep up with her as she yanked me out of the room, but by that time my convulsions had turned into hiccups.

"We'll splash some water on your face, and that will make you feel much better," she assured me as she led me into the guest bathroom. I did as she instructed, and the cool water did help me calm down.

"All this time, I was hoping Dan would come home, Sue Ann."

"I know, honey," she said, patting my back. "This is going to change things. Brad will investigate Dan's death, and this time he'll find out what happened to him."

I barely had the energy left to nod. I needed sugar. I needed chocolate. Then I remembered.

Stooping beneath the bathroom cabinet, I felt around until my fingers came in contact with the object of my intent. I grabbed that Tootsie Roll, unwrapped it, and popped it whole into my mouth. It was only a little hard—and fuzzy.

Sue Ann asked, "Did you hear all that about Fred stealing Dan's inventions?"

My jaw teeth became hopelessly embedded in the candy. I could only nod in response to her question.

"The battery charger has been worth a fortune. That could be a damn good reason for Fred to want Dan to disappear—so Fred could beat Dan to the patent office."

Again I nodded. My teeth wouldn't separate. At this rate, I wouldn't be able to speak until the candy dissolved, and considering how old it was, that might take weeks.

"Now that this is a murder investigation, we're going to have to be a lot more careful."

I nodded vigorously.

"Now that you've calmed down, are you ready to go back out there?"

I shook my head. Until I could talk again, I wasn't ready to go anywhere. I stuck my index finger in my mouth and tried to pry open my jaw.

"Still having hysterics?"

Whew. It came loose. "Hysterics? I never have hysterics. The candy was stuck."

"Honey, if that wasn't hysterics, I don't know what is. That séance stopped so fast, I almost got whiplash."

"I was crying."

"You were shouting, "Dead. Dead. Dead."

"I wasn't."

"Yeah, you were. What did you think happened?"

"I wasn't thinking. I was too busy reacting to Dan's spirit appearing. It's like a nightmare gone bad."

Sue Ann snorted as she led the way back to the dining room.

"Wait," I whispered, peeking into the room before the others saw us. I didn't want to go back in just yet, not if they were waiting for entertainment in the form of crazy Amy.

Liz was pale, as if she'd seen a ghost. Well, she sort of had. Jerome was in conversation with Brad, and by the annoyed expression on Jerome's face, I could tell he was upset about something. Whether it was because of my behavior or something Brad was telling him, I wasn't certain.

Karen and Dolores stood near the heavily draped bay window. Dolores, apparently back to her normal, abnormal self, spoke to Karen, waving her arms with broad gestures.

Thankfully, everyone seemed busy and didn't appear to be gossiping about me. When we entered, everyone grew silent, as I feared they might. It was better to get the humiliation over with in one fell swoop. I announced, "All better now."

"Good." Jerome crossed the room to join us. "I was worried about you."

He hadn't been the one comforting me when I'd left with Sue Ann, so I wondered how worried he'd actually been. He'd looked horrified, presumably by my actions rather than the whole visited-by-a-ghost situation. He seemed to take that pretty much in stride, maybe because all along he'd believed Dan wasn't alive. I let it drop.

"I guess the séance is over now." Only Fred, Dr. Elden, and Mrs. Mitchell were still seated at the table. Fred examined the tambourine in his hands, probably looking for wires.

"Karen suggested we disband for the night." Liz said. "Things got out of hand, and she's psychically drained from Dan using her as his vessel."

I started to say something about the vessel bit, but felt rather guilty because Liz didn't look like her usual self. She looked ashy beneath her healthy tan. She was subdued and timid, when she was normally boisterous and in good spirits.

Good spirits?

Now wasn't the time to get caught up on puns and wordplay.

That was when I noted Brad had his back to the wall. I raised my eyebrows. Was it normal cop behavior on his part—standing back and assessing the suspects?

Although I wasn't quite sure what he suspected the others of. After Karen's possession, I feared he might be even more suspicious of me.

I swallowed. Hard.

There had been no doubt in my mind that indeed Dan's spirit had been with us. And that he was no longer among the living. His behavior, through Karen, was entirely spot-on, even though they'd never met in life.

I wasn't quite sure what his death meant for my situation. The only clarity I had was his directive to get the insurance and thus save our—no, *my*—home. I'd grieved so entirely after his disappearance that I didn't think I could have anything left, but sadness enveloped me like a shield now. Knowing he had passed provided the closure that had been entirely missing in my life, yet his appearance at the séance added more questions to my list. First, I needed to know exactly what had taken him away from me.

Everyone seemed to be waiting for my next outburst, considering how they watched me from the corners of their eyes as if afraid I might catch them watching me. But I had gotten myself under control again and would act as if everything was normal, although nothing was or would ever again be.

I approached Brad, with Jerome following close behind. Brad's brow was knotted in thought. Placing my wrists together and extending my arms toward him, I asked, "Ready to take me in for questioning?"

"For what?" asked Jerome.

"Suspicion of doing away with my husband?"

"Not hardly," replied Brad. "No proof Dan's dead, much less murdered."

"What kind of proof do you need? You heard him, er, her. He's on the other side."

He shrugged. "That's not evidence."

"Come on, Brad. At least now you can maybe—look harder?"

"I'll be doing exactly that, Amy. There seems to be a whole group of folks who are happier with Dan gone." He nodded over my shoulder, toward the room. I turned and immediately knew exactly what he meant.

Dan's mother, Liz, and I were the only ones who mourned him. No one else in the room seemed to care one way or the other whether he was dead or missing.

Perhaps they'd each made their peace and moved on in a way I hadn't been able to—or perhaps, as Brad hinted, they had good reasons to wish him ill.

Jerome nudged my shoulder, and I glanced up at him.

"What is this I hear about another break-in at your house?"

The dirty look I shot at Brad could have felled lesser men. I shrugged and, in an effort to lessen the tension, said, "I guess all the locks in the world can't keep someone out if he's determined enough."

"How did he get in?" Jerome asked.

Brad answered, "Window."

"Any idea who's doing it?"

"Not much physical evidence, but we do have a partial footprint."

"I'm going to have to do a better job looking after you, Amy." Jerome placed a protective arm around my back. "C'mon. I'll drive you home."

"Can't. I drove."

"What? Your bike? It'll fit in my trunk."

"No. Even if I had ridden my bike, I wouldn't want it to mark up your nice car." I waved my hand toward Mrs. Mitchell, still seated at the table. "I drove Mrs. Mitchell's Cadillac."

Brad visibly shuddered. "Mrs. Mitchell? You gotta watch that woman."

"What do you mean?"

"Why do you think I'm standing with my back safely planted against the wall? It'll take a week for my bruises to heal." He made a pinching motion with his thumb and forefinger.

It took me a second, but then I realized he meant she had pinched him on his backside. I grinned. "When I'm her age, I'd love to have as much energy and vim as she does."

"I'd call it a general cussedness." Brad's expression was stoic, but I knew he was joking.

Our eyes met, but the joke seemed to go over Jerome's head.

"Come on, Amy. I'll follow you home."

"Okay. See ya later, Brad." I left the men and approached Mrs. Mitchell. "About ready to head out?"

"Suppose so," she said glumly. "Not much action here tonight."

"I thought it was more than enough action."

"Not the kind I mean." She gave a bawdy wink. "Let's roll."

"You got it. Let me say good night to Dolores." You had to hand it to Mrs. Mitchell. She was always entertaining.

She came with me over to the bow window, where I gave Dolores a hug.

"Thanks for setting up the séance tonight. Even though I'm not happy Dan has departed this earthly plane, I feel a sense of relief in knowing he's okay and moved on."

"It's never a good idea to call on the dead too soon after their passing. The time was finally right, and Daniel came through for us."

This was why she hadn't held a séance to contact him before. I guess spiritualists believe a spirit might get stuck on our earthly plane if they're contacted too soon. The spirit might want to stay with the people they love.

Dolores wrapped me in her soft embrace. "Having the séance tonight was the least I could do, hon. I know those stories about sex slavers ate at you."

I opened my mouth to object, but shut it. Tight.

She meant well. I gave her a gentle squeeze, then stepped back. "I'll see you in a day or two, then."

"Okay, hon. You'll be careful, won't you?"

"I'm always careful." You'd think everyone, especially my mother-in-law, would know that about me.

Karen spoke up in a low timbre. "Not as careful as you should be. My spirit guide tells me there's a sense of danger around you. Take extra precautions."

Concern cloaked Dolores' usually benign face, and an iota of doubt crept into my mind. Karen seemed to have a direct line to the afterlife. I should probably do as she suggested and be extremely cautious.

"Now, don't you worry," said Mrs. Mitchell. "Amy's beau and I are going to keep a good eye on her."

Just what I needed.

"You bet," said Jerome, joining us. "I'm making it my new mission to look after Amy."

"Watch after yourself, too," Karen told Jerome. "I'm sensing something about you, as well. Your time may be near, but it's not too late."

She reached out and touched his hand, but he quickly pulled it out of her reach.

"I'm not usually an alarmist," she said, "but you need to keep yourself on your own business. Don't stick your nose in where it doesn't belong."

Like Jerome could ever mind his own business? I snorted. Loudly. Couldn't help myself.

Their eyes all turned to me, and I tried to cover by faking a cough. "Time to go," I said and marched toward the entry, not concerned with whether any of them came along. I had Mrs. Mitchell's car keys and a ticket to ride.

A short time later, I pulled Mrs. Mitchell's Cadillac into her garage, rather pleased with myself that I'd managed to do it without hitting the boxes, tools, and other household debris piled up on the side of the garage.

"Thanks for letting me drive."

"No, Amy. Thank you for driving." She stepped out of the car. "Would you and your young man like to come in for coffee?"

Jerome had followed us as promised and parked at the curb in front of my house. I was itching to work on a new idea I had for a story about telephone psychics, and I knew Jerome was planning to search my house before giving me the go-ahead. "Can I take a rain check? It's been a long day."

She agreed and headed into her house as I walked to my door, where Jerome joined me.

"Good job driving," he commented, as if he were surprised.

"I guess it's like riding a bike. It comes back to you." I pushed the buttons to unlock my front door, and Jerome opened it.

"Let me check first to make sure you haven't had any visitors."

Bowing to the inevitable, I waved him ahead of me. "Knock yourself out."

One part of me was glad he was willing to make sure everything was okay in my home. Yet a new internal voice unexpectedly bristled with annoyance.

Most people would be filled with appreciation at his gesture, but since Sue Ann hadn't come to help me clean up after the last police visit, I felt otherwise. I'd done very little, other than remove the worst of the dust they'd spread everywhere. The floors hadn't been vacuumed or mopped, and fingerprint dust remained on most of the windows and doors, not to mention my usual state of household disorder.

Having Jerome witness my chaos was somewhat embarrassing. Yet nothing would discourage him from playing hero to my damsel in distress.

He quickly walked through my house, without commenting on the mess, thank heavens, and I followed close behind him. If someone was in the house, he might need my help.

He started in my bedroom, even kneeling to check under my bed and patting down the hanging clothes in my closet. Next he went to my office. Nothing appeared to be changed.

"Maybe you should start your computer to make sure there are no new messages?"

"Okay." I took a seat at my desk and fired up my desktop computer. It was neither a new nor fast computer, so it slowly began the process of loading. "It'll take a few minutes."

While I waited, Jerome checked the office closet, then went into my guest bedroom.

Just as the desktop finished loading, Jerome returned. "All clear."

I moused to my word processor, but there wasn't anything new. "All good here, too."

"Everything seems fine. I'll check the other part of the house before I go."

"Thanks." I stood and followed him through the living room and into the kitchen. I opened the door to the laundry room, where I'd set Chappy's bedding and litter box.

"Hello, cat," I said. "Ready for some kibble?"

Chappy came over and threaded himself through my legs. As I busied myself feeding him, Jerome looked on disapprovingly.

"Don't you like cats?"

"They're okay. I'm more of a dog man, myself." He took a chair at my kitchen table. "So, what did you think of tonight?"

"The séance?"

"The entire Karen-being-possessed thing?"

I shrugged, then lowered a saucer of cat food to the floor where I'd set a mat for feeding Chappy. "I have no reason to doubt it was Dan who came through and argued with Fred."

Jerome searched for the right words, soundlessly forming syllables, then closing his mouth. He probably didn't want to set me off again, yet I suspected there was some point he struggled to make. At last he said, "If Dan's . . . gone—"

He danced around what he wanted to say. I was a big girl, though.

I could handle it and strove to make it clear to him. "I said it tonight, Jerome. Dan's *dead*. I probably need a little time to process it, but deep inside, I know it's true."

Maybe I'd always known and hadn't wanted to admit it.

He looked me directly in the eye. "You'll be able to move on now."

Ah. So this was what he'd wanted to say. He was basically right, but not entirely. "I still need some closure. I still need to know what happened to him."

"It's good Brad was there tonight. While he didn't say so, I think the séance gave him an extra impetus to renew the investigation."

"That would be helpful." I stooped over and stroked my new cat. "I still worry I'm his suspect Numero Uno. The spouse is always the first person the police look at in suspicious circumstances, and you have to admit his disappearance was extremely suspicious."

"Brad knows you," Jerome quickly reassured me. "He knows you had nothing to do with Dan's disappearance—or death."

"I hope that's the case, because as long as Brad thinks I had something to do with what happened to Dan, Brad will continue doing nothing to find out what actually did happen."

Jerome stood and paced the few steps to join me where I kneeled beside Chappy. He placed a palm on the top of my head. "I'm glad you're finally coming to terms with losing Dan."

I stood. "Me, too. Once I learn what happened, I can truly start to live again."

Jerome's expression turned grim. "We may never know."

"If that's the case, I'll have to deal with it. But for now, I'm hopeful."

"I am, too." He wrapped his arms around me. "I'm extremely hopeful."

I smiled up at him, and he gave me a chaste kiss.

"I'd better head out. Let you get to sleep." A glint I hadn't seen before shined in his eyes. "Want me to tuck you in?"

Did the shine in his eyes indicate lust? If it was lust, I'd never seen it make a man look more dopey. Having him "tuck me in" was the last thing I wanted, but I didn't want to hurt his feelings, either. "I need to write tonight. It's my form of therapy."

"I admire that about you."

"What?" My ability to avoid having sex with him?

"That you can make things out of air."

My brow creased. O-kay. Nothing to do with sex. I hadn't realized, though, that he sat around thinking about me.

"Dan used his imagination to take physical things and combine them in unique ways. But you create something simply by the power of your mind. You make something out of nothing."

"I hadn't thought of it that way." I didn't see myself as an inventor of sorts. I sit around making up stories. "I think of it as selling my daydreams."

"And they do buy them."

I nodded. I enjoyed being paid for my work and, even more, I loved having readers. "They do. Speaking of which, I'd better get to it."

He gave me a final hug, then headed to the door. "I'll see you in the morning."

I didn't pay attention to what he said, because an internal monologue had already started up in my head. My latest short story began to play out.

Within minutes, I was seated at my keyboard, my fingers flying almost as quickly as the images in my head.

I'm not sure how much later, but my reverie was broken by a phone call. I thought I might have heard the phone earlier, but when I'd come out of the creative fog and answered, no one had been on the line. Now it rang again. I glanced at the time on my computer screen. Eleven o'clock. It had to be Sue Ann. No one else would call me that late.

I picked up the phone but kept typing. My heroine was in an argument with her husband, and I didn't want to lose the train of thought. "Hello?"

"You on for tomorrow?" asked Sue Ann. "I have time to take that trip to Belle Plaine if you do."

"Uh-huh." Interesting. My heroine didn't want to fight with her husband. She wanted to take a hot bath instead. But advancing the plot with her locked in the bathroom would be difficult.

"You're not listening to me, are you?"

"Uh-huh." I kept typing.

"Amy!"

Her yelling voice startled me and I realized I hadn't been paying attention to her. "Oh, I'm sorry. I was writing."

"I promise to only steal your brain for a few minutes."

With a silent sigh, I minimized the word processor. My heroine would have to wait. "What's up?"

"I've got the address for Gayla's shop in Belle Plaine."

"I thought she was a schoolteacher?"

"Not anymore. She opened a ceramics and local art shop about two years ago. Are you up for paying her a visit tomorrow?"

"Sounds like a plan. May as well make sure she doesn't know anything." Since I was supposed to be using Sherlock Holmes as a role model, I needed to return to my original intent to look for the woman. It had been sidelined by recent events, and Gayla Mullen might be the woman I needed to look for.

"Exactly. I thought I'd pick you up about 9:30."

A vague recollection surfaced: Jerome had said something about seeing me in the morning. I couldn't think or remember why. I must have misheard. "Yes, 9:30 is perfect."

"See you then. Get back to your story."

I already had.

CHAPTER TEN

When Love Walked in, i Walked Out

"I swear, Sue Ann, there's a really good chance if he doesn't leave soon, I'll kill him. Death by power tool."

Jerome had arrived early that next morning, and I had barricaded myself in the bathroom with my cell phone glued to my ear.

"I thought you wanted someone to take care of you."

"Not like this!" I raised my voice so I could be heard over the sound of banging in my bedroom—not the fun kind of banging, either. "Fort Knox, ha! I'll have better security than the White House."

"That's a good thing."

"No. It's not. This is way overboard." I lowered my voice and cupped my hand over the cell phone microphone so that she could still hear me when I dramatically whispered, "I think he's lost his marbles."

"Amy, you should tell him you don't want all the security measures. It's not like he's not speaking to you."

"He's not listening. That's the problem."

"It's your house. Tell him to stop—" She broke off for a minute, and I heard her muffled voice talking with someone. She returned to the call and said, "I've got to go, Amy. I'll be there before too long."

"Fine," I said, deflated.

"And stay away from those power tools!"

Snapping the phone shut, I decided to face the inevitable—a

showdown with Jerome. It was sweet he felt protective, but switching out all of my windows and adding a sophisticated security system surpassed all bounds. Before ordering the work, he should have discussed it with me.

I unlocked the bathroom door and peeked out. There had to be thirty workmen in my tiny house. I banged the door shut.

Chappy cowered in my bathtub, and his huge eyes seemed to scream with fear. I said, "I'm with you, babe."

A tentative knock sounded on the bathroom door. Sliding my moist hands down my jeans first, I opened the door.

It was Jerome.

I gave him the silent treatment as he stepped into the bathroom and closed the door behind him. "You doing okay?"

I nodded, not exactly sure how to approach the subject of ridding my house of workmen or whether to immediately start fussing at him.

"We need to talk," he said.

"Yeah, we do." My words were clipped, but he didn't pick up on my mood. As long as he'd known me, you'd think he would have.

"I have to go out of town for a few days, and I thought"—he paused, then took my right hand—"you should move in with me."

That had come out of nowhere. We'd never discussed the subject, and I wasn't prepared to, either. I opened my mouth to argue, but he cut me off.

"Wait, Amy. Hear me out before you turn me down."

The temptation to tell him I didn't want to discuss it at all was huge, but based on the intently serious expression on his face, I knew I'd have to hear him out. Then he could hear me out.

"After all of the break-ins at your home, I'd feel much happier, especially while I'm out of town, if you would move in with me."

"I truly appreciate the offer, Jerome. Don't you think if someone wants to get to me, they can break into your place just as easily as mine?"

"I feared you'd say that," he said on a long, drawn-out sigh. "Hence, the additional security measures."

Well, I had to hand it to him. He *did* know me, even if he couldn't read my moods. "About the security measures—"

My words were cut off when an especially loud boom sounded from the bedroom next door. Chappy meowed plaintively.

Jerome glanced in the bathtub, then back at me. "You can't keep that cat. You can't even take care of yourself."

I didn't want to get into an argument with him, not as he was leaving town. Considering the height my hackles reached, our discussion was heading into argument territory. "I make out okay."

He kissed my forehead in a totally condescending way, and I had to grit my teeth to keep myself from lashing out at him.

"You do manage, but a cat is a huge responsibility."

I turned and met Chappy's frightened eyes, then crossed my arms. "We understand each other. We'll be fine."

"Maybe I should cancel my trip."

Man. He was truly pushing it. "Why?"

"Might be because of Karen's dire warnings, or the recent events, but I feel a sense of—" He broke off and waved his hand, looking for the right word.

"A sense of my inability to care for Chappy and myself?" I took a seat on the commode, and the lid wobbled slightly under my weight.

"No. That's not what I mean."

"What do you mean then?" It dawned on me that perhaps I was wrong in trying to keep peace. A good argument might clear the air between us.

"Foreboding. I feel a sense of foreboding." He positioned his hands on the bathroom counter and looked into the wall mirror. "I can't believe I'm saying this. I can't rid myself of the thought that something is going wrong. The energy, as Dolores would call it, is off somehow."

It truly wasn't at all like him to discuss anything the least bit woo-woo, especially in a context indicating he might believe in it. "You're definitely reacting to what Karen said last night. She put the idea into your head. You know everything is going to be fine."

He straightened and smiled. "I'm sure you're right. This is merely a matter of my imagination running away with me."

Again, this was unlike him. He usually accused *me* of the overactive imagination. "Maybe I'm contagious?"

"You, my dear, are extremely contagious." He reached over to me and moved a strand of hair from my eyes.

No matter how much I wished, his touch didn't affect me the way Brad's did. Of course, Brad likely suspected me of murder. Jerome wanted nothing more than to protect me. He was very sweet, but there were no tingles; there was no sensual awareness. It might come with time? My relationship with Dan had been wonderful, but now I wanted more than I'd had before. I wanted the strong desire I knew existed between Sue Ann and her husband, the kind hinted at in movies and novels. Was I wrong to want more?

"You have to let me take care of you, Amy. I won't get any peace while I'm gone if you don't."

Even though he didn't say the words, this meant no more objections to the security system rivaling London Tower's. It was the least I could do for a man who tried so hard to be what I wanted and needed. "Okay."

"There's so little time to talk now, and this isn't the place."

I looked around my tiny bathroom. "You have a point. There isn't much space."

"When I get back, I've got something important to discuss with you." He bent and kissed me. It was pleasant and tender, and I kissed him back. But he leaned away too soon for me to find out if there might be a hidden ember of desire—although, if I had to look so hard, it probably wasn't there.

"I've got an important question to ask you. It will have to wait until I get home."

Oh, God.

He wasn't planning to ask me to marry him, was he? Now that we knew Dan was dead, did he think the timing was finally right? I sincerely and deeply cared about Jerome, but I was in no way ready to move our relationship onto the next level. I wasn't even sure if we had a relationship in our future other than friendship. At that moment I knew I wasn't in love with him, and I wasn't sure if I ever would be.

As discreetly as possible, I checked my watch. Sue Ann was due to arrive in ten minutes, and for sanity's sake it would be best if Jerome were long gone before then. I had no intention of telling him what I would be up to while he was out of town.

If he found out about our proposed trip to see Gayla, he'd probably insist on hiring me a personal bodyguard.

I needed to discourage him without hurting his feelings and get him on the road toot sweet.

I stood and gave him a quick hug. "You're too good to me, Jerome.

Too good for me, too. Let's go see what these workmen of yours are up to."

"You're too good for me," he replied.

We exited the bathroom, and I checked to make sure the door was closed so Chappy couldn't escape. We then headed down the hall. When we reached the living room, I saw the new windows were already in place. "These guys are fast and apparently very competent."

"I'm paying them to be."

"Looks like everything is under control here. What time do you leave town?"

"When I leave here." He looked around as if searching for something to do, but the men he'd hired didn't need supervision.

"You'll call me tonight?"

"You got it." He took my hand and tugged me outside. Though public, it still provided more privacy than my house. He took me in his arms and kissed me. Again, it wasn't exciting, even though I wished it were.

I pushed back. "Be careful while you're away."

He grinned. "Don't forget. We're going to talk when I get home."

Cold water splashed in my face. At least that was the effect of his words. It was my fault for giving him an inch. "Have a good trip."

He nodded and headed to his car, hesitating a moment, as if there was something more he wanted to say or do. Or something he hoped I would.

"I'll miss you," I called. I might not be able to use the *L* word he craved, but I could give him that.

"Hold that thought." He smiled, the lines around his eyes crinkling, as he lumbered into his Lexus then started it up.

I watched him drive off, giving him a small wave, but before I made it back inside, Sue Ann's SUV pulled up and parked where Jerome's car had just been.

Talk about cutting it close.

"Come on in," I said to Sue Ann when she exited her vehicle. "Jerome's hired a boatload of workmen to keep me safe. I need to let them know I'm leaving."

"What's he having done now?" Sue Ann wore blue jeans and the pretty coral shirt I like on her so much, with its twisty bow thing just below her bosom, making her assets appear inflated. Her streaked blond hair was pulled up in a clippy, with tendrils of curls escaping, framing her pretty face. Amid all the chaos, it was really good to see her, a solid and dependable fixture in my life.

"Could be worse, I suppose." Her leather flip-flops made that flip-floppy noise as she joined me and we walked inside.

The man I assumed to be the head of the crew of workmen watched over another man attaching an electronic panel near my front door.

"How much longer do you think you'll be?" I asked him.

"Shouldn't be too long," he replied, scratching his elbow. "Another couple of hours?"

He was asking me? I grimaced. "I need to run a few errands this morning. Think you can lock up when you're done?"

"I need to go over the security system with you. When will you be back?"

Sue Ann piped in, "We're going to be a while."

"Can we do the security system later?" I asked as politely as I could manage through clenched teeth. I didn't much like the way he seemed to expect me to shape my schedule around his.

He looked annoyed, like I was putting him out. "We've got another job in Coffeyville. I can't stick around."

"Neither can I. How about I call you to schedule a good time to go over it another time?"

"It'll mean not activating the security system when we leave . . . " He trailed off, I guess still expecting me to knuckle under and wait around for him to finish.

"That's not a problem," said Sue Ann, who evidently read my expression of extreme annoyance. "Amy will call you, and you can come show her all the bells and sirens at your *mutual* convenience."

With her emphasis on the word *mutual,* he got the point. "Let me get my business card."

He fumbled in his pocket for his wallet, opened it, and selected a card. "Here you go."

I took the card.

"Call the mobile number. It's the best way to reach me."

"Got it. When you leave, just close the door and it'll automatically lock up."

He nodded.

"I'll grab my purse," I told Sue Ann and headed to the bathroom where I'd hidden it under the sink.

Chappy appeared to have come to terms with all the noise in the house, because he had curled up on the rug in front of the commode. Not even my presence disturbed his slumbers. I whispered, "Be good."

Within minutes, I rejoined Sue Ann and we walked to her SUV. "Think we can stop at the bank on the way? I need to deposit a check."

"No problem," she answered, punching the button to unlock the car doors. "We've got plenty of time. Shouldn't take us over two and a half hours to reach Belle Plaine."

We climbed in her vehicle. I carefully buckled my seat belt, then voiced my hidden concern. "Do you think she'll be willing to talk with us?"

"I can't think of any reason why she wouldn't. Chances are this is a wild-goose chase. You know what they say—it's best not to leave any unturned stones."

I smiled, loving the way my best friend in all the world strung her words together. She's a heavenly mixture of smart-ass and plain good sense. You had to love her.

The drive to Belle Plaine went quickly. Sue Ann and I talked about our investigations into Dan's disappearance thus far. Or lack thereof.

Thanks to Dolores' séance, I was now convinced Dan had met his maker. Other than that, we were absolutely no further forward. "Did the séance turn you into a believer?"

Sue Ann laughed. "Not on your life."

Her response surprised me. I said, "I'm convinced that was Dan."

"You don't think Karen could have milked Dolores for information beforehand?"

"There were things said that Dolores wouldn't know. You should keep your mind open."

"I hate to admit it, but I was spooked." Her words came out slowly, indicating her reluctance. "I don't want to believe, but I tend to agree with you. I think Dan might have been with us that night."

"Wow." This was a huge admission on her part. She'd never

believed in anything paranormal. "Karen really got to both of us."

"Which means this is no longer a missing persons case."

The subject turned to our investigation. We had a few people we wanted to talk with, including Gayla, Dr. Elden, and Fred, all of whom were people who might know something about Dan's disappearance or who might be listed as potential suspects.

"It seems a stretch to believe any of them had enough reason to do away with him," I said.

Sue Ann never took her eyes off the road when she responded. "I think Fred is the strongest of our suspects. Look how Dan's spirit got into it with him."

If Fred had done it, that would mean my whole look-for-the-woman schtick was a total loss. "You're assuming Dan was murdered."

"What else could have happened to him? According to the *spirit* at the séance, we can completely rule out alien abductions."

"I don't know what to think. Let's face it. I've had seven years to come up with a theory, any remote theory, about what happened to him, and I've been unable to think of anything the least bit logical or reasonable. His disappearance never made sense, and his death is even more confusing."

The digital clock on Sue Ann's dashboard read 11:59 a.m., and we were just pulling into Belle Plaine.

"Do you know what time teachers get their lunch breaks?"

"Why do you ask?" asked Sue Ann.

"We're hoping to talk with Gayla and can't exactly interrupt one of her classes."

Sue Ann gave me a look, part exasperation, part incredulity. "I told you last night she has her own shop now. I knew you weren't listening. You get within five feet of your computer, and you flee to Planet Bozone."

"Ha-ha. Very funny." I gnawed my upper lip. "I can't help being how I am. I get lost in my stories. I do kinda remember now that you said something about her selling art."

"I know you can't help it. And you did remember about coming this morning." She smiled, not as upset with me as I feared. "Gayla sells ceramics and other products from local Kansas artists. She has a small Web site. Her shop looks totally trendy, with everything from paintings to handcrafted dishware to woodwork."

"Sounds like the kind of shop I love."

"It's definitely my kind of place." Sue Ann braked to allow a pedestrian to cross the street.

"With any luck, she'll have lunch with us and won't be too angry to let us explore her shop afterwards." I had no intention of accusing her of anything, but since we were digging for information, anything could happen.

"We'll find out soon. That's her shop over there on the left."

I looked to where Sue Ann pointed. The sign above the shop read, "Anything But Plaine."

Sue Ann quickly parallel parked, which is saying something considering the size of her vehicle. "Okay. What's our game plan?"

"We're supposed to have one?"

"We can't very well march in there and say we think she had something to do with Dan's disappearance."

"You're right. If I promise not to accuse her of murdering my husband, can we simply play it by ear?"

"Just be subtle." Sue Ann rolled her eyes as she unbuckled her seat belt. "Let's just ask her to lunch. We can work in our questions over burgers."

"Nice plan." I climbed out of the SUV and crossed the street with Sue Ann. The shopwindow displayed an extremely appealing set of sunflower ceramic platters, bowls, and plates. A gorgeous quilt with an intricate design of swirling color hung behind the ceramics display. "Sewing that had to have taken months."

"It would have taken me years." Sue Ann swung open the wood and glass panel door, and a bell jangled.

The shop was lovely and light, yet crammed with every imaginable kind of art. I noticed lace doilies, more ceramics with a myriad of designs, and rows of quilts behind the wooden counter at the rear of the store.

Gayla Mullen stood behind the counter. I'd forgotten exactly how pretty she was, with her round face, blue eyes, and head full of dark curls. Betty Boop personified. Other than her, the shop was empty of customers.

"Oh. My. Gawd," exclaimed Gayla with a squeal. "Sue Ann Livingstone and Amy Crosby!"

CHAPTER ELEVEN

My Secret Past Tore My Family Apart

Gayla ran out from behind the wooden counter and launched herself at Sue Ann, at first alarming me, but evidently intending to give her a tremendous hug. She did, then turned to give me a similarly effusive embrace, and I had to fight the urge to step back from her onslaught. Instead, I let her do her thing and gave her a light back pat.

"What brings you two to Belle Plaine?"

"I heard you had this shop, and it sounded interesting," I said.

At the same time, Sue Ann said, *"You do."* So much for subtlety.

"Wow. I'm so honored." Her smile was so broad that neither Sue Ann nor I could have any doubt of her sincerity. She was genuinely pleased to see us.

"Any chance we can take you to lunch?" I asked.

"What perfect timing! I was just getting ready to close for an hour. The shop hasn't been at all busy today. Let me grab my purse and, Amy, if you could change the sign on the door to say I'll be back at one o'clock, that would be perfect."

She entered the back room, still talking up a storm, something about how she'd known today was going to be lucky. She'd felt it in her bones.

I changed the sign, and by the time I was done, Gayla had returned. "You two girls look so great! You haven't changed at all!"

It was true that Sue Ann hadn't changed much. But what about me? I'd dropped twenty pounds since Dan's disappearance, and my permed hair could only be described as "afro on caffeine high."

That was when I recalled that Gayla Mullen had always been the type of woman who talked in exclamation marks and italics. Although I had never been in one of her classes, she'd arrived at Independence High School during Sue Ann's and my sophomore year. I think Sue Ann may have had her for homeroom during her junior year. Despite that, I was still surprised she remembered who we were, especially after so long.

I pondered how she could remember us so well as we walked the two blocks in downtown Belle Plaine to the restaurant Gayla recommended.

"It's the best in town," she said.

Gingham draperies hung in the windows of a tiny low-slung house that had been converted into a restaurant. Inside, there were only a dozen tables, all filled with people, meaning we'd have to wait.

A chalkboard listed the offerings for the day.

"There's no menu," said Gayla. "Everything they make is delicious. The owner, Fran Klein, moved from Belle Plaine to France to train at a fancy culinary school. But she got homesick for Belle Plaine. Definitely our gain."

The offerings on the limited menu listed on the chalkboard showed the owner's French training. Only five items were listed, each a Midwestern or Southern dish, yet with definite French twists. The aroma filling the air made my stomach growl in anticipation.

Within a few minutes, a bone-thin young man with colorful tattoos covering his arms seated us at the first available table, near the swinging doors to the kitchen. The room was noisy with voices and sounds from the kitchen whenever the doors swung open.

After we placed our orders, Gayla gave me a sharp look. "So, did you two really come to see me, or are you interested in local art?"

The eagle eye she trained on me was the sort used by generations of teachers when grilling their students, and I was no match for it. There was no way I could hide anything beneath that glare. My latent guilt rose up, and suddenly I wanted to confess everything. I would spill my beans one way or another. "To be honest, we're hoping you can help me."

"I will if I can, Amy."

"You know Dan disappeared seven years ago."

Gayla nodded.

"The police never learned what happened to him, and it doesn't seem as if they ever will. Sue Ann and I have decided to investigate ourselves. I need the closure."

"I don't blame you," said Gayla. "I'm not sure how you think I can help."

I glanced at Sue Ann, who seemed surprised at my directness. I shrugged and continued. "You left town around the same time Dan disappeared. We—I am hoping you might know something, even if you don't realize you know something. You know?" My phrasing was awkward because I wasn't exactly sure how to ask her if she'd run off with my husband without pointing a finger at her, and I doubted anyone would respond well to that. "If you know anything, it might help us."

Gayla's smiled dimmed. "If you're asking about my leaving town, it didn't have anything to do with your husband, Amy."

"That's good to know. But can you think of anything that might help me? Do you know anything about the night he disappeared?"

A flash of pain crossed her features, but it immediately disappeared. "I know some of the people in Independence have been gossiping like crazy about me—and I heard my name's been linked with Dan. It's not true. If you're asking if the two of us—" She broke off.

"She's not asking, Gayla," said Sue Ann. "She told me the rumors couldn't be true. But *I* am asking."

Gayla glanced down at her utensils that had been rolled in a paper napkin, then slowly unraveled them. She then looked me in the eye. "Dan is a good guy, Amy, wherever he is. He never would have carried on with another woman, much less with me."

My shoulders relaxed. "Told you, Sue Ann."

"I know you wouldn't have made this trip to see me if it weren't important to you, Amy. And I'll reassure you as much as I can. The rumors did have a morsel of truth." Her voice became a whisper, as if she were confessing a guilty secret, and I felt bad about putting her through a time that was apparently extremely painful for her to relive. "I left town so abruptly because of a bad breakup. But not with Dan."

My lips formed a silent *O*. Was she saying she had been involved with a married man? If she'd been dating someone who wasn't married, there would have been no need to keep their relationship a secret. Everyone would have known about the breakup.

Just then the skinny waiter returned with our orders, and all thoughts of romantic intrigue disappeared as we set about devouring one of the most delicious meals I've ever had the pleasure of eating.

By the time we finished, the three of us were giggling as if we'd been the closest of friends all our lives. While we waited for the check, Sue Ann returned to our earlier line of questioning. "You mentioned a bad breakup. Who were you seeing?"

"It wasn't my finest hour, and it's not something I want to discuss." Gayla shook her head. "Now, I'd be happy to tell you about my new boyfriend. He owns the Ready To Wear Dry Cleaners on Main Street."

Gayla batted away any other attempt we made to find out more about her leaving Independence. While she remained friendly, there was no way to ask her more.

Once we returned to the shop, Sue Ann and I spent several pleasurable hours, and lots of her husband's cash, on the artwork offered by the shop.

When Sue Ann finished paying for her purchases, Gayla handed her the receipt. "Thanks so much for coming today. I don't know when I've had so much fun. And, like Fran at the restaurant, I'm a little homesick. Independence is a lovely town."

"You could come see us sometime," I offered.

But Gayla was already shaking her head. "I'm sorry, but there are too many bad memories. As you can see, I'm doing okay here in Belle Plaine. I've got a good life now. However, I'd love it if you two would come see me again."

"You can bank on it," said Sue Ann, with a jiggle of the shopping bags in her arms.

I said, "If you remember anything that might help me find out what happened to Dan, please call and let me know, okay? Nothing's too small."

"I did think of one little thing. I'm not sure if it's big enough to help you or not."

"Even if it's little, it might be a big help."

"I'm not 100 percent on this, but I think I may have seen Dan as he was leaving the Independence Tavern the night he disappeared."

"Really! As far as I knew, there weren't any witnesses to him leaving the Tavern. Was he with someone?"

She shook her head. "No. I saw him leave the Tavern alone and begin walking in the direction of your house. We—the man I was with and I—were arguing, and we headed in the other direction. That's why I think it was the night of Dan's disappearance. That argument was pretty heated. I think Dan was going to say good night, but thought better of it after he realized we were having a disagreement."

"Do you remember about what time that was?"

"I'm sorry, Amy. I told you it wasn't much. It was late, probably around one in the morning, but I can't remember well enough to give you an exact time."

"Thanks for telling me this much."

If Gayla remembered the right night, at least it appeared Dan had intended to come home.

A short time later, we were back in Sue Ann's SUV, headed toward home. "Did you believe her?" asked Sue Ann.

"I had a mixed reaction. On one hand, I felt she was being truthful—as far as it went. On the other hand, she never told us who she was having an affair with, and it does seem an odd coincidence."

"I don't think we can take her off our list of suspects, even though I like her so much. She seemed very sincere, and I don't want to suspect her of anything bad. She feels guilty over whatever happened in her past, and it seems like she's straightened out her life since then."

Gayla was a very likeable woman, and it was hard to imagine her doing anything to harm anyone. But maybe she was just a very good actress who gave us only enough information to make us believe her. "You're right. She remains on the list. What about our other suspects?"

While continuing to drive, Sue Ann ticked off the suspects on her fingers. "There's Gayla, the entire readers' group membership—"

The car swerved.

"God, Sue Ann, can you keep your hands on the wheel?"

"Oops." She grabbed the wheel and righted the car, then returned to listing suspects. "Dr. Elden, and we added Fred Cook."

Few people got along with Fred. He was a difficult man, and the events at the séance certainly put him at the head of my list. "Fred is probably the person most likely to have something to do with Dan's death."

"We need to talk with him. After taking today off, I don't have any free time for days. Have to play catch-up. Think you could go without me?"

I grimaced. Fred had never been pleasant to talk with. After the other night, he'd probably throw me out of his house. "Don't make me do it alone," I whined.

"You're a big girl. You can do this."

I'd been busy insisting to Jerome I could take care of myself, and here I was resisting the idea. I straightened my shoulders. "You're right. I can do this."

"Good. Go tomorrow, and call me afterwards to let me know what you learn."

"Will do. What do you think is the best way to approach him?"

"You could ask about the invention Dan's ghost thinks he stole."

My brows rose. "Don't you think that seems a bit confrontational?"

"No conversation with Fred could be considered anything but."

"Excellent point." My stomach churned as I told myself, *No problem.* I could do this. I was quite capable of taking on the man who stole from my husband and, thus, stole from my pocketbook. If he hadn't taken whatever it was he took, perhaps my house wouldn't be close to foreclosure.

That reminded me. "You know how I asked you to have your husband stop proceedings to have Dan declared officially dead?"

"Yeah?"

"I think he should go ahead."

Sue Ann chewed her bottom lip. "I have a confession to make."

Something about Dan? What could she know and not have already shared with me? We'd been best friends for almost ever, and we never held anything back. "Go ahead. Confess. It does a body good."

Sue Ann's lips scrunched to one side at the bad attempt at a joke.

"It's not like you wouldn't tell me anyway."

"You know when you asked me to talk with Ron?"

"Uh-huh."

She bit her lip, reluctant to continue.

My mind raced, but I realized what it was she didn't want to tell me. "You didn't tell Ron to stop the proceedings?"

She nodded. Her gaze darted toward me as if she were accessing my reaction; then it skittered back to the road again.

I couldn't believe it. All this time I thought the declaration procedure had been put on hold—and it hadn't been. I felt betrayed; my trust violated—for about thirty seconds. But this was Sue Ann, my dearest friend in the entire world. "Okay. Why didn't you talk with Ron?"

"I knew your situation and, despite the blackmail note, you had to move ahead."

"Don't you think you might have discussed that with me?"

"I didn't think you'd be receptive."

"Well, you got that right. So you made the decision without me."

"I was looking out for you. It was in your best interests."

Had I spent the last seven years totally unable to take care of myself? Was that why everyone important in my life acted without talking with me? Maybe it was true. Maybe I had been so frozen I wasn't truly dealing with my own life. I could think of a dozen times when someone had stepped in and solved my problems for me in the past year. And dozens more over the course of my life. I was like a kid masquerading as an adult.

But not anymore.

"Sue Ann . . ."

"Yes?" Her gaze again darted toward me, then back to the highway.

"I'm not that girl anymore."

"What do you mean?"

"The girl who couldn't take care of herself." I wasn't sure how to word what I wanted to say, but the words came tumbling out. "From now on, I'm no longer a girl. I'm a woman. An independent woman who not only does a great job taking care of herself but can take care of others, too. I even have a cat now. You know what I mean?" There. I'd said it, so it must've been true. I ignored my queasy stomach. It was time to make a stand, and I'd stick to it.

"I know exactly what you mean. It's a good change, Amy. And I'm glad. It might be hard, though, you know?"

"Yeah, it is hard. It's a change I need to make."

She gave me a reassuring smile. "You've always been able to accomplish anything you set your mind to. But you may have to be patient with me at times. Stepping back won't come easily. Watching out for you is second nature to me."

"All I'm asking is that you try to let me fend for myself."

"You got it." She patted the steering wheel, and I feared she was going to start ticking names off again, but she kept the vehicle under control.

She asked, "So what's your plan for finding out what happened to Dan?"

Oops. I'd forgotten that taking care of myself meant exactly that. From now on, I'd make my own decisions—and while I could consult others, the decision would be mine alone to make. This included finding out exactly what had happened to my husband.

"I'll start with Fred tomorrow morning and move on from there."

After arising the next morning, I wandered into the kitchen to the sound of scratching and mewing coming from the laundry room. Chappy wanted out and made no bones about it. I opened the door. "Time for breakfast."

He galloped out the door before I fully opened it, then tore through my kitchen and into my bedroom, sending the rug on the living room floor sailing. Within seconds, he'd returned to sit at my feet. "Meow."

I moved over to the sink. On the floor below it, his food bowl sat empty. I picked it up, then washed it out. After toweling it dry, I added two scoops of dry food and placed it on the floor for him. He dashed over to the bowl.

While he ate, I prepared coffee. I figured I'd need quite a bit of caffeine for the day ahead. I'd thought about it long and hard the night before. I had two goals after completing my daily writing quota. First, I had to talk Mrs. Mitchell into allowing me to borrow her Caddy. Second, I had to go see the man I thought might have murdered my husband.

Yes, it would be a fun time for all. Not.

Three hours later, I'd written, dressed, shut the cat in the laundry room, and was kinda ready to face the tasks ahead. Well, almost. This looking out for yourself business was not for the faint of heart. But everyone else seemed to do it just fine, and I'd get the hang of it before long. My chest constricted painfully. It was merely the stress of having to confront two people, and I'd never been comfortable with confrontation. I'm sure some people wear it naturally.

But my unnatural sass rose up and kicked me in the patoot, launching me out my door toward Mrs. Mitchell's house. Once I arrived on her porch, I slowly exhaled, releasing my anxiety, then knocked.

She opened the door almost before I completed the first knock. "Morning."

"Good morning." I tried smiling ingratiatingly, but it wasn't a natural expression for me. And Mrs. Mitchell could tell.

"You want something. Out with it."

"I wondered if you might let me borrow your car."

"Thought I made it clear I wouldn't lend it to you."

"What if I beg?"

She looked at me consideringly, with a tilt of her head. Then she nodded, having come to a conclusion that I hoped was in my favor.

"How about we agree to a trade."

It wasn't a question, for good reason. I had no bargaining power. I inhaled deeply. Suspiciously. "What do you want?"

"I have a car and need a driver. You can drive and need a car."

"Where do you want me to take you?" I hadn't intended for my voice to sound more like a low growl, but it did. I truly wanted to be able to use her car and reminded myself I'd better get busy sucking up. "You know, I'd be happy to help out whenever you need me to."

"Whatever." She wasn't buying my bull, and I didn't blame her. But this was a new me.

"I mean it. I get tired of being cooped up all the time," I said.

"Your friends tired of you freeloading rides?"

"No. I'm tired of the lack of freedom."

"Excellent. So, I'm thinking it would be lovely to have you take me to Wal-Mart this afternoon."

Oh. My. Gawd.

Mrs. Mitchell's trips to Wal-Mart were things of legend. She not only spent hours putting items in her cart; she spent an equal number of hours removing them. This was so not good.

"Sure you wouldn't rather go to the grocery store?"

"Take it or leave it, kiddo."

Sold.

Thirty minutes later, I pulled up at Fred Cook's home. It wasn't quite midafternoon, so his wife would still be at work. Hopefully Fred would be alone and willing to talk. I just hoped he didn't think I'd come to chase after him.

He lived a little out of town, off a dirt road. A wide, chalk driveway was wedged between a large outbuilding and his house, which sat further back from the road.

As I approached the house, I considered my goals in talking with him. While I was somewhat disappointed my chief suspect wasn't a *femme*, I'd be satisfied if Fred held the answers to what had happened to Dan.

If that was the case, my main aspiration had to be to get him to tell me whatever he knew.

And that was a problem.

All of our prior interactions had primarily focused on his and Dan's rivalry, which hadn't exactly been friendly. I'll never forget the hours Dan spent trying to one-up Fred and the crazy inventions resulting from their competition.

If Fred had done something to Dan, or even if he merely knew something, I couldn't come up with a motivator to get him to tell me anything.

What did I have to offer other than being a sounding board for his guilty conscience? At least I had to try to make friends with him.

I nervously wiped my palms down my jeans and stepped onto his front stoop. My heart knocked as I rapped on the glass- and steel-paned storm door.

Despite the ruckus raised by my yammering insides and pounding fist, there was no response.

Maybe I'd lucked out. I didn't feel prepared to face him and had no idea what to say to get things rolling. Sue Ann could come with me the next time I tried to talk with him. Two heads would be better than just my one, and she might have a better clue of how to get him to talk.

I turned and walked toward the Caddy. But before I made it all the way, I heard a male voice saying, "What is this? Good cop, bad cop?"

Huh?

The loose rocks under my feet crunched as I spun and saw Fred standing in the doorway of the outbuilding. The large metal structure could have been a barn or garage, but I knew it had to be the workshop for his inventions. Especially since he wore a welding mask. He lifted the clear shield from his face, and it hovered over his head like a crown.

"Good cop?" I asked.

"The poor, desolate wife come to beg?"

This was not starting out well. What was he talking about? "I'm sorry, Fred, but you lost me somewhere around cop."

"Nice try, Amy. Liz got here before you."

Liz had come to question him? Was she trying to find out what had happened to Dan, too? Surely she would have said something to me if she were investigating? My best response to Fred would be something vague until I learned what he meant. "What does Liz have to do with cops?"

Fred didn't reply for several long seconds, taking his time to study my face, and probably hoping to make me uncomfortable.

He succeeded.

The man was the closest thing to a complete misogynist I'd ever known, although the fact that he was married indicated otherwise. Fred didn't much like women.

I was tired of feeling bullied and in the dark. Two could play his game. I stared him down.

"You didn't know about Liz's visit?" He broke first, and I gave myself an imaginary high five.

"No clue." I remained halfway between my car and his outbuilding, and the steady Kansas sun beat down on my head. Tiny beads of perspiration formed on my forehead, and the smell of drying grass filled my lungs.

"She suggested we join forces."

"I'm not sure what you mean."

"Team up in the invention business. I'd continue doing the inventing, and she'd be my partner as she had been Dan's, handling the money and the administrative side of the business."

"Hmm. That's not a bad idea. She's really good with money."

"Other peoples'," he gruffed.

"I presume you told her no." The conversation was going nowhere and was unlikely to lead to the answers I sought. I looked down at the keys in my hand and considered making a run for it. I was totally unsuited for questioning him, or any suspects for that matter.

"Told her she had sixty seconds to get off my property before I had her arrested for trespassing."

"I'm sure she loved hearing that." I couldn't keep a wry grin from my face.

He grinned back, which was something new between us. Usually he scowled or threatened to have me arrested. It was probably coming any time now.

"You can come in if you're not here to talk me into partnering with Liz."

Wow. Totally unexpected behavior. My self-doubts about getting him to tell me anything lifted a little. I held up two fingers. "Scout's honor."

He led me into his workshop and pointed toward an area near the rear that had been set up as a kitchenette. A black iron bistro table circled by three chairs sat next to a bright orange countertop containing a sink and mini-fridge, with brown cupboards beneath it.

The workshop was air-conditioned, and the coolness soothed my heated skin. The bulk of the high-ceilinged workshop held the materials he used for his inventions. Unlike Dan's work tools, everything was neatly organized, with tall storage cabinets and bins for all of Fred's supplies. He drew off his welding mask and tossed it onto a metal table as we passed it, creating a loud *thunk*. He turned and asked, "Coffee?"

"Sure. Thanks."

A few minutes later, he handed me a steaming mug and joined me at the table where I had taken a seat in one of the chairs.

Lest I give the wrong impression, while clean, this was not a trendy setup. Two of the chairs had all four legs, but neither of them was steady. The third was missing its fourth leg, but managed to totter on only three. Dried paint splashes and nicks made up the top of the table. It had seen better days.

But the coffee was delicious. Between sips, I said, "Good."

He nodded. "Grind my own. Columbian with a Kona chaser."

Another surprise. Was it possible my prior assessment of him had been wrong? I would have banked on his being a Folgers kinda guy.

"Dan's business in financial trouble?" he asked as he took a seat on the three-legged chair, immediately tilting it back on only two of the legs. It seemed to be a habitual gesture he made without thinking about it. Guess he didn't need that fourth leg.

After having me promise not to discuss business, his question seemed out of place. Was he testing me? "Not going there. You promised no business."

"Touché." With a flash of a grin he said, "Can't blame me for testing you. So why *are* you here?"

The moment I'd worried about had finally arrived. What could I say? I searched for something reasonable that wasn't too inflammatory. "The séance the other night."

"You honestly believe that was Dan?"

I nodded. "You believe it wasn't?"

"You're smarter than that. A two-bit con artist puts on a show, and you're believing everything she dishes out."

She'd been entirely convincing. I shrugged. "Seemed like you thought it was him at the time."

"I've had time to reflect," he said sheepishly.

"Me too." I gave him the same attempting-to-be-ingratiating smile I'd used on Mrs. Mitchell. "What do you think happened to Dan?"

"Theory or fact?"

"Fact. I'd really like to know anything you can tell me."

"Whoa." He held up his hands, and his chair hit the floor. "You're implying I know something I haven't told previously."

I had to hand it to him because the chair didn't even wobble on those three legs. The man had good balance. "I guess I am, but I don't mean it the way you make it sound. I just want to know if you know anything."

"Let me get this right. You came here today because, after that trickster fed us her line of bull, you now think I had something to do with Dan's disappearance?"

"I didn't say that."

"You sure implied it."

"It wasn't my intention." I sought a way to explain how I'd decided to come to him. "Sue Ann and I drove to Belle Plaine yesterday and—"

"That's enough," he cut me off and angrily rose to his feet. "What are you getting at? What the hell do you want?"

While we weren't exactly best buds now, I thought we'd been getting along fairly well—until he thought I was accusing him of murdering Dan, which I had sorta kinda hinted at. Fred was almost frothing at the mouth, and the skin around his neck and face had turned bright red. He must not like being accused of things. "I just want to know what you were doing the night Dan disappeared."

Within seconds, the red in his face dissipated and he grew pale. "Out."

I looked at him in confusion. Things were moving too fast.

He pointed toward the door. "Get the hell out."

CHAPTER TWELVE

I Shot My Neighbor for Being Late

With as much dignity as I could muster, I exited Fred's workshop and got in the Caddy. Quickly starting the engine, I pulled out of the driveway and headed toward home.

How had things gone so bad so quickly? I'd never been kicked out of anywhere before and it was a humiliating experience. I'd once been kicked off something—the girls' softball team. I'd agreed to leave, as the coach had asked, "for the good of the team." This felt much the same.

Even though I hadn't accused Fred of anything specific, I must have implied more in my line of questioning than I'd wanted to. At the very least, he probably felt I didn't believe him. I didn't much enjoy having my ethics questioned, either, but evidently it had set him off.

Or maybe he had a great big guilty conscience. There was no way to know for sure, unless I could lay my hands on some truth serum. Once I could chew things over with Sue Ann, hopefully I'd get a better perspective on what had transpired.

It didn't take long to return home and park the Caddy in Mrs. Mitchell's driveway. There was no point in garaging it since she met me in the driveway and I knew exactly what she wanted.

"Took you long enough," she said.

Checking my watch first, I said, "Only an hour and a quarter."

"Seemed like longer." She held out her hand and wiggled her fingers.

I handed her the key ring. "How does seven o'clock sound?"

"For?"

"Shopping."

Relief that she didn't expect to leave right away swept through me. It would give me plenty of time to talk with Sue Ann, check my e-mail, and play with my cat. "Seven o'clock it is."

"Meet me here and don't be late," she said, spinning on her heel and heading back to her door.

Nothing like pleasant social interactions to make my day complete.

When I entered my house, Chappy nearly escaped between my legs, but I managed to grab him in time. "What are you doing in the living room? How'd you get out?"

I closed the door and allowed Chappy to wriggle out of my arms. Then I sensed it. Maybe it was simply a matter of being certain I'd locked Chappy in the laundry room before leaving. Or maybe it was sensing something being out of place. But it felt more like ESP, because small hairs stood up on my arms.

Something was wrong.

I stood still, listening for any unexpected noise, but all was silent. My gaze darted from the entry to the living room, then down the bedroom hallway. Nothing.

Should I leave and call the police? What could I report? My cat escaped?

Why hadn't I made arrangements with the security company to go over the new alarm system? If I had, I wouldn't be afraid to enter my own home. Where had I put that man's card? I couldn't remember.

I allowed Chappy to leap from my arms, and he made a dash for the kitchen.

The only option left to me was to pluck up my courage and make sure everything at my house was okay. If someone had broken in again, I hoped he was long gone.

With my nerves on high alert, I stepped into my den, and from there I saw that the laundry room door was ajar. There was every possibility I hadn't closed it all the way, allowing Chappy to make his escape.

Or he could be part alley cat, part Houdini.

I took a deep breath before taking the few remaining steps into my kitchen. Chappy sat in front of the sink, his meow demanding food.

Scanning the rest of the kitchen, I saw nothing unusual and placed my handbag on the counter. The voice mail light on my phone on the counter flashed, but I decided to wait to listen until after I'd finished checking for another break-in.

It didn't take long to walk through, and by the time I finished I'd calmed down. I'd found no new messages on my computer, no blackmail notes, and no Post-its.

Chappy continued waiting for me by the sink.

"You've got food in the laundry room." I reached to pick him up and put him back in there, but once he saw where I was headed, he fought me.

One of his claws connected with my arm.

"Ouch." I dropped him, and he immediately skittered from the room and ran for the den. But I knew how to lure him out. Turning, I opened the refrigerator and pulled out a bowl of leftover chicken salad. He'd licked my saucer clean when I'd given him some the night before. Scooping a little onto a saucer, I placed it on the floor below the sink and called, "Kitty, kitty."

He came running. Once he reached the saucer, he sniffed it then abruptly hissed. Next he clawed at the ground as if he were attempting to bury the food.

Hmm. I picked up the remainder that I'd intended for my late lunch and sniffed it. It did seem a little off, but I'd only just made it the night before. It couldn't go bad that quickly. Could it?

A niggling thought about the possibility that someone had been in my home took hold. It was silly to think someone would attempt to poison me—wasn't it? One of the reasons I'd become a writer was that I have an incredible imagination that simply doesn't turn off, and my biggest challenge is sorting between what's real and what's imaginary. I had to be overreacting about the chicken, but I decided it was better to be safe than sorry.

I picked up Chappy's saucer and dumped the contents in the sink, along with the rest of the chicken salad in the bowl. After running the disposal and thoroughly cleaning the dishes just in case they were poisoned, I punched the button to listen to voice mail, feeling a little queasy about the idea of eating anything. It would probably be a good idea to avoid any open containers in my house.

There was only one voice mail, a message from Jerome. "My cell is beeping, so my battery is running low, but wanted you to know I got done early and I'm heading back to town. See you tonight at the Independence Tavern. The book clu—" The message abruptly cut off, and I supposed his battery had faded.

I couldn't attend the book club meeting tonight. I had to take Mrs. Mitchell shopping. I dialed his cell number, but it went immediately to voice mail. I explained why I wouldn't be there and hoped he'd get the message. I then called his home voice mail and left the same message.

A short time later, Mrs. Mitchell and I hopped in her Caddy convertible, top down, and sped toward her favorite shopping destination. The parking lot at the Wal-Mart Supercenter was filled to overflowing with after-work shoppers. Ultimately, I dropped Mrs. Mitchell at the door, then ventured to the outermost recesses of the lot before finding a place to park her boatlike car.

By the time I reached the door, Mrs. Mitchell was nowhere in sight. She'd obviously started without me. Not that it was a bad thing.

Considering her reputation as a choosy shopper, I felt the less I was involved the better. I took my time seeking her out, dawdling in the automotive aisles because she was unlikely to be found there. Maybe my Gremlin would look good with a pair of fuzzy dice dangling from the rearview mirror. Or the cool rhinestone, heart-shaped bling might look nice in the back window.

After half an hour of blissful reverie, I heard my name being called over the intercom. "Amy Crosby, please meet your party at the information desk. Amy Crosby, your party is at the information desk."

Could I be more humiliated? Reluctantly leaving the safety of the automotive department, I briskly walked to the front of the store, where I found Mrs. Mitchell in conversation with the store manager.

"Sorry. I couldn't find you," I said.

"Paging you wasn't my idea," Mrs. Mitchell said with an evil look directed at the manager. "She insisted on finding whoever brought me."

"What's up?" I asked.

"If you don't mind, I'd appreciate it if you see to it that she doesn't leave items scattered throughout the store. If you take a cart with you, she can place her unwanted items in it and then I'll put them back where they belong."

Ohh. Got it. With my perkiest smile, I said, "No problem."

"Come along, Amy," said Mrs. Mitchell with her haughtiest tone of voice. "Let's shop."

She turned on her heels and pushed her empty cart toward the women's clothing section. Grabbing the cart offered to me by the manager, I ran to catch up. When I did, I asked, "Are you looking for something in particular?"

"I could use a couple new outfits. I saw a pair of slacks and a blouse I really liked. Over there." She pointed toward a rack of clothing. "What size do you wear?"

"Six. Why?"

"Curious is all." She found the items she wanted, but I noticed she'd taken two of each. Maybe she wasn't quite sure of her own size.

You had to hand it to her—she was good with a shopping cart, wheeling it between racks and people-crowded aisles like a pro. I, however, wasn't quite so good at it. I bumped into racks and had to stop to apologize to people I accidently rammed while trying to keep up with her.

Eventually we landed at the dressing rooms. The two attendants wore identical expressions of dismay when they saw Mrs. Mitchell. It was obvious they recognized her from prior expeditions. She began to wheel her cart into the dressing area, but the younger of the two attendants stopped her. "There's a limit to what you're allowed to take back. I can hold the rest for you."

"That's okay. Amy's with me, and she can bring in whatever's over my allotment."

Great. Just great.

She bundled a load of clothes into my arms. "These are for you, dear."

What could I do? Refuse? Drop them to the ground? She wanted to bring in more than the quota, and evidently it was my job to help her get away with it. With my back figuratively against the wall, I took the items and followed her back into the dressing rooms.

"You take that one and I'll be right next door," she said, stepping into the cubicle of her choice.

I hesitated. Had she forgotten the clothing I was holding for her? "Don't you need these?"

"Oh, no, dear. Those are your size."

I gave her a blank stare.

"You'll try on the same things so I can see how they look on the body—in 3-D. I hate getting home after trying on clothes and realizing they aren't right. This way I'll be able to see the full image."

"Oh, no. I don't think—"

"No need to think," she interrupted. "You're such a nice girl, catering to a sweet old lady's needs."

More like a manipulative and evil old lady's needs.

I remained in place.

"Just do it," she growled, then pushed me into the cubicle. "Humor me."

I couldn't understand why she wanted me to try on the same clothes. The 3-D thing didn't make sense. The clothes weren't suited to someone my age, but maybe she thought she was doing me a favor by getting me to update my wardrobe. Or maybe she truly did want to see how they looked on someone else.

"Get busy in there," she ordered from the next room. "Remember—it's quid pro quo. You scratch my back and I loan you my car."

I was doomed, doomed to don flower-embroidered cardigan sets with matching elastic-waisted double-knit slacks. I yanked off my T-shirt and jeans and pulled on the outfit.

"All set?" she asked.

"As ready as I'll ever be," I replied.

"Come on out."

"If I have to." I opened the door and stepped out. She stood before me, almost like a mirror image. It was like one of my worst nightmares.

"Ohhh, that looks very nice, Amy."

"Glad you think so."

"But it needs something else. Stay right there." She shoved me back into my dressing cubicle. "Don't take it off and don't go anywhere."

I took a seat on the tiny ledge in the cube. What on earth did she have in mind now?

It didn't take long for me to learn.

"I'm back, Amy. With accessories!"

I peeped out the door, and she stood there holding two flowered hats, a number of necklaces, several long silk scarves, earrings, and bracelets. I started to slam the door closed, but she wedged herself in before I could.

"Put on the hat and let's see how we look," she ordered.

Had I died? Was this hell? It certainly felt that way when she plopped the outrageous hat on my head. I looked like something out of a *Gone With the Wind* satire. She put the identical hat on her head and cocked it as she glanced in the mirror then back at me. "The outfit needs a bit more pizzazz."

Two minutes later I'd been draped in jewelry and scarves, and Mrs. Mitchell was admiring her image in the full-length mirror at the rear of the dressing area when my cell phone rang. Thank heavens. With any luck, it would be Sue Ann and she'd come up with a way I could get out of this madness. I didn't recognize the number she was calling from, but I couldn't resist answering, "Insane asylum."

"That's not a very nice thing to say," said Jerome. His voice came out a little distant, most probably because the signal in the store wasn't very strong.

"Well, it's kinda true."

"Where are you? I thought we were meeting here at the Tavern."

"I left you a message, but I guess you didn't get it."

"What's that you said? Your voice faded out."

"I left you a message."

"Oh. Cell phone died. I'm calling from a pay phone."

"At the Tavern?"

"Yes."

The store intercom boomed, something about needing help in the grocery section, and I couldn't make out what Jerome was saying.

"What's that noise?" he asked. "Where are you?"

"I had to take Mrs. Mitchell shopping."

"We need to talk."

"Ouch," I cried when Mrs. Mitchell pulled one of the necklaces from my head and it caught on my hair. "Hang on. Hang on."

Mrs. Mitchell yanked, and I wondered if I'd have a bald patch.

"There, honey. No harm done." She waved the deadly necklace at me.

"Sorry, Jerome," I said into the cell, but realized I'd come back online in the middle of one of his sentences. He hadn't heard that I'd put down the phone, and evidently he'd continued talking.

" . . . as Dan's executor. I couldn't believe my client had one."

"What are you saying? I couldn't hear you for a minute."

"I'll tell you later," he said impatiently, then added, "I didn't know about the blackmail note."

Oops. Caught red-handed in the sin of omission. "I was going to tell you."

He sighed. "How long before the court proceeding to declare Dan officially dead?"

"I'm not sure. Sue Ann's husband originally said about four weeks."

"That's fine then. The readers' group should finish up in about an hour, and I'll come over to your place so we can discuss what we need to do next."

Did he mean something about Dan, or was he planning to propose? Before I could ask, Mrs. Mitchell attacked the cardigan I was wearing and began unbuttoning it. "Hold on, Jerome."

"What are you doing? Can't you wait a second while I talk with Jerome?"

"Just take off that sweater."

"Fine." I exhaled heavily, then stripped off the cardigan. "Happy?"

"Much better," she said.

I returned to my call, but all I heard was a dial tone. Evidently Jerome's three minutes were up.

CHAPTER THIRTEEN

Sex Slavers Kidnapped My Boyfriend

Forty-five minutes later I managed to pry Mrs. Mitchell out of Wal-Mart. I couldn't believe it, but after all I'd been through she'd ultimately only purchased one pair of earrings. Earrings I hadn't tried on.

No wonder the store manager wanted help with restocking the items Mrs. Mitchell selected. After checking out, I got her out of the place fast. I scurried out to the parking lot, started the Caddy, then quickly drove to the front of the store to pick her up.

Jerome was due at my house soon, and it would probably be a good thing if I was actually at home after standing him up earlier. Plus I'd come up with a great new idea about being a store clerk, and my muse was anxious to get started writing it.

When we pulled into her driveway, Mrs. Mitchell said, "Thanks so much, doll, for taking me."

Unsure how to reply—*my pleasure* certainly wouldn't work in this instance—I concentrated on driving the Caddy into her garage. Since I was hoping to maintain driving rights, I finally said, "Glad to help out."

"Nothing like a little shopping to put a spring in a girl's step."

"Uh-huh." I would never describe what I'd been through as *a little shopping,* and my steps were anything but springy. The woman was positively bubbly, and I didn't know how she did it. "Want me to put the top up?"

"Might as well keep it down. It's safe in the garage."

I climbed from the car and inched away from the garage. Time to make my escape. "Well, I'll see you."

"Ta," she said, walking toward her back door.

Did she think she was British now?

I did my best to put the whole incident from my mind as I punched the buttons to enter my house. The writing muse had bitten, and I couldn't wait to get to my computer.

After releasing Chappy from the laundry room, I went into the kitchen and found an unopened jar of peanuts to munch on. I hadn't eaten lunch or dinner, and my stomach rumbled.

Before long my head was filled with characters yammering, and I typed as quickly as I could to keep up. While putting the finishing touches on the then-completed short story, I glanced at the computer clock. Three in the morning? How could that be?

I turned and checked the wall clock behind me and it confirmed the time. I could have sworn Jerome was supposed to come over after the readers' group meeting ended. Running through the brief phone conversation in my mind, I grew certain he was supposed to be here.

Hopefully I hadn't been so absorbed I hadn't heard his knock. I saved the file and pushed my chair back, then headed toward the front door.

Switching on the porch light, I looked out but didn't see any sign Jerome had been here. Stretching out the stiffness after the long hours at my computer, I turned and walked into my kitchen to check voice mail. Maybe Jerome had called and I hadn't heard the phone.

There weren't any messages.

I picked up the phone and checked caller ID to see if he'd phoned without leaving a message.

There hadn't been any calls.

My latent psychic abilities kicked in, and I knew deep inside that something was very, very wrong.

It was extremely unlike Jerome to not show up, especially without calling. Wishing it weren't too late to consult Sue Ann, I began pacing, trying to decide what to do. Jerome was an early riser, and I ultimately decided to wait the three hours until he got up before giving him a phone call to fuss at him for worrying me.

The only problem was that I knew I'd be unable to sleep in the meantime. My brain was foggy from the intense writing jag, and my stomach growled because I hadn't been good about eating.

There was a reason for that, though. I was afraid to eat anything in my house. I probably should have called the police when I'd first suspected the food might have been tampered with, but it hadn't occurred to me at the time. At least then I'd know if I was overimaginative, as so many people have accused me of in the past, or if my fears were justified.

My stomach rumbled.

I looked in the refrigerator for something safe to eat, in case there truly had been a vicious poisoner on the loose in my house. Hard-boiled eggs should be safe.

I grabbed the carton, removed two eggs, and placed them in a saucepan. I ran a little tap water over them and set the pan on the stove to boil. As I waited, again I went over Jerome's phone call. He'd said something about being Dan's executor. I'd kind of known that but hadn't much thought about it since his will hadn't kicked into effect and wouldn't until after the court proceeding.

That would be coming up before long, so Jerome was probably trying to get his ducks lined up. What had he said about his client? About him having one? One *what*? I couldn't figure out what having something or not had to do with Dan's will, so perhaps I'd misunderstood.

The eggs were done, so I spooned them from the water and placed them on a saucer. Time moved too slowly. It was only a quarter after three, and I didn't know what I'd do to keep myself occupied until dawn. I spent the next few hours nibbling my eggs and making notes about what my investigation into Dan's disappearance had yielded thus far.

It wasn't much, but it was something to go by. I listed potential suspects and ranked them according to how likely or unlikely it was they might have had something to do with the disappearance. A chill crept down my spine as I looked over the list of names. Had I been spending time with a murderer?

There was Fred Cook, Dan's inventor rival who'd thrown me out of his workshop. Dr. Mary Elden, Dan's chess competitor, who I'd been unable to rule out. Gayla Mullen, who I wanted to believe was innocent of any wrongdoing, yet mystery clung to her. The list included unlikely people, such as Jerome, Brad, Dolores, Liz, and Mrs. Mitchell. I couldn't leave anyone out, no matter how illogical it might seem.

At last, six o'clock arrived and I made a beeline for the telephone. I punched in Jerome's number and waited anxiously for him to answer. After five rings, his voice mail kicked in. My stomach clenched.

He was a light sleeper, so why didn't he answer the phone?

I tried his cell phone. It went immediately to voice mail. He must have turned it off, or the battery was still dead.

It was too early to borrow Mrs. Mitchell's car, and I considered whether I should try riding my bike to Jerome's house. It was on the other side of town, but not too far from where Brad lived.

Maybe I should call him.

My fingers hovered over the phone's keypad as I hesitated, unsure what would be my best course of action. But this was definitely not like Jerome, and the feeling of dread I'd been blocking for the past three hours came back in full force.

This was eerily like the night Dan had disappeared. Once the thought hit me, I immediately dialed the number Brad had given me, which I'd accidently on purpose committed to memory.

He answered on the second ring, his voice heavy with sleep.

"I'm sorry to wake you, Brad, but I'm worried."

"Someone trying to break in?" he asked, the tone of his voice suddenly alert.

"No one is trying to break in. I'm worried about Jerome."

I heard the sound of sheets ruffling, as if he had climbed from bed. "What's up?"

"He was supposed to come over last night and never showed." Now my tone sounded odd as it climbed an octave. "I've tried calling him, but he doesn't answer."

"He seemed fine at the Tavern last night."

"You saw him? He called and said he was coming over after the book club meeting broke up."

"It ended late. When I left, the group was still at it. He probably thought it was too late to call you."

"Then why doesn't he answer now? He always gets up at six."

"Maybe he's in the shower." His annoyed tone said it all.

"You think I'm overreacting, don't you?"

He blew out a sigh. "You've had a lot on your plate lately."

I guessed he didn't want to confirm my fear. My shoulders slumped in discouragement. "I know it might sound silly to you, but I've got a bad feeling about this, Brad. I keep reliving the night Dan disappeared, and—"

I broke off, trying hard not to sob. I wasn't going to let him hear me having a breakdown.

"Here's what we'll do, Amy."

I loved the sound of *we* from his mouth. I wasn't in this alone. "What will we do?"

"We'll wait a quarter of an hour for him to get out of the shower, and you'll call him again. If he doesn't answer, and I'm confident he will, call me back and I'll head over to his place."

"Thanks, Brad. I really appreciate it."

"No problem."

"Go back to bed. I'll only wake you if Jerome doesn't answer."

"You got it." He ended the call, and I placed the phone on the kitchen table in front of me. I only had to wait fifteen minutes. Jerome was in the shower and I was overreacting, I told myself. But that little voice inside me remained on high alert. I jumped from the chair and decided to take a shower of my own. It would clear my head since I'd been up all night, and I'd feel better and more assured afterwards.

By the time I'd wrapped my wet hair in a towel and dressed, twenty minutes had passed. Jerome would definitely be out of the shower by now. I returned to the kitchen and dialed his number, expecting his early-bird-gets-the-worm voice to answer at any second.

But he didn't answer. Voice mail came on instead.

I hung up and tried the number again, only to have the same result.

My fingers trembled so hard when I dialed Brad's number that I thought I might punch the wrong number, but the call went through and he answered on the first ring. "Amy?"

"He didn't answer, Brad. I'm scared."

"Don't be. He probably slept in after a late night. I'll get dressed and head over there. I'll have him call you once I rouse him. Okay?"

"Sounds good. Thank you again."

"No prob."

I hit the end button, then dialed Jerome's house again. This time when his voice mail kicked in, I left a message for him to call me as soon as he received it. The feeling of panic remained as I went into my bedroom and toweled off my hair. I grabbed the afghan my grandmother had crocheted and wrapped it around me before returning to my den and collapsing on the sofa, where I waited to hear from Jerome.

Where could he be? Why wasn't he answering my calls?

Chappy jumped onto the sofa beside me and purred as I stroked his soft fur. His tiny paws kneaded the afghan, and the feeling of his warm body comforted me as I waited for word. At some point, I dozed off.

The sound of knocking at my door woke me. At first I was confused. But then clarity returned as the knocking continued, and I leapt from the sofa. I threw the door open, and Brad stood there looking sober and somber.

"Where's Jerome?" My words came out in a rush.

He shook his head. "Can I come in?"

"Sure." I stepped back a couple of paces and opened the door wider so he could enter.

"Do you have any coffee?"

His question alerted me to the fact that he wasn't telling me something. I searched his face, but he gave nothing away. "I can make some. Instant okay?"

He nodded, then followed me to the kitchen, where I pulled out the stash of instant I kept for Jerome. It reminded me of the other morning when the workmen had installed my new locks and I'd made coffee for Jerome. Don't think of that, I told myself as I put the water on to boil.

Brad soundlessly watched my efforts. I swallowed, then went into the living room and pulled down my shelf of teacups and selected a cup covered in tiny bluebells. It had been my grandmother's favorite, and it gave me comfort—a rare commodity lately.

I couldn't stand the silence anymore. When I returned to the kitchen, I asked, "Were you able to wake Jerome?"

The skin around Brad's mouth tightened. "No. He didn't answer the door and believe me, I knocked loud enough to raise the dead. I reconnoitered his house and checked the garage. His car wasn't there."

I grabbed the back of a chair to steady my shaky hands.

"Not home?"

The kettle whistled, and I glanced at it with annoyance for interrupting. "One sec."

"It'll wait," he said.

I moved to the counter and quickly prepared our beverages. Within seconds, I returned to the table with the cups and took a seat. I had a feeling I was going to need it.

"Do you have any idea where Jerome is?"

He shook his head. "I drove over to the Independence Tavern. His car was still in the lot."

"What?" Dizziness now made my head spin. This couldn't be happening. Not again.

CHAPTER FOURTEEN

Handcuffed in Front of My Children

My head continued spinning, and my heart hammered painfully when Sue Ann arrived. "Thank goodness you're here. How did you know to come?"

"Brad called." She scooted beside me on the sofa and wrapped an arm around my shoulders. "Jerome is fine. Don't you think, Brad?"

"Most likely he made other plans for the night," he said, his brows drawn in that tremendous scowl of his.

Sue Ann laughed. "What a way to put it."

I shook my head. "It's not like Jerome to not call."

"Amy," Sue Ann said, her voice tender, "he's hinting at the possibility Jerome went home with another woman."

"Are you nuts?" I asked. "That's what people insinuated when Dan disappeared, too, and we both know that was a load of hay."

"I think he went home with one of his buddies at the Tavern," Sue Ann reassured me. "Probably not sober enough to drive. He'll call when his head clears."

"I suppose it's possible. Jerome would never drive if he was the least bit tipsy."

"He had a long day, what with driving back to Independence, then the readers' group meeting." Brad sat to my other side. "It wouldn't have taken much to make him impaired."

My heart slowed to a normal pace. "Okay. I won't panic now. But you'll keep looking for him, won't you?"

"It's too soon to file a missing persons report, Amy," Brad said. "But I'll try to track him down. I'll call some of the people who were at the meeting and see if any of them recall when he left or who with."

"That's a very good idea."

He got up, ready to leave.

"Thanks, Brad." The dizziness abated and my head cleared. "I can't help but worry. This is so much like what happened to Dan, and with all the break-ins and the blackmail note and the snake and the poison—"

"What poison?" both Brad and Sue Ann said in unison.

"Maybe not poison. I'm probably just being silly." I explained about the chicken salad, hoping they would dismiss my fears.

"It's too bad you threw it out. We could have sent it to the lab. Did you at least put the bowl in a safe place?"

"No. I washed it. I was sure it was simply my overactive imagination."

"It may have been," Sue Ann said, "but considering everything going on, it might not have been."

"If anything else happens, imaginary or not, Amy, I want you to call me right away," Brad said. "And don't do anything that will destroy evidence."

There was no point in arguing with him. The chicken may or may not have been poisoned, and I had been creeped out. "Okay."

He nodded. "I think Jerome's disappearance is simply a coincidence, but I *will* find him. You've got my word."

❧❦❧

Three days later, there was still no sign of Jerome. He'd disappeared just as completely as Dan had. Both men had been on their way to me, and neither had made it. Sue Ann and I had talked with members of the waitstaff at the Independence Tavern, Brad had talked with readers' group members and other patrons, but no one had seen him leave.

No one knew anything.

Or at least they weren't talking.

I spent much of the time dialing Jerome's phone numbers over and over because I couldn't find my usual escape in writing.

Maybe somewhere near the Independence Tavern was a mysterious triangle, like in Bermuda. It certainly felt that way.

Between bouts of depression, I tried to go about my normal business but found it impossible.

Even worse, people who weren't close friends avoided me, and those who were close acted far too nice. Sue Ann practically lived at my house, to the point that I had to send her home to her husband. Brad stopped by or called every day to report his lack of progress and to check on me. Liz brought me a casserole Dolores had baked. Needless to say, I didn't eat it. No telling what Dolores had laced it with: tequila, fairy dust, floor polish.

The one bright spot was Chappy. He didn't treat me any differently. He didn't know anything was wrong. All he knew was that he didn't want to be cooped up in the laundry room anymore. So I finally gave in and let him have the run of the place.

That morning, he was in the middle of darting from the bedroom to the kitchen and back when someone knocked on my door. I opened the door to find Mrs. Mitchell. "Hi?" I said, more as a question than a greeting.

"How are you today?" she asked, with a phony smile plastered on her face. Not another person trying to be nice.

"I'm fine. What can I do for you?"

She cocked her head to one side. "I thought you might like to borrow my car."

The offer of her car was suspicious in the extreme. "You don't need to go to Wal-Mart, do you?"

"We could if you're up for it, but maybe we could just run to the grocery store?" She dangled the keys toward me. When I didn't immediately grab them and sprint for her car, she added, "We could go for a joyride first, if you like."

"Now you're talking. I'd like to go check on my Gremlin, if that's okay by you?"

"Dolores told me you had visitation rights, but I didn't believe it. If you want to go look at that heap of junk, that's fine by me."

I smiled. Broadly. It was my first smile in days, and it felt almost uncomfortable on my face. Guilt nibbled at me. How could I feel excited about anything? But the idea of fresh air and seeing my car won out. "Let me go grab my purse."

When we arrived at Eck's garage, Mrs. Mitchell waited in the Caddy. Eck personally greeted me. "I thought you'd forgotten us."

"No way."

"Come around back. I've been making some progress."

Oohh. Progress. As we rounded the corner, I saw my Gremlin. It was no longer sitting on cinder blocks. Now it stood proudly on all four tires. "Oh my gosh! Is she ready to go?"

"Not quite, but it won't be long."

I was so excited, I ran and stroked her hood. I wanted to climb in and toot her horn, but the fear of snakes held me back. "No reptiles?"

"Not a one."

I swung open the door and climbed in. "Will she start?"

"She'll go just fine. It's the stopping that's the problem."

"No brakes?"

He shook his head. "Shouldn't be long now."

I could grow used to this people-being-nice-to-me thing. I tooted the horn, and it blasted nicely. Climbing out, I said, "You'll let me know as soon as she's ready?"

"I'll bring her to you myself."

"How much longer? Next week?"

"Might be sooner. Might be later." His gaze met mine. "But I promise to bring her to you as soon as she's ready."

"You'll deliver her?"

"You can count on it."

That was the best I'd get from him, so I gave him a hug and hurried back to the Caddy to drive to the grocery store with Mrs. Mitchell.

It was early afternoon before we returned home. Evidently I have a lot in common with Mrs. Mitchell, because I put all kinds of items in my cart before having to go back and return a number of things. We had a good time together, and we were in good spirits as I pulled onto our street.

Nearing our houses, I saw Brad parked in front of my house. "Do you think he has news about Jerome?"

"Could be." She scrambled in her handbag, then pulled out a lipstick and quickly applied it. "How do I look?"

"You look very nice." She didn't seriously intend to flirt with Brad, did she?

I pulled the car into the driveway instead of the garage since we each had a number of bags of groceries to unload. Brad got out of his car and joined us. "Can I help?"

"Oh, that would be so lovely," cooed Mrs. Mitchell. "A big strong man to bring in my bags. Have I died and gone to heaven?"

But Brad was no fool. After their last encounter, he didn't let her anywhere near his nether regions. "You go on in ahead of me. Wait here, Amy. I'll be right back to help you."

Yeah, right. Like Mrs. Mitchell would let him out of her house once she had him in her clutches? I didn't think so. I grabbed three bags and climbed the stairs to my front porch. Before I finished punching the buttons to open the door, Brad joined me, carrying the last of my items.

"How did you escape so fast?"

"Police training sometimes comes in handy."

I smiled and swung open the door. "Why don't you go first?"

He snorted and gestured for me to go first. Guess police training included mind reading because I'd definitely planned to get in the pinch denied to Mrs. Mitchell. Thwarted, I hurried to the kitchen with my groceries, and he followed closely behind, shutting the front door behind him. I began unpacking the items I'd purchased. "Do you have news?"

"That's why I'm here. Let's get this all put away first, though." He pulled a roll of paper towels from one of the bags he'd brought in and placed it on the counter.

This couldn't be good news. Otherwise, he'd tell me straightaway.

I wasn't ready to hear it. I needed more time to compose myself. I was unable to keep my hands from shaking as I finished putting everything where it belonged. Since my cupboards had been practically bare after tossing away anything that might have been poisoned, I truly needed these groceries. After stowing the milk in the refrigerator, I looked under the cupboard and pulled out the bottle of whiskey Sue Ann kept on hand. "Am I going to need this?"

"You might."

Whatever the news was, it was going to be hard. Based on his procrastination in telling me, it was going to be hard for him, too. "Are you on duty?"

"I'll take mine on the rocks."

That wasn't reassuring. I pulled out two glasses and sloshed in the brown liquid, then added ice cubes. Brad grabbed both glasses, then walked to the kitchen table and took a seat.

I joined him. Horrible pictures sprang into my imagination. Hit and run. Kidnapping. Organ theft. I couldn't bear it. "Out with it. I can't stand waiting any longer."

"I told you I'd find Jerome."

I nodded. Every part of my body had tensed.

"I did. It's not pretty, Amy."

I chugged a gulp of whiskey, then squeezed my eyes shut. Unsure what to expect, I presumed the worst. "He's dea—" I couldn't say it.

"We found his body in the Verdigris."

"Damn. Damn. Damn." While I hadn't expected to discover he'd gone on a binge, I hadn't expected anything this awful. "How did he get there? Did he drown?"

"The coroner says no. It was murder."

My mind couldn't quite grasp what he was saying, and my stomach alternated between churning and clenching. "Someone killed him?"

"Looks that way. The best we can piece together is that he suffered blunt trauma to the head and, afterwards, the killer dumped the body."

"Why would anyone do that to Jerome?" For a moment I feared I'd lose the contents of my stomach, whiskey and all. "He was the nicest guy ever."

"I don't understand it myself—but I will. Right now we're trying to sort out where the murderer dumped his body. It's been in the water for several days, most likely since the night he didn't show up here."

"I should have paid more attention when he called, but the connection wasn't good. Mrs. Mitchell and I were in Wal-Mart, the call kept cutting in and out, and she kept interrupting me." I sorted what I remembered he'd said through my mind. "He said something about being Dan's executor. Do you think that's a clue?"

"I'm going to need to take your statement about everything you remember from that call. Maybe Mrs. Mitchell's statement, too." He looked at me sadly, and I knew he was hurting as badly as I was over Jerome's death. "It gets worse, Amy."

"You keep saying that. How much worse can it get?"

"You're Jerome's beneficiary and—this is straight from the police chief—that makes you our prime suspect."

CHAPTER FIFTEEN

i Confessed to a Murder i Didn't Commit

I glanced around my house, at the new windows, at the new locks, at the new, as yet inactivated, security system. Jerome had done all this to protect me, when instead I should have gone all out to protect him. While I had done nothing to directly harm him, what I hadn't done stole my breath away.

I looked Brad in the eye. "Do you think I had something to do with Jerome's death?"

"Absolutely not."

I believed him.

His gaze met mine and held. "But my boss does."

"So what can I do? I have to find out who killed Jerome."

"Whoa." Brad pushed his chair back from the table. "That's my job, not yours."

"With the police thinking I'm guilty of killing Jerome, it just became my top priority."

"Amy, this is an order. Stay out of it."

He didn't understand how important this was to me. Not only did I need to avenge Jerome, but it might point to what happened to Dan, as well. Even if the chief of police didn't suspect me, I had to find out. "There's nothing you can say or do to stop me."

"Don't push me." He pulled handcuffs from behind his back and rattled them at me.

"You wouldn't dare."

"Try me."

His tight posture and serious expression led me to believe he meant business. "Look, Brad, I have to do something. I'll go crazy if I have to just sit here doing nothing. I feel responsible for Jerome's death even though I didn't have a hand in it. If he hadn't been involved with me, I'm certain he'd be kicking and breathing right now."

"If you won't stay out of it, I could hold you for questioning. The chief wouldn't object."

"You want to force me to be secretive? Not tell you what I'm doing?"

"I'm trying to keep you safe. There's a murderer on the loose, and there's every chance he's struck more than once. Do you want to be next?"

"It's time for me to take responsibility for my own safety." After what had happened to Jerome, it wasn't safe to allow anyone else to look after me. I needed to do it myself. "I want to make sure the murderer is behind bars so he can't strike again." Or she. I hadn't forgotten my look-for-the-woman plan.

"Both men were on their way to you. Both men were linked to you romantically. Don't you think this is a sign the murder has something to do with you? Dammit, Amy, be *practical*."

I hated that word. I hated the situation. I hated being at odds with Brad. "I'm not going to hide under a rock like a cockroach. I'm in this, Brad. I'm already involved. No matter how much you order me to stay out of it, it's impossible. Even if I wanted to, the murderer won't let me."

"I'll deny this if you ever tell anyone, Amy, but do you know what this has done to my insides? I'm sworn to serve and protect. I just pulled my best friend out of the river, and I've been useless in looking after you. I'll never forgive myself if something happens to you."

"What the hell am I supposed to say to that? You'll feel bad if something happens to me, but I'll be dead. I have to look out for myself. I can't just sit here on my duff any longer. I've done that too long."

The scowl he directed my way would have previously filled me with guilt, but now it was nothing, a whisper falling on deaf ears. I knew what I had to do. I had to find out who killed Jerome. I just needed some private time so I could grieve for a man who'd only wanted the best for me.

"Here's something you can do. Come down to the station and give a statement about the last time you saw Jerome and the last time you spoke with him."

"When do you want me to go?"

"No time like now." He stood and pocketed his handcuffs. "I'll drive you."

Obviously I wasn't going to be granted any time to grieve for Jerome. Maybe staying busy would forestall the shock I felt coming on. I blinked my eyes and took a deep breath. "Fine."

I grabbed Brad's untouched glass and my half-empty one and walked to the sink. I turned back. "You're not going to cuff me?"

"Not this time."

Snatching my purse from the counter, I followed him to the door. But when I opened it, Chappy escaped through my legs. "Chappy!"

He didn't turn back. He ran for cover in my bushes. I chased after him, but he saw me coming and darted like a bat into Mrs. Mitchell's yard, then over her fence. "I don't know what to do."

"He'll come back," Brad reassured me. "He likes to eat."

"I'm afraid he'll get lost." I turned to go after him.

Brad hooked my arm. "Amy, sorry, but there's no time. I go off duty shortly. Once you've given your statement, I'll come back with you and help you look for him. I bet he'll be waiting for you."

I hoped Brad was right, but it didn't seem like I had a choice other than to go with him now and look for my cat afterwards.

He opened his Tahoe's passenger door, and I climbed in. A short time later, we arrived at the police station, where Brad led me through a door labeled *Detectives.* It was a reasonably large room furnished with tables and desks. Brad indicated his desk and had me take a seat beside it. I glanced in front of me, and there was a mirror on the wall beneath another desk. "Is that one of those secret window thingies?"

"Yeah, but no one is watching. We hardly ever use it. I'm turning on the recorder now to keep a record of your statement. I have to ask a series of preliminary questions first. Then we'll take your statement."

"Okay."

Once the preliminary questions were completed, Brad said, "Tell me when you last saw Jerome."

"It was the morning he left town on business. That was when he had the security system installed."

"Did he say anything to indicate he might be in trouble of any kind?"

"No."

"Did he ever indicate he might be having financial problems?"

"No. In fact, he seemed to be doing very well."

"You're his beneficiary. Did you know that?"

I shook my head. "Not until you told me. He never said anything. He wasn't old enough for me to think about inheritances, but even if I had, I would have assumed his aunt Patty would be his beneficiary. She's his only living relative."

"Are you aware there was a substantial life insurance policy on him?"

That was news to me. Just as he asked that question, the door to the small room opened and Police Chief Jeff Kane entered. He nodded at me, then asked Brad, "How's it going?"

"We were just getting started." He didn't seem happy about the intrusion, and I wasn't very happy about it either.

Chief Kane took one of the extra chairs from the table and slid it toward the wall. "Don't mind me. Continue."

Brad cleared his throat. "Tell me about the phone call."

"Okay. I was shopping at Wal-Mart with Mrs. Mitchell." I stopped, my cheeks heated from embarrassment at having the chief in the room and the knowledge he suspected me of something so evil.

"And Jerome called?"

"Uh-huh."

"About what time was this?"

"Probably about 7:30-ish. We can check the caller ID on my cell to get the exact time."

"We'll do that. And what did he say?"

I sighed, knowing what the emotional cost of reliving the phone call would be. "It was a bad connection. I couldn't hear him very well."

"Tell me about the conversation."

"He said he was coming over after the readers' group meeting ended."

"Anything else?"

"His cell phone died, and he called from the pay phone near the restrooms, so it was rather noisy. He wanted to know why I wasn't at the Tavern. I'd left a message on his home and cell phones explaining

I couldn't make it because I had to take Mrs. Mitchell to the store, but I guess he hadn't checked his messages."

"What else did he say?"

"I can't recall his exact words, but he said something about being Dan's executor. He also mentioned the blackmail note."

Chief Kane said, "The blackmail note?"

"Yes. You know, it just occurred to me. How did he know about it? I never told him." I glared at Brad. "Did you?"

"It never came up. But that's interesting about him mentioning it. Who else knew about the note?"

"Sue Ann. You. Maybe Peggy. Maybe Sue Ann's husband, Ron. Other than the police, that's all I know of. I kept the information about it to myself."

Brad's brows drew together as he made a few notes on the legal pad on the table in front of him. "You didn't mention him saying anything about the blackmail note before."

"I'd forgotten. Mrs. Mitchell was snatching clothes off me—"

Brad looked uncomfortable and squirmed in his chair.

I realized what I'd just said and unintentionally implied. "It's not what you think. She had me try on the clothes she was interested in buying. I was only listening to Jerome with half an ear because of the chaos."

This was much harder than I'd thought it would be. "I wish I'd listened more carefully. I wish I'd told him to hang on while I stepped outside."

"Is there anything else you forgot?" asked Chief Kane.

"I don't think so. I told him to hang on while I took off a sweater for Mrs. Mitchell. When I came back on the line, he was no longer there. I never spoke with him again." My throat felt swollen shut, and it ached. "He did say some other stuff, but I couldn't hear him clearly."

Chief Kane asked, "And he never made it to your place?"

"No. I so wish he had. I so wish I had more information. Chief Kane, I know you think I had something to do with his death, and I want to reassure you I didn't. I want the murderer caught even more than you do."

Again Brad cleared his throat. I must have said something I shouldn't. He stood and reached out a hand to shut off the recorder.

"Hold up," directed the police chief.

Brad turned to look at him, but the chief didn't notice. His eyes were only on me.

"Did you know you were Jerome's beneficiary?"

"Not until Brad told me today."

"You're about to inherit a tidy sum. His business, his house, and a million-dollar life insurance policy."

The blood drained from my face. "A million—" Wooziness overwhelmed me. "Surely not. Surely you're wrong."

Chief Kane left his chair and came to hover over me. "As far as I'm concerned, you had well over a million reasons to see to it that Jerome never arrived at your house."

"That's enough," said Brad, switching off the recorder. "I'll get your statement typed, and you can come back later to sign it."

Pushing back my chair, I realized Brad was saving me from the wrath of Genghis Kane. The only problem was that Brad had driven me to the police department, and I didn't have a way home. On the upside, I hadn't been locked up. Judging by Chief Kane's attitude, I should be extremely grateful for my freedom.

Brad gestured for me to leave the room ahead of him. Once I did, he didn't follow. Instead, he closed the door. As I stepped away, I heard his raised voice. Apparently, he was having a few words with his boss.

I hoped he didn't lose his job on account of me.

As I climbed the steps to leave the basement-level police department entrance, I pulled my cell phone from my purse and flipped it open. After punching in the speed dial for Sue Ann, I paced the sidewalk outside the building.

She answered on the third ring.

"Any chance you can come and get me?"

Less than ten minutes later, Sue Ann's SUV pulled to the curb and I quickly jumped in.

She pulled away from the curb and into traffic. Not bothering with niceties as usual, she got right to the point. "What were you doing at the police station?"

"I had to make a statement about the last time I talked with Jerome." I wasn't quite sure how to break the bad news about Jerome to her. Even though she never thought Jerome was the right man for me, he'd been part of our social circle for many years, and she'd always liked him. "I have bad news."

She glanced my way, then back at the road. "Bad news about Jerome?"

"Yeah. I'm sorry, Sue Ann."

"What happened?"

"They found his body."

"No. No. No." She pounded her steering wheel in dismay. Her SUV came to a halt in the middle of the road, and her eyes filled with grief as she turned to me. "What happened to him? Where did they find him?"

"Sue Ann, Brad told me Jerome was murdered. They pulled his body out of the Verdigris."

"I can't believe he's gone." Tears burst from her eyes, and she fought to gain control of her emotions. She reached over and grabbed me in a fierce hug.

As soon as she touched me, I lost it too. The shock of the news of Jerome's murder had apparently worn off and the full impact of his loss hit me. Sue Ann and I cried so hard it was almost impossible to breathe. I'm not sure how long we sat cradling each other for comfort, but eventually a car came up behind us and honked.

Sue Ann leaned back and pulled her vehicle to the side of a road. She grabbed some tissues, handed me one, then wiped the tears from her face. At last she asked, "Are they sure it wasn't accidental drowning?"

"Not according to the coroner." I bit my lip, wondering how much to tell her, but I couldn't hold it back. "There's more. The police think I did it."

"Brad would never—"

"Not Brad. Chief Kane."

"That's a crock, Amy."

"Well, he has a pretty good reason. Jerome named me as his beneficiary and took out a huge insurance policy."

"I told you . . ." She trailed off, but I knew what she was going to say.

She'd told me Jerome was going to ask me to marry him, and I think she was right. He planned to do it the night he was murdered.

Since he assumed I'd say yes, it made sense that he named me as beneficiary. "Yeah. You told me."

"Chief Kane should still know better." She steered her SUV back onto the road.

"He seems pretty intent."

As she drove the rest of the way to my house, I filled her in on my recent grilling. She pulled into my driveway. "They didn't read you your Miranda rights?"

"I don't think they needed to. It wasn't an official questioning. I was voluntarily making a statement."

"I don't like it."

"Me neither." I sighed. "I'll let you in the house, but I need to hunt for my cat. He escaped when Brad and I left."

"Why didn't Brad bring you home?"

"I think he was too busy yelling at Chief Kane. I hope he won't get into any trouble on my behalf."

"He knows what he's doing."

We walked to my door and I let her in, all the while glancing around, hoping to see Chappy. No luck. "Go on in. I'll be there in a sec."

Turning, I walked over to Mrs. Mitchell's side yard, calling out for Chappy. I even peeked through the slats in her privacy fence but didn't see him. Giving up, I returned to my house to find Sue Ann straightening my den. "Don't worry about that. Let me tell you more about Jerome."

She reluctantly joined me in my kitchen for a cup of tea. After we got situated and sipped our tea, I filled her in on the details I knew about Jerome's death. She took it hard because she'd truly liked him.

"I can't believe someone would do that to him. Did they say what he was hit with?"

"No. Brad told me they'd know more once the coroner completed the autopsy. As much as I want some time to sit and mourn and just plain react to his death, I don't feel I have that luxury. I need to find out who did this to him. I feel totally responsible."

"Well, you're not. Some crazy person did this, and we'll see to it that whoever it is will fry."

I reached to the baker's rack behind my chair and pulled out my list of suspects. "Let's go over the list and see if we can rule anyone out—or in."

Diary of a Confessions Queen

"Good thinking."

We put our heads together over the list, but since we weren't sure who was there and who wasn't, it was impossible to rule anyone out entirely. "We need to ask Brad who was at the Tavern that night."

I made a note to that effect. "I should call Dr. Elden and set up that chess lesson. Maybe she'll say or do something that will let us strike her from the list."

"We know for certain that most of the readers' group members were there for the meeting. I'm cleaning Helen's house tomorrow and will see if she remembers anything that'll be helpful."

Helen was the detail-oriented (some said anal-retentive) president of the group. If anyone had any information, she was most likely to. "Hmm. She's not on my list. Should I add her?"

"If Helen wanted to off anyone, she'd stage it as an accident and no one would ever find out."

Sue Ann was right. Helen was extremely effective. "Okay. I'll put her at the very bottom of our list."

Someone knocked on the front door. I left the kitchen and answered the door.

Brad stood there, looking very cute in khakis and a polo shirt. He'd obviously changed clothes since going off duty. He held something behind him.

"Hi."

"Hi." He grinned and pulled a twisting and hissing ball of fur from behind his back. "Missing a cat?"

CHAPTER SIXTEEN

i Checked My Mate. and i'm Not Happy with What i Found

Having my cat again filled me with gratitude. Brad, Sue Ann, and I were seated at my kitchen table, watching Chappy gobble canned tuna. "Thanks for finding him."

"No prob." He reached out and picked up Sue Ann's and my list of suspects. "What's this?"

There was no way I could tell him what it was without receiving another lecture about staying out of it. "Sue Ann and I are thinking about having a party."

His expression was doubtful. "Isn't that a little out of place considering Jerome's death?"

Sue Ann emitted a nervous giggle.

"Did I say *party*? I meant wake." The words tumbled out of me, and I kept my eyes pointed anywhere but near Brad. I've never been good at lying, but the situation seemed to call for a little truth-stretching. "A wake for Jerome."

"Seems an odd list." He looked up at me, and I knew he knew I knew he knew what the list darn well was. "You're inviting the readers' group to his wake?"

"Of course." I shrugged, not willing to back down from my fib. "They're all his friends."

"I wouldn't exactly call him friends with Fred Cook."

"He went to school with Fred's wife, Yvonne." I hoped that was true. They were pretty close in age, so it likely was, even if they weren't in the same grade.

"So, Brad," said Sue Ann, effectively taking his attention off me. "Who all was at the Tavern the night Jerome disappeared?"

Whew. Hot seats are extremely uncomfortable.

He cocked a suspicious eyebrow. "Why do you ask?"

"So we'll know who to avoid," she replied, fluttering her eyelashes.

"You two are so transparent." He shook his head. "I shouldn't tell either of you a thing."

"I'm your chief suspect," I piped in. "You owe me."

I was really pushing it, but what else could I say? I needed the information he had, and he darn well better dish it or he'd have to guard some other area of his body besides his derriere.

He cleared his throat and tapped the list, changing the subject. "Interestingly, everyone on this list was at the Tavern the night Jerome disappeared. Fred Cook was there with his wife, Yvonne. Dr. Elden attended her first readers group meeting. Even Dolores and Liz were there with their woo-woo psychic medium pal. Go figure."

Karen? Go figure, indeed. Perhaps I should add her name to my list because I hadn't considered her before.

"I was thinking, Amy. The two men you were involved with both disappeared."

"This is news?" Maybe I'd given him more credit than he deserved. With such perceptiveness, it's no wonder he'd never found Dan. He needed all the help he could get. Then I realized what he might be thinking. "Are you linking them together? Do you think someone murdered Dan, too, but his body simply hasn't turned up?"

He nodded. "It's a possibility."

"I think it's damn likely," said Sue Ann. "What else could have happened to Dan?"

"Is there someone who wants his competition out of the way?" Brad frowned my way. "Someone who has a fixation on you?"

"No one has a fixation, or crush for that matter," I replied. "I don't have a stalker. I don't even know anyone who'd have a chance to fixate on me. I don't get out much."

"That's true. You should get out more," said Sue Ann.

"If you think of anyone who might fit the bill, let me know," Brad said. "I need an angle to pursue on this that doesn't involve you being a black widow."

"I just thought of someone fixating on me."

"You did?" Sue Ann asked expectantly.

My answering grin was bitter. "Chief Kane."

After Brad and Sue Ann left, I placed a call to Dr. Elden to ask her about chess lessons. She agreed to get together the next afternoon after she got done at the veterinary clinic. So it was with not the least trepidation that I went next door and asked Mrs. Mitchell if I could borrow her Caddy for the night.

"Buy your own car," she said, then slammed the door in my face. The whole people-being-nice-to-me thing crashed to the concrete on her front porch.

What had I said? What had I done?

I sighed heavily and walked back to my house. Because Sue Ann would be busy at Helen's, she wouldn't be able to drive me. I really didn't want to ride my bike after both Dan and Jerome were waylaid somewhere between the Tavern and my home, especially with the break-ins that had occurred at my house. I didn't feel personally threatened, but to the best of my knowledge, neither of them did either.

Last choice, I could see if Officer Friendly would like to give me a ride to the police station on some pretext. I could ask for a copy of my statement, and the Tavern was walking distance from there. I wouldn't dare ask him for a ride to the Tavern, though, because he'd probably make good on using those handcuffs to keep me out of the investigation. I just needed to time the phone call appropriately.

In the meantime, I finally had a few quiet moments to think about Jerome's death and how much I would miss him. I headed to the altar in my bedroom, lowered my head, and sent good thoughts out into the universe. Then, hedging my bets, I genuflected, then made the sign of the cross and began saying the Our Father, with a few Hail Marys thrown in.

When at last I raised my head, it was too late to call Brad for a ride. I wandered into my office and fired up my desktop. Somewhere between my opening scene and a series of *aaaaaaaaaaaaaaaaaaa*'s, I fell asleep on the keyboard.

The next morning, I wondered if the imprint of the keyboard would ever fade from my face. I looked like something out of *Hellboy*. After I took a quick shower, Chappy led me into the kitchen for his breakfast. Once I fed him and made myself some tea, I gave Sue Ann a quick call.

"I'm meeting Dr. Elden after she gets off work today."

"That's great. I think it should be fairly easy for you to rule her out. I can't see how she could have anything to do with Jerome's death. I don't think she had a crush on him, and I doubt Jerome saw her in any insinuating circumstances."

"That's right. I hadn't thought of that before, but ruling at least one person out would be a step forward. I'm tired of not making any headway on this."

"You and me both. I'll chat with Helen and see if she knows anything helpful."

"I imagine Brad already talked with her, but she might tell you more."

"And he might not have asked the right questions."

"Speaking of the devil, I'm asking him for a ride to the station this afternoon to pick up a copy of my statement. Mrs. Mitchell won't let me borrow her car, and I can walk from there to my meeting with Dr. Elden."

"You couldn't promise Mrs. Mitchell Wal-Mart?"

"Not on your life! But something was odd—she practically slammed the door in my face."

"What's up with that?"

"I don't know, but it's not like her."

"Maybe she's mad because Brad's crushing on you and not her."

"Heaven forbid. And I've told you a zillion times, Brad doesn't have a crush on me."

"If he didn't, don't you think he'd have already arrested you for Jerome's murder? I do."

"Suspicion isn't the same thing as proof." I sighed. "A crush or lack thereof is the last thing I want to think about right now. I want to find out who killed Jerome and probably my husband. I just wish I had a better idea of how to go about it."

"Footwork."

Late that afternoon, Brad pulled up to my house. I quickly left the house and shut the front door without allowing Chappy to escape. This took some doing, involving sticking my foot in the crack and quickly yanking it back before slamming the door on my leg. I hopped into Brad's car. "Thanks for the ride."

"Protect and serve."

"Have you made any headway on the investigation?"

"Even if I had, I couldn't tell our chief suspect."

"Very funny." I hate it when my own words are thrown back at me. "Have you heard from the coroner?"

"Report confirms blunt trauma to the head. Wound created by cylindrical object. He said the weapon could have been anything from a tree branch to a table leg—something big, rounded, and heavy. Jerome was definitely dead before being thrown in the river." He suddenly stopped speaking, then added, "Don't tell anyone you got this information from me. Chief Kane is already *anxious* about my personal involvement in this case."

"Basically you're saying my source of info has dried up."

"Like the Mojave." He pulled into the lot behind the police station. "But that doesn't mean I'm not determined to find out what happened to Jerome. I am, and I will."

That was reassuring. "Thanks, Brad. I won't ask anything that might jeopardize your position. It's not worth it."

"That's where you're wrong," he said, unbuckling his seat belt and putting his car into *park* all in one fluid motion. "I'm determined to find out what happened to Jerome. But I'm not in any danger of losing my job."

He led me down the steps to the front door of the station, and it took a minute for my eyes to adjust after being in the sunshine outside. It didn't take long for him to get me settled with a copy of my statement.

"I have some paperwork to do," he said. "But I'll give you a ride home as soon as I'm done."

Uh-oh. "Oh, I don't want to put you out."

"You won't. I'll be heading home."

"It's not necessary." He wasn't backing down, but I wasn't yet ready to divulge where I was heading—not with Mr. Buttinsky. "I have other plans."

He narrowed his eyes, but didn't ask more questions. Thank heavens. He simply spun on his heels and walked away.

For a moment I felt guilty, but then I gave myself a mental kick. This was Brad. While he was being very helpful, if I gave him an inch, he'd take the mileage to Kansas City and back. However, I wasn't about to stick around to give him the chance.

Within minutes I was out on the sidewalk, walking the two blocks to the Independence Tavern where I would be meeting Dr. Elden shortly. The day was clear and sunny, and the temperature was warm without being hot. A perfect day for walking. Since I still had a few minutes before it was time to meet Dr. Elden, I took my time and enjoyed window-shopping along the way.

Twenty minutes later, I arrived at the Tavern. As before, my eyes took a few minutes to adjust to the lack of sunlight. Once my vision cleared, the first thing I saw was Dr. Elden sitting in a booth—with Brad.

I marched over and joined them. "How did you know where I'd be?"

"Amy, I'm a detective. I detected." He smirked as he stood, allowing me to take a seat in the booth.

"What did you do—call Sue Ann and ask where I'd be?"

He looked a little uncomfortable as he pulled up his pant legs, then took a seat in the booth beside me. I figured I'd hit the nail on the head when he said, "Nice work, Sherlock."

I scooted over as far as I could in the booth. His body heat disturbed me. It was going to be truly difficult to get my questions in with him watching my every move—or, for that matter, feeling my every intake of breath, considering how close he was sitting.

"So why are you here?"

"I thought it would be nice to learn to play chess, too." The grin he directed my way was very toothy.

"I'm sure Dr Elden won't—"

"Don't worry. She already invited me to join you. Didn't you, Mare?"

Mare? He called her by a nickname instead of Mary or Dr. Elden? This time my eyes narrowed. How well did they know each other?

"I hope you don't mind, Amy," she said.

I dredged up what I hoped would pass for a sincere smile. "Of course not."

But under the table, I swung my leg sideways, connecting my shoe with Brad's shin.

The tabletop had a chessboard embedded on it, and Dr. Elden pulled out a case filled with chess pieces. She set them up on the table-top. "This is how you set up before starting a match."

She then began explaining how each piece moved, starting with the pawns. "They aren't very powerful, but at times they can make the difference in a game. Never underestimate the power of the little guy."

Next she picked up the queen and demonstrated how she could move. "She's the most powerful piece on the board, kind of like a pawn hopped up on steroids."

The last of her words were drowned out by the sound of singing coming from the Tavern's back room. It's there the readers' group some-times met, and considering the sound of "Sweet Adeline" lyrics coming from that direction, it's where a barbershop quartet met as well. For a moment, the singing died down, but then as Dr. Elden started to speak again they started back up with a flourish, even louder than before.

"This may be difficult, Dr. Elden," I yelled in her direction, hoping she could hear me over the quartet.

"Call me Mare," she shouted back.

I shot Brad an I'm-one-of-her-intimates-too grin. "Okay. Mare, maybe we should move to another seat."

"Chessboards are only set up back here."

Finding out whether she had something to do with Jerome's murder or Dan's disappearance would be impossible in this racket. She could barely hear me, much less answer questions I could hear.

"Want to try a test match?"

"Sure. Brad, you go first." At least with him busy, I could sneak away and do some investigating on my own. I wanted to check out the restroom and phone area to see who all might have been able to overhear Jerome talking with me the night he was murdered. It also wouldn't hurt to speak with a few of the Tavern's employees, on the off chance they might have remembered anything suspicious.

"Ladies first."

I shook my head. "No, you."

"I insist."

The man must be a mind reader. He simply wasn't about to let me get away with anything. "Fine, but I need to visit the powder room first."

He scowled, but stood.

With as innocent a smile as I could muster, I rose from the booth and headed to the restrooms. The entrance to the meeting room was to the right in the same back hallway, which ran east to west behind the main dining room. The door to the immediate left was the men's room. Following it in the middle was a pay phone, and at the far end to the left was the ladies' room. The hallway dead-ended straight ahead at the kitchen entrance. This meant anyone—from a guest, to a restaurant employee, to a readers' group member—could have overheard Jerome. Assuming he'd said something to me on the phone that had gotten him killed might not be correct, but at least it was a starting point in trying to piece together what had happened that night.

I stepped into the ladies' room. The manager of the Tavern, Tara Lewis, stood inside, washing her hands. Tara was an interesting character. Her hair was flaming red and extremely—tall. She had no patoot to speak of, and had one hell of a rack. And you never saw her without a wad of chewing gum in her mouth.

She greeted me between gum smacks. "Hey there, Amy. I heard about Jerome. I'm so sorry."

I nodded. "Me, too."

"How you holdin' up, hon?"

"I think okay. But I sure wish I knew what happened to him."

"I've been thinking about that night. You know, I remembered something I haven't mentioned before."

"What's that?"

"I saw your mother-in-law standing just outside this door with her head bent in deep conversation with Jerome. Might be nothing, but I thought I should mention it."

"You saw Dolores talking with Jerome?"

She nodded. "They were standing by the pay phone."

"I don't suppose you remember what time that was."

She shook her head, and for a moment I thought the skyscraper of hair might topple. It wobbled left. It wobbled right. If it fell, would she hit the ceramic tile floor? But her hair teetered back into place without physical harm. Tara continued, totally unaware of her near-disaster, "I've tried to remember, but I'm just not sure. Might have been early. Might have been late. No clue."

"Thanks so much for telling me. If you think of anything else, I'd truly appreciate you letting me know." Since she didn't remember when she saw them talking, there was no way to be certain their conversation took place after Jerome called me. It could have happened at any time.

"I'll let you know if I remember anything else, hon. Do you think I should tell Brad? It didn't seem important enough to me, but you never know."

I was certain Dolores wouldn't harm a hair on anyone's head, and the last thing I wanted was for Chief Kane to go after her. He might, given how quickly he jumped to conclusions, no matter how innocent her conversation with Jerome may have been. Dolores' hold on sanity was feeble enough as it was, without Kane driving her even more insane. "It's probably nothing. I wouldn't."

"I'm sure you're right." She gave the Empire State Building that was her hairdo one final poke, then turned to leave. "Gotta get back to work now."

"See you later," I said, watching her sashay out the door. Glancing at myself in the mirror, I wondered if she had some sort of wiring structure in her hair to keep it in place. And hair spray. What brand did she use? If I was coming into the kind of money Chief Kane told me about, then I might want to invest in the manufacturer.

I dawdled in the bathroom as long as I could, hoping Brad would have given in and started a game with my new bosom pal, Mare. But when I exited the hallway and my gaze focused on them, they weren't alone. Sue Ann had joined them and was seated beside Mare.

"Hey," she called as I approached the booth. "I got through early and thought I'd join you guys. Are you a chess pro yet?"

The quartet was evidently on break, because all I could hear from the meeting room was the sound of men's mumbled voices. Thank God.

Not that I dislike music. Or quartets.

I just like them to be in tune.

"We were just getting started," said Mare. "Do you want to learn, too?"

"Oh, no. I'm no good at games."

Brad stood, allowing me to take my seat again as he studied the chessboard.

He and Mare had been playing a game, and he reached over and moved his queen. "Check."

Mare looked startled as she glanced at the board; then she moved a pawn and scooped up his queen. "Checkmate."

CHAPTER SEVENTEEN

Serial Cheater

The chess lesson finally ended, thank heavens, but the four of us were still seated at our booth chatting.

Our waitress, Heather, strolled up. "Do you guys want anything? More coffee? Dessert?"

"I'm up for pie," said Sue Ann, who loved dessert.

"Sounds good." Brad leaned across me and pulled the plastic-cased menu from behind the napkin holder, then scanned the list of desserts.

Even Mare got in on the sweet-tooth action. "I'll have strawberry cheesecake."

I was the only holdout, not being so much in the mood. Knowing what had happened to Jerome after leaving the Tavern only days earlier left me gloomy.

Sue Ann read my thoughts. "Thinking about Jerome?"

I shrugged. "He's never far from my thoughts."

She reached across the table and patted my hand. "We'll figure this thing out, won't we, Brad? You're going to find the jerk who did this and bring him to justice."

"I'm determined to apprehend Jerome's murderer."

We all looked at the equally determined expression on Brad's face as Heather returned with the desserts. She placed a cookie on a saucer in front of me.

"I didn't order anything."

"I know you didn't, Amy, but from your expression, I thought you needed some chocolate." She bobbed her head and flounced away, leaving me staring at the chocolate and walnut cookie.

What the hey. I broke off a piece and ate it. Heather was right. I needed chocolate.

Mare pointed her whipped cream–stained fork in my direction. "I was thinking, Amy. First Dan disappeared, and now Jerome's dead. Is there some man getting rid of his romantic rivals?"

"I don't think so."

"Come on. Surely there's some guy with a crush on you."

Mid-bite, Sue Ann stopped eating her chocolate cream pie and turned to meet my gaze. Simultaneously, we both turned to look at Brad. I couldn't help myself, and Sue Ann apparently couldn't either.

Red heat climbed my neck into my face, and I quickly looked down at my cookie. But not quickly enough.

Mare, who'd watched our every move, immediately looked at Brad, too.

"What?" he asked with furrowed brows. He glanced at each of us in turn, when enlightenment dawned. Then an irate scowl covered his features. "I don't—I mean—how could you think that? Jerome was my closest friend."

"Think what?" asked Sue Ann in her most innocent tone.

He pushed back his plate. His next comment was directed at me. "Don't go getting any ideas."

"What? I didn't say a word."

"You didn't need to."

When I glanced away from Brad, I noticed Yvonne Cook and, based on the direct look she gave me, she was heading my way. She had great timing.

Yvonne was medium height, a little bit chubby, in a truly cute way. Her hair was honey blond and neatly styled. She always wore suits as part of her job, and I'd never seen her in anything else. Since I always wore jeans as part of my job, I always felt underdressed when she was nearby. That night was no exception.

I nudged Brad as Yvonne arrived at our booth. "Hi, Yvonne."

"Hi, everyone," she said through thinned lips. "Sorry to interrupt, but can I talk with you, Amy?"

"Sure."

Her gaze darted around the table before meeting mine, and she fidgeted where she stood. Considering she was the high school administrator, this wasn't her usual bossy behavior. She added, "Alone. I need to speak with you alone."

My brows rose. "Okay."

Brad scooted out of the booth to let me get out. I was anything but graceful, my legs sticking to the plastic seat covering, but eventually I slid out.

Yvonne and I walked together a few paces toward the back room where the quartet met. It sounded as if they were breaking up for the evening, and I wondered how private my conversation with Yvonne would be.

She must have been of the same mind, because she began to speak rapidly in a whisper. "Fred said you came to see him."

I nodded. It wasn't easy to hear her, so I moved a step closer and said, "Did he tell you he told me to get out?"

"I don't honestly blame him. How dare you accuse him of having something to do with Dan's disappearance?"

"I didn't. I just hoped he might know something about that night."

"Amy, I heard the news about Jerome, and before you go siccing the police on my husband, I figured some straight talk is in order."

Straight talk. I sure liked the sound of that. "Honest, Yvonne, I didn't accuse Fred of anything."

"If you repeat what I have to say, I'll have the high school football team toilet paper your house. Got it?"

"Yes." At least she wasn't threatening me with hit men. Compared with everything I'd been through lately, her threat was almost laughable.

"The night your husband disappeared, my husband was with another woman."

"Ohh." I didn't say anything else, and there was a moment of silence between us. At last, enlightenment dawned. "He was with Gayla Mullen."

Yvonne lowered her gaze.

My thoughts raced, putting everything into place. "So that's why Fred told me to get out—"

"You'd been to Belle Plaine. Yes. I don't like the idea of you trying to blackmail him."

"Blackmail? Who said anything about blackmail? I honestly didn't know. It was a coincidence. Sue Ann and I have been trying to find out anything we can about Dan's disappearance, so we've been talking with anyone who might know anything."

It was Yvonne's turn to look uncomfortable. It had been unnecessary to air her personal dirty laundry. But once she had, she evidently liked having someone to talk to, because she continued. "I told Gayla to get out of town before I had her fired from her job. She saw the wisdom of my words."

Whoa. I sure wouldn't want to mess with Yvonne—not to mention her husband. She meant business and didn't willy-nilly around. No time wasted beating around the bush. Gayla must have been crazy to have become involved with Fred.

"I'm sorry, Yvonne. It's not nice to learn bad things about people we love."

She tossed back her hair. "It was one of the hardest things I've ever faced. After dealing with juvenile delinquents, you'd think something like that would be easier to deal with. But it's not. Nothing prepares you for it."

"How did you find out?"

"Fred came home the night Dan disappeared and told me. Someone saw Fred with Gayla, and he wanted to confess before someone beat him to the punch."

"Do you know who saw them?"

"It wasn't important."

It might not be important to her, but it might be extremely important to me. "Do you think you can find out?"

She shook her head. "I'd rather not reopen the can of worms. Fred was genuinely ashamed of himself, and I've made sure ever since that he wasn't in situations where it could happen again."

"I can understand your reaction. So why tell me? Why now?"

"The night Jerome was here at the Tavern, Fred and I were here, too. But let me make this point clear. Fred and I left here together. Alone."

Message received. She and her husband had nothing to do with Dan's disappearance or Jerome's murder. "Well, thanks for telling me.

It's good to rule—" I broke off, not wanting to admit I had thought Fred might have offed my husband. "It would have been great if Fred knew anything that could help us find Dan, but at least now we know he doesn't."

"Now you go tell your policeman boyfriend that Fred isn't a suspect."

"He's not my boyfriend."

"That's not what Maureen at the Clip 'n Curl says, and she knows everything."

"She's wrong this time. Brad and Jerome were close friends, and Brad's determined to do whatever it takes to find out who killed his friend."

"Whatever." She waved her hand as if it was unimportant. And it probably was, to her. But it was a literal matter of life and death.

"It's true."

"Just make sure Brad's aware we're out of this. I'm tired of police sniffing around, asking questions about things that are none of their business."

I wondered why she didn't tell Brad herself. However, I realized if I did a favor for her, perhaps she'd return it. "I'll tell him what you said. And if you should happen to learn who saw Fred and Gayla together, please let me know."

With an abrupt nod of her head, she turned and walked away, without any good-byes or pleasantries. I'd been dismissed. Memories of being seated in the principal's office during middle school assailed me. (Sue Ann and I chatted too much in class.)

After a moment, my thoughts cleared enough to return to the booth. This time Brad scooted over and let me sit on the edge. Guess he was tired of letting me in and out.

"Boy, she left fast," said Sue Ann. "What did she want?"

"She wanted me to tell Brad neither she nor Fred had anything to do with Jerome's death or Dan's disappearance."

Brad's eyebrows rose so high, they almost disappeared into his scalp. "Why wouldn't she tell me this information? Why you?"

"It's a woman thing. I told her I'd ask you to scratch her off your list of suspects."

"That's not exactly how it works." He pulled out his small police notebook. "I'll bring them in for questioning."

"I wish you wouldn't." Reaching out, I placed my hand on his arm. "Seriously, Brad, I don't think they had anything to do with either event."

It took him a moment to respond while he looked into my eyes. At last he blinked, shrugged my hand off his arm, then flipped his notebook closed. "I'll wait to contact them."

"Thanks." I beamed at him.

"For now." He enunciated the words carefully.

My smile died. At least he'd given me that much. "Thank you."

He cleared his throat. "You about ready to go? I'll drive you home."

I wasn't sure what to say. "Sue Ann is planning to—"

He shook his head and said, "You're not going home without me checking it first."

"I'm sure that's unnecessary." I was definitely beginning to wonder if he was my stalker. What if Brad had wanted me to himself? What if he was some crazed guy, and I'd never realized it before? He certainly had the knowledge needed to have made Dan disappear without a clue. "Sue Ann and I have something to plan for the . . ." I searched for something we had to do together.

"The Neewollah Festival." Sue Ann broke in fast. It's lovely having such a wonderful friend who knows when I'm desperately trying to get out of something. "I'll make sure she's fine," she said, nodding toward me.

"Why don't you talk here now? I insist on securing your place, Amy."

"Fine. I'll call you in half an hour, Sue Ann. If you don't hear from me by then, call the authorities." I tried to say it like a joke but knew my grin was sickly.

Sue Ann's eyes widened. "Okay. You've got half an hour, or the Mounties come to the rescue."

During the ride home, I was anything but calm. I kept shooting nervous glances at Brad out of the corner of my eye. When the topic of someone being fixated on me had come up earlier, I hadn't taken it that seriously. But now that I was alone with Brad, I couldn't seem to rid my mind of the idea. What if I was alone with the man who killed my husband and Jerome? What if I was next on his list?

I clutched my purse tightly in my hands, hoping the karate training I'd begun while writing a confession about being a karate master would come back to me. The only problem was that I hadn't practiced any maneuvers useful while sitting in a car.

I was being silly. This was Brad. I was just freaked out over everything that was happening. It was no wonder I'd begun to suspect him—I suspected almost everyone I knew.

"You're not harboring a fugitive, are you?" Brad asked.

What an odd question. Did he think I might have someone hidden in my house to help me? "I don't think I know any fugitives to harbor. Why do you ask?"

"You're nervous about something. Illegal drugs?"

I snorted. "I wish. I've got aspirin if you have a headache."

Now why had I said that? Thankfully it was dark out, so he couldn't see the blush that had traveled to my cheeks. Even though I knew it was silly, I couldn't help but think if I kept him laughing, I wouldn't be the next victim on his list.

At last, he pulled his car into my driveway and parked. As he climbed from the car, inspiration struck. "Why don't I wait out here while you check things out?"

That way, if he had any murderous impulses, I wouldn't be nearby. With any luck, it wouldn't take him long to search, and I could find a way to get him out of my house and me in.

"Lock the doors," he ordered curtly, then stopped. "You have to unlock the door."

Rats. Rats. Rats! "Okay, but I'm coming back out here after opening it."

He didn't say any words, but I thought I heard him making chicken noises under his breath.

He was right. I was a coward. I had no reason to suspect Brad of anything, but emotion rather than logic ruled my thoughts. I dashed out of the car and past him to the front door, quickly punching in the number to unlock the door. Once I swung it open, he joined me and I motioned for him to go inside. "Let me know when it's safe to come inside."

He entered, shaking his head like I was nuts. And I was nuts. Nuts to get away from him. I ran back to his car and locked the doors.

Then I realized he had his keys. Maybe waiting in his car wasn't such a great idea. I quickly exited, having decided to go to Mrs. Mitchell's. I didn't get further than three steps away, when I heard his voice.

"Amy!"

"What?"

"Where are you going?"

"To Mrs. Mitchell's."

"Good idea." His voice came out strained. "Stay inside, and don't let anyone without a badge in."

I started to nod, but stopped when I realized what he meant. "Has someone broken in again?"

"You could say that."

That made me pause. "What did you find?"

"Signs that someone broke in through a broken window. I've called into the station, and a team will be here shortly. Go inside Mrs. Mitchell's, and stay there."

Great. Just great. How much more fun was tonight going to become? I just hoped my cat hadn't escaped again. "Can you check on Chappy, please? Make sure he's okay?"

"Will do. I'll bring him over to you once the team arrives."

I approached Mrs. Mitchell's and knocked. She opened the door slowly, rather than with the speed of light as usual. "What do you want?"

"Can I please come in? My house has been broken into again, and Brad asked me to come stay here while they check everything out."

She didn't answer immediately, but then I remembered what Sue Ann had suggested about her being jealous of my friendship with Brad. "Brad said he'd come over soon."

She smiled and the door swung open like magic. "Come on in."

By the time I'd taken a seat on her sofa, she'd warmed up as if she hadn't shut the door in my face the day before. We sat chatting about her Pilates class when someone knocked on the door.

"That must be Brad." I stood up to go open the door, but Mrs. Mitchell gestured me back.

"I'll get it." She smoothed her skirt and patted her hair as she walked to the door. When she swung it open, it wasn't Brad. Instead a uniformed officer stood there with my cat in his arms.

"Is Amy here?"

I jumped from the sofa and sprinted to the door. "Where's Brad?"

The officer looked nervously over his shoulder toward my house.

A number of police vehicles were parked in my driveway and on the street.

"Detective Tyler asked me to tell you that things are a little more complicated than he'd first thought," said the officer. "He asked me to bring you your cat and tell you to find a place to stay for the night."

My forehead furrowed. "A place to stay?"

"It'll be a while before you'll be allowed back into a crime scene."

CHAPTER EIGHTEEN

My Life is a Crime Scene

The idea of my home being a crime scene again shouldn't have freaked me out, but it did. After I questioned the officer further, he revealed it was now a vandalism case. That got me very worried, but when I tried to go over to find out what was happening, Brad came out of the house and ordered me back to Mrs. Mitchell's.

Naturally, I didn't take that well. "Just tell me what's going on."

"Some of your things were broken, Amy. I'll be over to tell you all about it once things here are cleared up."

"Why do I need to spend the night somewhere else?"

"We're taking fingerprints and photos. It'll be a few hours, so you might as well get some sleep. I'll have the officer bring your cat's litter and food as soon as possible."

"What happened? What was vandalized?"

"I'll tell you later."

"You're making it worse, you know. I'm imagining all sorts of horrible things."

"I just don't have time to go into this now."

I grimaced and tried to sidestep him, but he blocked my path.

"Can't you make things easy just once?" he asked.

"Fine." I crossed my arms. "Just tell me—is my computer okay?" Since I make my living using it, my computer's unvandalized state was important.

"It appears to be. Look, I'm going back to work so we won't be here all night."

"You're off duty."

"Not now." He didn't seem as annoyed. I could tell he was weakening.

"You'll come over as soon as you're done?"

"It might be dawn. I don't want to wake you."

"Believe me, I won't be asleep."

"Don't say I didn't warn you." He pivoted and walked toward my front door, then turned back, obviously waiting for me to return to Mrs. Mitchell's.

By this time, she was standing at the front door. I could tell she was thinking about sprinting over to talk with Brad, too, so I quickly joined her. "We have to wait inside."

Her expression was mutinous, so I added, "Brad says he'll come over as soon as they're done."

She eyed me, then glanced over, looking for Brad. By then he'd disappeared into my house. With a shrug, she led me back into her house. She was awfully quiet at first, and I could see the wheels turning in her head. At last she asked, "Want some warm milk?"

She must have hoped I'd be fast asleep when Brad returned. "There's no way I can sleep. How about some coffee instead?"

Somewhere around three in the morning, I heard a rap on the front door. I'd called Sue Ann earlier and filled her in about what Tara had told me as well as about what was going on at my place, or at least as much as I knew about it. Mrs. Mitchell had fallen asleep in her recliner and was softly snoring. I tiptoed to the door and quietly swung it open. Brad stood there, looking exhausted. Stubble covered his jaw, and his eyes were puffy. Let's just say he looked even cuter than usual, and his usual was very, very cute.

I stepped outside and pulled the door slightly, not closing it entirely since I didn't want to lock myself out. All of the police vehicles were gone. Only Brad's Tahoe still sat in my driveway. "All done?"

He nodded. "Just about."

"What do you have left to do?"

"Take you back in to check your computer for any messages—and do a walk-through with you."

"Okay." It must have been time to learn what had been vandalized. With everything going on, I didn't want to leave Mrs. Mitchell with her house unlocked, so I went ahead and closed her door the rest of the way as silently as possible, then joined Brad on the walkway.

It was still dark out. Crickets chirped, but otherwise there was little noise besides the sound of our footsteps. The only light came from a streetlight a few houses down the block. My house was dark, leaving it looking like a large, black face. The sky must have been overcast, because I couldn't make out any stars overhead. I shivered, glad I wasn't walking the few feet between our houses alone. I glanced up at Brad beside me, feeling he was the only solidity in my chaotic world right then. At least with whatever I had to face in my house, he was with me. I wouldn't have to do this alone.

He'd closed the door, so I had to key in my number to let us in. As the door swung open, I momentarily closed my eyes, worried about what I'd find. At first I didn't see anything except the entry area, but then I looked to the left. There, where smooth carpeting should be, I made out small jagged shapes on the floor. I didn't understand what it was until I reached over and switched on the overhead light.

Immediately, I wished I hadn't, not quite able to take in what I observed. Shards of broken pottery circled the room. Not pottery. China.

My glaze lifted, and I saw the shelving Dan had so carefully installed dangling at odd angles from the walls.

Nana's china. Her beloved teacups.

I dashed over, forgetting Brad, forgetting anything except the memories of sitting with Nana at her table, sipping tea and sharing secrets. My parents' deaths had frozen me. When Nana had brought me home from the cemetery, she'd observed me quietly but hadn't dismissed my feelings. To her, death meant a new beginning, so there were no tears from her. Only a light of love shining in her warm blue eyes.

The two of us were alone; she'd turned away all visitors.

"Go change your clothes and wash your face," she'd said matter-of-factly. "It'll make you feel better. Then come join me in the kitchen."

Wordlessly, I'd done as she asked.

When I entered her tiny kitchen, she was seated at the aged, dark wooden table, the china hutch behind her wedged into the corner like crayons in their box. China teacups sitting on the hutch shelf circled behind her like a halo.

The aroma of freshly steeped tea assailed my senses, the bitter fragrance matching my mood. Perched on the table were two beautiful teacups on saucers, steam from the beverage rising like something from a witch's brew.

My parents had talked of Nana's peculiarities in hushed tones, as if she were someone to be ashamed of, but I'd always adored her and she, me.

Yet my eyes had widened. What if the substance in the teacups truly was a potion?

Her words rushed over me. "Take a seat and drink up, Amy. It'll help for now, and time will heal the rest."

She was right. Time had healed the rest, but that was because Nana had freely shared her love. A love that now choked me as I viewed the unnecessary destruction.

I brushed back the memory, as well as the moisture threatening to spill from my eyes. Now Nana's teacups were gone. Lowering to my knees, I picked up the closest shard. It was the lovely violet pattern. Nana's favorite.

I glanced around the devastation, then began gathering the pieces, hopelessly thinking I might be able to glue them back together again. There had to be some way to repair them.

But there were too many shards, too many broken memories. I leaned back on my heels. "Nana."

Brad came over and lightly touched the back of my neck. "I'm so sorry, Amy."

I wouldn't cry. Fighting tears, I couldn't look at him. I wouldn't let whoever did this have the satisfaction of seeing my pain, even if the jerk never knew. A huge lump formed in my throat, and I thought I wouldn't be able to breathe past it, but at last I managed to suck air into my lungs. More composed, I asked, "Who did this?" My words came out in a roughened rasp, as if forming words was foreign to me.

Brad cleared his throat, probably buying time. I barely noticed.

The china looked as if it had been run through a blender, with pieces so fragmented it was impossible to tell their original design.

Anger sledgehammered through me. "Someone destroyed my memories. Someone who knew how important these cups were to me came in and deliberately smashed them to bits."

My gaze flew to his. He studied me, his expression calm and calculated. I didn't back down. I didn't look away.

He drew in a deep breath, then slowly released it. "There was a slip of paper buried beneath some of the pieces. We think it fell out of his pocket while he broke the cups. We've brought him in for questioning."

"Him?" Again the raspy sound I didn't recognize. All this time, I'd thought the killer was most likely a woman. *Cherchez l'homme* didn't have the same ring to it. "Who?"

At last he looked away, but his words were clipped. "Amy, it's not definite."

I swallowed past the lump in my throat and found my voice. "Tell me who."

My words came out strong. Insistent. Demanding. Brad's woeful expression told me he knew I wouldn't stop insisting until he'd told me all he knew.

"The paper could have been planted here, Amy."

The gentle tone of his words did nothing to soothe me.

He added, "It's not concrete evidence."

"I'll accept that. It's not concrete." Even if he wasn't certain, the odds were the man who had done this, the man who had sought to slash me to my core, had been apprehended. "I want to know who you've brought in for questioning. You have to tell me."

"Fred Cook. The paper was a drawing of the battery charger—the one Dan's spirit accused him of stealing."

"But Yvonne—"

He interrupted. "Don't you find it odd she came and ordered you off his trail?"

"While I didn't expect her to react the way she did, I find it even odder that she would draw attention to Fred while he was here"—I waved my arms at the devastation—"doing this."

"Perhaps she didn't know. Perhaps he took advantage of her absence to come here, looking to harm you, and when you weren't home he took it out on the objects you most love."

"How would he know that?"

"Amy, are you being deliberately dense? Dan built custom shelving, created an invention, just for your teacups. Anyone coming in your house would know how special these teacups are—were—to you."

"He's never been in my house."

"That you know of. What about the break-ins?"

I gnawed my lower lip. Could Fred have been behind all of the recent events? Could he have destroyed his competition by killing my husband? Could he have murdered Jerome? I couldn't think of a reason for him to do any of these senseless things. And it made no sense at all for him to have blackmailed me. Unless . . . "Do you think he stole more of Dan's inventions?"

"Perhaps. Jerome was Dan's executor. Dan's will is due to be executed soon, and Jerome would have audited everything. Jerome was extremely thorough, and he would have checked every book, every record, every note relating to Dan's inventions."

There were no other arguments I could make. It felt almost anticlimactic.

While I'd desperately wanted to know what had happened to my husband, who had killed Jerome, and why I had been blackmailed, the solution simply didn't resonate within me. My shoulders slumped. It was all too much. The broken china, the debris from the police investigation. I didn't think I could face clearing away more fingerprint powder. I hadn't slept at all the night before, and the exhaustion was catching up with me. "I need to clean this all up."

"I'll help. Where's your broom?"

Broom? I didn't think I owned one, but then I remembered the long push broom in Dan's workshop. "There's a push broom in the garage."

"I'll get it and see if there's some lumber to board up the window he came in through."

"Okay. Let me get the key." Using a hand, I started to push myself out of the kneeling position. Brad reached to help me, his touch reassuring and steady when I stood. I gave the broken china a last, regretful gaze.

"I'll get the key," offered Brad.

"You'll never find it. It's in the kitchen junk drawer." I stepped into the kitchen and crossed the floor to the last counter before the laundry room. First opening the drawer, I dug through all the detritus I'd collected in the many years since Dan and I had moved into this house. At last, my fingers closed on a key ring. I pulled it out, selected the correct key, then handed the bundle to Brad. "There you go."

While he went to fetch the broom and boards, I went into the bathroom. I washed my face and brushed my teeth, hoping that would make me feel more alert. At the sound of Brad returning, I went out to join him. But he stood there, looking worried, carrying some lumber but no broom.

"Couldn't find it?"

"When was the last time you were in the garage?"

"I'm not sure. It's been a while. Several months at least. Maybe even a year."

He scowled and settled the lumber on my counter.

"Why?"

"Someone smashed the lock and has broken in."

"Not more." I couldn't believe this. Wasn't smashing Nana's teacups enough?

"I walked through and didn't see anything amiss, but you need to come out and look to see for yourself whether anything is missing."

I sighed, but acquiesced, wanting this to be over. Wanting to move on with my life. Wanting to push the fast-forward button, putting all of this behind me. But for now, I didn't have that choice.

We went out through the back door, and it swung closed behind us. The sun had risen since we'd last been outdoors, and early-morning sunlight streaked the sky as if it had been tie-dyed. Bits of broken concrete and gravel crunched under our heels as we neared the garage, and from the distance it didn't look as though the lock had been broken. However, as we neared, I saw it had been removed from the doorframe, then pushed back into place. The hinge hung loosely from the doorjamb.

I stepped inside, my eyes slowly adjusting to the darkness. Brad reached in front of me and switched on the overhead light. A bare bulb dangled from the center of the work shed where Dan had kept all of his inventions. My gaze shot to his workbench, but it didn't seem as if anything had been tampered with or removed. "Do you think Fred took something?"

"Could be."

I slowly circled the small room, but nothing jumped out at me. "I don't see anything."

"Let's check the garage." He swung open the slender door separating the work shed from the garage, and as soon as I looked inside I immediately knew what had been taken.

"The tarp," I cried, pointing at Dan's car.

"Tarp?"

"The one I kept over his car to keep it from getting dirty." I pointed at his odd invention. "Someone took the tarp off the car."

"Check to see if anything else is missing."

Again I circled the room, and again I didn't notice anything. "As far as I can remember, that's it. Just the tarp is missing."

He nodded and radioed into the police department. While he did so, I grabbed the broom, then returned to my house, leaving him in the garage. My brain was churning so hard, I couldn't think straight. Why take the tarp?

A few minutes later, he joined me in the living room, where I had begun sweeping up the mess. He soundlessly extended his hand for the broom, then took over for me.

"The officer who came last night will be here shortly. Once he arrives, I'll update him, but then I need to get some shut-eye before going back on duty this afternoon."

"That doesn't seem like much sleep," I commented.

"Comes with the territory." He began sweeping the shards into a dustpan. "Now tell me what you remember about the tarp. What color was it?"

"It's blue. Bright blue."

He finished cleaning up the broken china while I filled him in on all the details I could recall about the tarp, including the way Dan had stenciled his initials in the lower right corner. By the time we were finished and Brad had boarded up the window in my spare bedroom, the uniformed officer arrived.

As Brad left with the officer, he said, "I recommend you get some sleep, too."

Cleaning up all the fingerprint dust seemed daunting. A nice nap was just the ticket. "Good thinking."

CHAPTER NINETEEN

Paging Detective McSexy

Once I awoke from my nap, I immediately checked the time. Eight o'clock. I couldn't believe I'd slept so late but it wasn't too late to run next door and pick up Chappy. I slid on my favorite pair of sandals and rushed over, worried Mrs. Mitchell would be upset since I hadn't come to claim Chappy earlier.

I tapped on her door.

It took her so long to answer, I thought she might be out. As I turned to leave, the door slowly swung open. "Hi, Amy."

"Hi." I turned back. "I thought I should come claim my cat."

She didn't move, holding the door open only wide enough to stick her head through. "I heard about what happened at your place. I was so sorry to hear about your grandmother's china."

The news sure traveled fast. "Believe me—I was, too."

When she didn't make a move to let me in her house, I wondered if she had a visitor she didn't want me to see. "So—my cat?"

"About Chappy. Do you think he'd be safe at your house with all that broken china?"

"Brad cleaned up most of it. I think Chappy will be fine."

She grimaced, but finally stepped back to let me in. "He's doing just fine here."

When I walked into her living room, I saw Chappy curled up on top of the recliner where Mrs. Mitchell had slept last night. Extending my arms, I approached him. "Hey, Chappy."

"He's a nice kitty," cooed Mrs. Mitchell.

Chappy awoke and purred at Mrs. Mitchell. Then he noticed me. He hissed, spat, and leapt from the chair, then scurried around the corner and out of sight.

"Hmm. He doesn't seem very happy to see me." Definitely not the reaction I'd expected. He usually rushed right up to greet me whenever I walked into a room.

"You know how animals are, dear. They get attached to a human and don't want anything to do with anyone else."

I blinked. Chappy should be attached to me, not her, but it seemed rude to contradict her. "Maybe he needs to use his litter box. Where is it? I'll bring it home."

She pointed in the opposite direction of where Chappy had fled. "An idea just occurred to me. Why don't I keep Chappy until you have everything settled at your place? It'll be safer for him. I hate to think what might have happened to him last night."

I hadn't considered his safety. What kind of kitty mother was I? Chappy had probably hidden while the killer destroyed the china. Smart cat. But I didn't want to take chances with his safety. Until the culprit was behind bars, maybe I should allow Chappy to stay with Mrs. Mitchell since she seemed to like him. He apparently liked it here. And he'd be out of smashing range. "Just don't let him out of the house, okay?"

"I absolutely won't." Her grin was enormous. She'd apparently become very attached to my cat. "I'll take good care of him."

Glancing around what I could view of her house, I didn't catch any sign of the animal in question. "Tell him good night for me. I'll get back to work."

She led me to the door. "Another confession?"

"Yes. Tonight I'm researching wrestling moves."

"Sounds interesting, dear," she said, but her tone said otherwise.

Not wanting to further bore her, I said my good-byes and headed home to write. I wasn't likely to be able to sleep after my long nap.

Way too early the next morning, Sue Ann arrived at my house with her cleaning supplies since she didn't have to work.

The sound of her knocking woke me, and I cracked open the door. I'd slept, for the few hours I could manage, on the sofa in the den. Feeling anything but perky, I asked by way of greeting, "What are you, the early bird?"

"Yup. And I'm after some worms." She toted a bucket up my porch steps. "Let me in, brat."

For the first time in what seemed like forever, a sense of peace engulfed me. I was totally lucky to have such a wonderful friend who not only tolerated my grumpiness, but came simply because she knew I needed her.

After she came in and I closed the door, she dropped her bucket and gave me a hug. "We'll get your place back to normal, Amy. Then you'll feel more normal, too."

"Thanks. I appreciate it, and you."

I led her to the living room. While Brad had swept up most of the shards, Dan's telescoping shelving hung drunkenly from the walls, like some nightmarish version of crown molding. Brad hadn't been able to get up all of the dust from the broken china, plus the signs of the police dusting for prints decorated every surface like a black dusting of snow.

"Go get dressed while I get started." Sue Ann had come equipped with her own super vacuum, and she went right to work on the living room floor.

Feeling guilty for not helping, I did as she requested.

"I simply don't believe Fred did it," she said as she wiped down my kitchen table. "It's not logical that Yvonne would turn up at the Independence Tavern the way she did."

"That's what I told Brad, but he said maybe she didn't know what Fred was up to." I grabbed a paper towel and rubbed at the front of my refrigerator. Since it didn't have any cleaner on it, the dust only smeared.

"The woman has kept him entirely under her thumb for the past seven years. After all she knew about Gayla, trust me, she knew exactly what he was doing. And another thing. What possible use did he have for your tarp? I'm not buying that Fred did this." Sue Ann picked up a bottle of cleaner and moistened my paper towel.

I turned and went through the motions of cleaning the refrigerator door. The liquid cleaner was fairly good at removing the fingerprint dust. "What possible use does anyone have for my tarp? If they wanted one, they're cheap at Wal-Mart."

"You know what I think?" Sue Ann moved over to the kitchen counter and began scrubbing it. "I think the killer took it, intending to use it later. Maybe intending to implicate you in something?"

"I'm not following you. How could the killer implicate me with a tarp?"

"It's just a thought that came to me this morning." She warmed up to her theory. "Think about it. He planned to put it somewhere to make you look like you were guilty of something or to cover his tracks."

"I still think it's Fred," I said stubbornly.

"*Cherchez la femme*, remember? I bet you if the police don't charge Fred, that tarp will show up somewhere. Mark my words."

Just as I made the mental effort to mark her words, my phone rang. The caller ID revealed the call came from the police department. When I answered, Brad said, "I've got news."

"Good news? Did Fred confess?" It would be nice if he made it easy on everyone, although, given his personality, it wasn't likely.

"The opposite. Fred's been released."

"What?" I dropped the paper towel I'd been pretending to use, shocked by his words.

"He and his wife claim he was sitting in the car while she came into the Tavern and talked with you. She says she was with him not only that night, but also the night Jerome disappeared."

I couldn't believe it. It seemed so clear that Fred was the guilty party. How could the police have released him? "So you just let him go?"

"We couldn't do otherwise until we find evidence his alibi doesn't hold up. Right now we're looking for witnesses to Yvonne's visit to the Tavern."

"I wish I'd looked out the door." I turned to Sue Ann. "Did you ever look outside the Tavern that night?"

"No. Why?"

"Fred claims to have been sitting in the car while Yvonne was talking to me."

"Is that Brad on the phone?"

"Yeah."

Before I knew it, she'd removed the portable from my grasp and was speaking with him. "You know that tarp is going to show up now, don't you? Fred isn't the killer, and whoever it is will try to frame Amy with it now."

When Sue Ann got on a roll, there was no stopping her. While they talked, I put the kettle on the stove, but when I turned to get a teacup, there weren't any. I'd forgotten. There were a few mugs in my cupboard, so I pulled one down and decided right then I'd replace the broken cups. They might not be exact duplicates, but new ones would be better than none at all. Otherwise, I'd go on reliving what happened to Nana's china, and I couldn't bear the thought of the destruction staying with me for a lifetime. Maybe if I searched the Internet or antique shops, I could find some that matched Nana's.

After a few more *uh-huh*s, *yeah*s, and *okay*s, Sue Ann punched the disconnect button and replaced the phone on the charger. "Brad's coming over later. He's got more evidence and wants to show us something."

By the time we'd finished cleaning, repaired Dan's shelves, and I'd showered and called the locksmith to repair the garage lock, Brad arrived.

He didn't come empty-handed. As I swung the door open to welcome him, he thrust a paper sack bearing the name *Yesteryears* at me.

"What's this?"

"Saw it in the window."

The gravelly tone of his voice alerted me to his uneasiness. Although he didn't urge me to open it, I could tell he was anxious for me to see what was inside. "Come on in the kitchen with Sue Ann and me, and I'll see what you brought."

I led the way, and it wasn't long before the three of us were seated at my table. "Look, Sue Ann." I wiggled the bag at her. "It's from Brad. Should I be worried?"

Her gaze shot to Brad, then back to me. "Probably. You know what they say about geeks bearing gifts."

"It's just a little something. Not enough to count as a gift," Brad said.

Now I was truly curious. I unrolled the top of the sack, no neat folds for a man like Brad. My fingers came into contact with tissue paper and, beneath it, a thin, hard surface. I drew the item from the bag, instantly realizing what he had done.

While I carefully unwrapped the paper from the gift, my gaze met his. What a truly nice man he was. I lowered my eyes to the beautiful china teacup and saucer he'd bought for me.

It was lovely, with tiny blue flowers and green vines on a bone white background. "Oh, Brad, you shouldn't have. But I'm very glad you did. I love it."

"Amy, I tried gluing one of the broken cups back together, but the fragments were too small. I hope this'll do."

Words failed me. All I could do was lean from my chair and wrap my arms around him. When I released him, his face was red, but whether it was with embarrassment at my actions or happiness, I wasn't quite sure. I found my voice. "Thank you so much."

Sue Ann beamed at him. "Amy had to use her Pennzoil mug this morning, and I could tell the tea didn't taste quite right. Now all we need is for you to put the killer behind bars."

"The entire Independence Police Department is working on that. All we need is a witness who saw Yvonne's car while she was inside the Tavern talking to Amy. If the car was empty, Fred's whole alibi will tumble like a baby learning to walk."

"I wish he'd made it easy for all of us and simply confessed."

"He maintains he's innocent."

Sue Ann nodded. "He is. I'm certain you still haven't apprehended the killer. Otherwise, why would anyone take the tarp?"

"I'm not certain the tarp is relevant."

Sue Ann bobbed in her chair. "I'm certain the killer stole the tarp in order to frame Amy. You'll see. It'll turn up."

"Anything that links Amy to Jerome's murder won't go down well with Chief Kane."

It sure wouldn't. With the chief's attitude toward me, it had felt as if it was only a matter of time before he ordered Brad to bring me in on murder charges. If evidence were to turn up linking me to a crime, my remaining hours of freedom were numbered.

The three of us sat in silent contemplation for a few minutes. I glanced at my new teacup, then realized I hadn't offered Brad anything to drink.

"Would you like some coffee, Brad? Sue Ann, do you want anything?"

"I'm already full up," Brad said while Sue Ann shook her head.

He leaned back in his chair and stretched, then pulled an object from his pocket.

"Is that Jerome's cell?"

"One like his."

"Why the duplicate?"

He shrugged. "There's a chance the killer might react to it, thinking it might give him away."

"Where did you find it?" asked Sue Ann.

"In his pocket. We dried it out and recharged it. Fortunately, we were able to activate it despite it being underwater for so long." He cradled the identical phone in his hands. "At first we were most interested in the phone logs, but then one of the guys got the idea to look at his files. It's a pretty fancy device."

"Did you find anything helpful?"

"Not sure. But we did find one thing that seemed peculiar, given Jerome's personality. I'm not sure anyone else would have noticed besides me."

"What's that?"

"We found a photo he took the day before he returned to Independence. It's the object that seems odd. I uploaded the photo to this phone." He punched a few buttons, then turned it so I could see the display.

Depicted was a toilet. "Why would he take a photo of that?"

"I wondered the same. Look at it more carefully." He held the phone closer to my face. Then I saw what he meant.

"It's one of Dan's self-cleaning toilets." I could just make out the little mouse thingy. "I don't understand."

"Neither do I. But I will." He drew back his arm, then turned off the phone. "Do you have any idea why he might have taken the picture?"

I shook my head. "Do you have any idea, Sue Ann?"

"Beats me."

"Maybe he thought it was cute."

Brad frowned. "Guys don't think toilets are cute."

"I think it's cute. Were there any other photos or files that might give you a clue?"

"There's some financial information stored in it, and we've sent it off to be looked over. Might have a clue." Brad pocketed the phone. "If you ladies hear of anyone who might have seen Fred in Yvonne's car, tell them to get in touch."

This was apparently his way of giving his blessing to our continued investigation. He'd never say it outright, but the hint was definitely there.

As he stood to leave, there was another knock on the door. My, I was having far more visitors than usual. Not exactly Grand Central Station, but enough foot traffic to probably be up there with the Independence Chamber of Commerce offices.

I opened my front door to find Dolores. Judging by the skunk struggling in her arms, this wasn't one of her better days.

CHAPTER TWENTY

Caught in the Act

One look at Dolores, and Brad said, "I'll check back later, Amy. Nice to see you, Dolores." Being no fool, he promptly skedaddled to his car and drove off, leaving Sue Ann and me to deal with Dolores. And the skunk.

Sue Ann joined me at the door. "Hello, Dolores."

"Morning."

"What's that you've got there?" she asked, pointing at the skunk.

"Amy's grandmother."

Had she lost it entirely? I should probably chat with Liz to make sure Dolores wasn't zanier than usual. In the meantime, it was best to play along. No telling what her nutty bats would do otherwise. But I couldn't quite make myself act as if it was usual to claim my grandmother was now a skunk. "I don't see the resemblance. Nana's hair was gray, not black and white."

Dolores gave me an impatient glare. "I'm not talking about how she looks. This is her, reincarnated."

Stymied for a response, I simply stared at her. She didn't look crazier than usual. Her short salt-and-pepper hair was neatly styled. The slacks and tunic she wore were well coordinated. Even her leather shoes matched.

"What makes you think it's her?" Sue Ann bit her upper lip, and I could tell she was desperately trying to keep from laughing.

Me? I didn't find it so humorous.

"I think she turned up in my yard this morning because of what happened to her china teacups. Lordy, she was proud of them."

"You found the skunk in your yard?" I asked.

Before Dolores could answer, Sue Ann spoke up. "She let you catch her?"

Dolores nodded. "I just scooped her up from where she sat waiting for me on the front porch."

The entrance to her historical home included a large concrete porch. I couldn't imagine what a skunk was doing there in the first place. "Dolores, what makes you think it's Nana?"

"She always promised that when she reincarnated, she'd come back as a skunk and get even with a few folks around here. She didn't like it when people poked fun at her."

Made sense to me and sounded exactly like something Nana might say.

It was a good thing Dolores had a stranglehold on the skunk with the way she kept trying to get loose. "Let us in, and maybe she'll tell us whatever it is she's trying to say."

I didn't step back. "What about the scent? My house has been through enough lately. The last thing I want is skunk spray."

"It has been bad for you, hasn't it?" Dolores bobbed her head. "But it's another confirmation, don't you think?"

It took me a minute to catch up with her train of thought. Although anything was possible with the way her mind worked. "The skunk hasn't sprayed you?"

"Not once. And look at her squirm. It's evident she's eager to give us a message."

The skunk looked more eager to get out of Dolores' arms than to tell us anything. "She must be an escaped pet. Her spray box was probably removed."

Dolores had lost patience with me, and she sighed heavily. "You going to let us in or make us stand out here all day?"

If it had been anyone other than my mother-in-law who wanted to come into my house with a skunk, I would have shut the door in their face. But this was Dolores, and I couldn't ever deliberately hurt her. "If it's all the same to you, and no offense meant, but I'd rather not take the chance on it." If I thought cleaning up after the police was problematic, no telling what would be required to eliminate skunk scent. "Although, if you need something . . ."

"No, dear. I didn't really need to come in anyway." She held up the animal's face to her own. "It was Nana's idea. Right, Nana?"

The skunk didn't appear to agree. She continued struggling, and I definitely wasn't buying her as the reincarnated soul of my grandmother. Nana would have found some way to escape Dolores' clutches.

"Well, guess we'll be heading back to my house then." She stepped toward the driveway and her car, but turned back. "Oh, dear, I almost forgot. I wanted to tell you both I'm having another séance tomorrow night. You won't want to miss it. Karen will be conducting it again, and Nana here will be our guest of honor."

"We'll be there," Sue Ann answered for both of us. I was still too busy trying to envision a skunk on the loose in Dolores' home and how it would behave at a séance.

"It sounds like something I wouldn't want to miss." My answer was completely truthful. It was going to be very interesting. But in the meantime, I wondered how Liz would deal with the new addition to their household. "You might want to get her a cage."

"Nana would never hear of it." Dolores firmly shook her head. "Seven o'clock tomorrow. Don't be late."

"I'll try to arrive a little early." She might need my help with the skunk. "Do you want me to bring anything? Potato salad? Cookies?"

Dolores raised her chin, evidently offended. "This is a séance, not a picnic."

I had no response to that. I waved as she got in her car and drove away.

Sue Ann jiggled her car keys. "Get your things."

"Why?"

"We're going tarp hunting. It's better if we find it before the police do. Then we can prove our point."

"Our point?"

"Of course." She walked with me back into the house, where I grabbed my purse. "Where do you think the tarp will be?"

"Wherever Jerome's body was dumped into the Verdigris."

Her logic was sound. If the murderer wanted to implicate me, using my tarp for Jerome's body would put the legal heat on me. It was incredibly difficult not to feel completely overwhelmed. If the killer was as sly as Sue Ann believed, I was going to have to think faster and smarter than I ever had before if I didn't want to end up in prison for a crime I didn't commit.

I glanced over at Sue Ann, who stood by the front door watching me. Feelings of gratitude welled up inside me. If she hadn't been thinking for me, I would have been clueless about the murderer's attempts to frame me. "Thanks, Sue Ann."

"For what?" she asked, opening the door for us to leave.

"For being you and for being the best friend ever."

She grinned. "Back atcha, BFF."

We climbed into her SUV, and she asked, "Where shall we look first?"

"We start at the Tavern and fan out from there. I think it's logical to decide where we would go to dump a body. I can think of several locations private enough to minimize the chances of being seen and where the terrain would be suitable for dragging a body. Want to start at Riverside Park? It's not far from the Tavern."

"Great idea." She headed the car north, and it didn't take long to reach the park.

"Let's head toward Shulthis Stadium. There are some shelters behind it just above the river."

A few minutes later we reached the area of the park I'd indicated. A small side street led behind and above the stadium to several remote shelters. The street ended in a graveled area and while it might be possible to drive a car down it, I was afraid the SUV would get stuck. "Let's park by this shelter and walk down instead."

It didn't take long to rule out the area as a dumping spot, so we left the park and headed north. We drove along Morningside Drive and back into the subdivision. While there were many ponds, we didn't see anything to indicate the body could have been dumped in that location.

"How about the old Burns Street Bridge?" It was east of the Tavern and just down the corner from Dolores' house. Hopefully she wouldn't see us. "If I wanted to quickly dump a body, that's where I'd go. Even though it's on a residential street, it's a quiet one and fairly remote by the old bridge. No one would notice anything."

"You're right. We should have checked it first."

Soon we reached Myrtle Street and headed east to where it

dead-ended at Burns Street. Sue Ann pulled her SUV onto the bit of crumbling pavement that once led to the bridge. Overgrown brush nearly covered the metal gate closing off what remained of the bridge.

"Stay here," I suggested. "I'll go see if it's possible."

I exited the SUV and walked the few feet to the bluff above the Verdigris. Although there was a drop-off, it definitely could have been used as a location for the murderer to rid himself of a body. Miscellaneous trash littered the small bluff, as well as a few beer and pop cans. However, there was no sign of *anything* blue, much less my tarp.

I strolled back to the vehicle and got inside. "I'm not sure, Sue Ann. I didn't see the tarp, but it's a great place to dump stuff."

"Want me to go take a look, too?"

I nodded, depression eating at me. Was this where the killer had disposed of Jerome? "I'll stay in the car."

While she went to look, I considered some of the other locations where the killer could have taken Jerome's body.

Sue Ann returned to the SUV. "You're right. It's a good location for it, but there's no sign of the tarp or of anything being dragged."

"I thought of another place we should check." It was outside the city limits, but it wasn't that far. The main advantages to the location were its remoteness and easy access. "Let's go check the bridge on Old Highway 160."

In less than ten minutes, we reached the turnoff to the old suspension bridge. It wasn't well traveled, but it led to a number of homes and farms. Sue Ann pulled to a stop in the middle of the bridge.

"You could do it from here, but lifting the body would be kind of difficult."

"It's much easier to drag." I pointed to the right shore. "But down there it would be simple. It's just past where 4410 Road meets 4175."

Sue Ann accelerated and we reached the corner in minutes. She made the turn onto the loose gravel road, then slowed when it reached the bend. Directly to our left was the Verdigris River. She turned onto an old access point that ended in a gate only a few feet off the road.

But I wasn't paying much attention, because I'd seen a flash of blue just beneath a pile of deadwood and brambles. "Look."

Within seconds, she was out of the car and running toward it. I quickly joined her. Mostly buried beneath the deadwood was blue fabric that looked very much like the tarp that had recently covered Dan's car. I bit back an expletive.

Having turned up nothing so far, I'd hoped Sue Ann had been wrong about the tarp.

But she hadn't been.

Only feet away, on the ground to our left, were signs something had recently been dragged toward the water's edge. It made far too much sense.

This was my tarp, and the killer had used it to dispose of Jerome's body.

Sue Ann kneeled and looked more closely at the tarp. "There—I think it's blood."

I glanced where she directed and observed a small, brown stain. It very well could be dried blood. Jerome's blood. It was smeared across the corner of the tarp bearing Dan's initials.

Memories of the last time I saw Jerome, of how he'd done his best to protect me, swam before my eyes. He'd succeeded in keeping me safe, and the cost had been his life.

A desperate need to find vindication for him rose. The killer would be found and brought to justice. I stepped back to her car in order to get my cell phone. "Let's call the police."

"Wait a second, Amy."

I spun back. She remained kneeling, and anxiety underscored her facial features. Her lips were drawn and tight. A white line punctuated the middle of her forehead. "What's wrong?"

"If the authorities see your tarp here, you'll rise to chief suspect, Amy. I'm not sure that's smart, especially considering this is out of Brad's jurisdiction. The County Sheriff's Department will be involved."

"I don't see what difference that makes."

"It makes a world of difference." She slowly stood. "Don't you realize that Brad's the one who's kept you from being brought in for questioning? Once the county sheriffs are involved, your safety net is gone. I should take the tarp and burn it."

I couldn't believe she'd make such a suggestion. "You can't. That's tampering with evidence."

She didn't immediately reply. Instead she stood frozen in thought. At last she said, "It's your call, Amy. But I think it's best."

I considered her suggestion. I didn't want to go to jail. I didn't want the authorities distracted from finding the real killer. But I simply couldn't do it. There might be necessary evidence on the tarp that would lead to Jerome's killer and, more than anything, I wanted him or her apprehended. As I opened my mouth to tell her, the need for me to decide was taken out of my hands.

A sheriff's cruiser drove up and parked behind Sue Ann's SUV, blocking us from leaving. A deputy sheriff exited the vehicle and paced toward us.

I didn't recognize him, and apparently Sue Ann didn't either. "Look what we found, Officer."

He strolled over and glanced at the tarp beneath the branches, but he didn't seem to understand its importance.

"This is my tarp," I explained, "stolen from my garage."

He rubbed his chin in thought. "You want to report you found it?"

We needed Brad. Fast. He'd know what to do. I opened the door to the SUV, grabbed my cell, and phoned him. "We found the tarp."

CHAPTER TWENTY-ONE

i Stole My Lover Back

Standing in my kitchen, I looked out the window toward Mrs. Mitchell's house, wondering how my cat was faring. The balance of the day before had been spent talking with one law enforcement official after another. The fact that I wasn't currently behind bars surprised me. The police and sheriff's department now seemed certain that the location was where Jerome's body was dragged into the river. It had been implied that I hadn't discovered the tarp—that I'd merely returned to the scene of my crime.

At last, Brad told me to go home and stay there.

My house was too quiet, and I jumped at every noise—the sound of wind blowing through the trees, a distant car honk, barking dogs. I had two sets of fear. One was that the murderer would return and smash me like my china. The other was that I would be arrested and the true murderer would never be found. Every sound set my teeth on edge as I waited for the arrest that seemed inevitable.

Sleep had been nearly impossible and, when it did come, was filled with nightmares. I couldn't summon the sass, natural or otherwise, to help me deal with my current dilemma. Despite Sue Ann's assurances, I hadn't felt this alone since the death of my parents. Like then, now I had no choice but to continue soldiering on and holding on to the faith that this, too, would pass.

I reached for the kettle and set it on the stove to heat. Perhaps the mundane daily routines would see me through. While I waited for the water to boil, I decided to work on my next short story. I needed to do more research on professional wrestling, so I had checked out some library books on the topic. Maybe reading one of them would help keep my mind occupied while I waited.

I went into my office to fetch one of the books, returned to the kitchen, and began to read.

Some of the professional wrestling moves in the book seemed impossible, and it was patently obvious I needed something to practice on since I was short on humans at the moment. The kettle reached a boil, and I poured water over a tea bag to steep.

I searched my mind for something to practice wrestling moves on. Dan once won a huge stuffed bunny for me at a county fair, and I thought it might be in the closet of the guest room, so I went to go look for it.

Emerging from the guest room victorious, I then returned to the kitchen with my bunny. Since it had arms and legs, it was perfect for sparring against. After drinking my tea, I went right to work in the den, pushing the coffee table back into the sofa so I could create an area to practice in.

Two hours later, I was able to complete some of the moves without consulting the book. Now ready to begin writing my confession about being a professional lady wrestler, I checked the clock. I hadn't been arrested, the murderer hadn't returned, and there was just enough time remaining for me to write the opening to the story before I needed to get ready for Dolores' séance.

I'd gotten my opening written and hated to stop work for the day, but I'd promised Mrs. Mitchell I'd drive us both to the séance in her Cadillac again. For once, I was early getting ready, so I took a little extra time and blow-dried my hair in the hope of taming some of the curls. I thought it might give me the confidence I needed to make it through the coming hours. Although my hair didn't turn out exactly smooth, it was somewhat better, and I looked a lot less like a dark-haired Carrot Top. As I applied a finishing dab of lipstick, a loud car honk sounded and the tube hit my teeth. Squeegeeing it with my forefinger, I turned and darted for the door. I was late, and the horn had to be Mrs. Mitchell's.

I was right. Mrs. Mitchell had backed her car out of her garage, the engine was running, and the top was down. Now she sat shotgun, and a colorful scarf covered her head, presumably to save her hairstyle. Wishing I had thought of that myself, I sped to join her.

"How are you tonight?" I asked.

"Wonderful. Chappy and I are getting along like two birds of a feather."

It was great they were getting along, but I missed having him around. I backed the Caddy out onto the street, then turned it in the direction of Dolores'. "I was wondering how he was getting along. Is he eating okay?"

"Absolutely. He's such a darling kitty and so cute. This morning when I made my coffee, I found him sniffing the pitcher of cream. He hadn't gotten to it, mind you, but if I hadn't seen him, I'm sure he'd have lapped it up. I gave him a little, and he just loved it."

We chatted about him during the short drive, and I battled a case of jealousy. Chappy seemed very happy with her, but he was my cat. I wanted him back home with me, but until I was certain he'd be safe with me, he truly was better off with someone who adored him as much as I did.

When I turned onto Myrtle Street, I realized parking would be difficult. Not only were there the usual cars from the guests, but I noticed a police cruiser parked directly in front of Dolores' house.

Surely they wouldn't arrest me in front of a group of my family and friends?

Brad's car was parked across the street, and I had to believe that was a good sign. Surely he wouldn't allow them to arrest me. I doubted he could entirely stop them, but he would look out after me as well as he could given the circumstances.

"Why don't you get out here, and I'll go look for a parking space?" I suggested to Mrs. Mitchell. She readily agreed and stepped from the car. There was room to park on Burns, but I couldn't face the idea of parking so near the river. Instead, I turned the car around, which wasn't an easy feat in such a huge car, and parked on a block on the other side of Dolores' home.

The walk up the block gave me the time I needed to calm my fears. While I didn't know why the police were there, I was convinced it couldn't be because of me. If they wanted to arrest me, they would have come to my home. I ran my hand down my now windblown hair in an attempt to smooth it and climbed the steps to Dolores' large front porch.

Just as I raised my hand to knock, I heard a scream coming from inside the house.

"Skunk."

I smiled. Dolores had made good on her promise to make the animal guest of honor. The sound of scurrying and raised voices penetrated the door before it opened. Liz stood there, looking the worse for wear. "Welcome to the zoo."

I laughed. "It sure sounds like one."

"It's not too late to turn back. You could say you suddenly came down with the flu." She smiled, but I could tell she was half-serious.

"I wouldn't miss this for the world." I entered the house and followed Liz to the dining room.

"Don't say I didn't give you fair warning," she muttered as we entered the room where pandemonium ruled.

The skunk had taken up residence under the dining table and Dolores, Brad, and Mare were half under it, trying to get the animal out. The image of their backsides sticking out from under that table would live with me for a lifetime. I looked for Sue Ann, who would have shared the humor in the situation with me, but she hadn't yet arrived.

Karen remained seated in the same chair she'd occupied during the last séance, but even she didn't appear to be calm. She wiped her forehead with the tail end of one of the scarves draped around her neck.

Fred and Yvonne stood on the far side of the room, and I suspected each was searching for a means of escape. The fact that they were in attendance at all was something of a shock. They had to be aware that most of the people in the room thought Fred was a cold-blooded murderer. While I wasn't convinced of his guilt, especially after finding the tarp, I couldn't bring myself to approach them.

Odds were, someone in this room had killed Jerome. My gaze flickered over the people gathered together, and I wondered why they each had agreed to return for another séance. It was logical to suppose Fred and Yvonne hoped some evidence of his innocence might come to light. But why had Mare come again? Why would the friendly veterinarian agree to participate? Maybe she liked the paranormal? Or maybe Nana the skunk was now her patient?

Mrs. Mitchell couldn't stand being left out of anything, so I never doubted she'd want to come when I'd asked her about driving. Liz was a captive audience, as was Brad. He would definitely want to be here in case something occurred that would help in his investigation into Jerome's death.

My gaze landed in the back corner, where an off-duty police officer positioned a video camera seated on a tripod. So that's why he was here. I'd have to ask Brad about it once he emerged from under the table.

Mrs. Mitchell hovered near Brad's backside, and I figured he was going to be in serious trouble because he wasn't in a position to defend himself.

It would be best if I distracted her, so I walked over to join her. "I forgot to warn you about the skunk."

"Best fun I've had all year," she said, but her gaze wasn't directed at me.

I glanced down at the group wiggling under the table. No wonder she was having a good time.

Her hand lowered toward her intended target.

"Got her," cried Brad, wedging himself out from beneath the table, just in the nick of time. When at last he came out, Mare moved to take the skunk from him. The animal's sharp claws were embedded in his shirt, and Mare had to pry each one loose.

"Nana, you bad girl," said Dolores. "If you can't behave, you'll have to go back into your cage."

"You're not turning her loose again," said Liz. "I'll go get the cage."

Dolores began to argue, but Mare spoke up. "It's best for her. She'll feel safer and more comfortable."

Dolores mulled it over for a moment. "What do you think, Karen?"

"It's best to do as the doctor suggested," she replied.

Dolores looked at the others, but no one met her eyes. She looked at me, and I nodded my head in agreement with the vet. Since she wasn't receiving any support for giving the animal free rein of the house, she finally capitulated. "If you think it's best."

Liz returned with a large metal birdcage, and I guessed she'd been forced to improvise. How had she coped with having the skunk for a housemate, the latest in a line of *Adventures with Dolores*? No wonder she looked frazzled. "Here you go."

Dolores, however, positively beamed. She was in her element—and she, of course, hadn't been forced to deal with the practicalities of having a skunk in the house. Finding a cage, feeding the animal, and tending to her bathroom needs had probably been up to my saintly sister-in-law. Dolores was extremely fortunate Liz hadn't moved away long ago.

"Set the cage on the chair next to me," Dolores ordered, and Liz quickly did as she asked. Mare didn't lose any time caging the skunk.

The doorbell rang and I knew it was Sue Ann. "I'll get it."

I opened the door and whispered, "You missed all the fun."

"What happened?" she asked as we walked to join the others.

"The skunk was loose, got trapped under the table, and everyone was squirming under it trying to catch her. Brad almost got pinched by Mrs. Mitchell. You would have loved it."

"I'm sorry I missed it." By then we'd reached the dining room, and she called out, "Hi, everyone. Where's Nana?"

I snorted. "Safely in her cage."

Dolores pointed to the cage by the table.

"Can I sit next to her?" Sue Ann asked. She probably was trying to think of some way of setting the animal loose again.

Dolores shook her head. "I'm sorry, but everyone will need to resume the same seats they had during our last séance. The spirits will be more receptive that way."

Sue Ann's crestfallen expression was priceless, and I nudged her with my elbow.

"Now if everyone will take their places," Dolores directed. "Yvonne, if you'll sit beside Nana, that would be lovely."

For a moment, I thought Yvonne might refuse, but Fred made a shooing motion at her and she took the indicated chair.

"You'll notice Brad's friend in the corner behind me. He'll be filming our proceedings in order to document evidence of the paranormal." Dolores gave an animated wave toward the off-duty officer. I imagine she relished the idea of becoming the star of her own TV program.

Brad leaned over and whispered, "Or make sure there's no hanky-panky going on with the items on the table."

Dolores couldn't hear what he said, but her suspicious gaze landed on him, as did Karen's. "Brad, can you please dim the lights?"

Brad stood and did as she asked, then returned to his chair beside mine. My heart skittered with the knowledge we'd soon be holding hands again, and I wondered if the electric zings between us would return. Or had it merely been a fluke?

Eeriness settled over the room. How peculiar to be back at Dolores' table, gathered for another séance. Yvonne was seated in Jerome's chair. His absence loomed over the gathering, and my heart ached. It felt surreal going on without him, but that was a lesson I'd learned well in my life. I knew firsthand what it was to continue living, even when your heart was shattered to dust. Nana would have chided me if she'd been able to hear my thoughts. She'd have reminded me about the joy I'd experienced as a result of having someone in my life.

But every death compounded the loss. First my parents, then Nana, then Dan's disappearance, and now Jerome. It added up to more than I could calculate.

Although the room was dim, it was possible to make out the same objects in the center of the table as the last time. The tambourine, writing utensils, and glass of water sat patiently, waiting for an otherworldly spirit to make use of them.

"Everyone join hands," began Karen in a singsong voice. Her tone was soothing, monotone and half made me want to fall asleep. Brad's hand on mine kept the other half of me alert. Hormonal teenagers had nothing on my reaction to his nearness. The sound of his breathing, the heat of his palm, and my awareness of his simply sitting beside me sent my senses into overdrive.

My focus on him was so acute, I was nearly unaware of what happened around me. I struggled to take my mind off him and pay attention to what Karen was saying and doing. At last, a metallic clink drew my attention. Was the tambourine about to spring to life?

The sound of several indrawn breaths indicated that some of the others thought the same, and the room drew quiet. Silence beckoned like a lover's hand, and my eyes strained to penetrate the darkened room. I could only view the other guests' shadowy faces until I glanced down and saw Karen's palm clutching my left hand and Brad's my right.

A tiny beam of light reflected off the tambourine—enough to reveal it wasn't moving, at least not yet.

"Daniel Crosby, I call upon you to join us here tonight," whispered Karen.

Again a metallic clink, but nothing else followed.

"My poor dead son," moaned Dolores, "must not have enough strength to fully join us tonight."

"If he ever was here," said Yvonne with an angry sniff. "He's probably too much of a coward to show himself after the world of trouble he caused. He's afraid to face me. All of you should be ashamed of yourselves, using all of this to implicate an innocent man."

Dolores jumped in with both feet. "Don't you dare accuse my son of being a coward."

"Yvonne," barked out Fred. "Remember why we're here."

"You think any of these people want to see your name cleared?" Yvonne's voice shook with anger.

"If Dan's spirit truly was here, he would want to see my name cleared," Fred said. "That's why we're here tonight. Now hush."

Karen cleared her throat, then started again. "We call upon your spirit to join us, Daniel."

I couldn't help wondering about Yvonne's outburst and Fred's quick response. If Dan's spirit wasn't here and in fact had never been, did Fred plan to make it appear that Dan was with us? As an inventor, he was certainly capable of creating something to give that effect. This was so emotional for me, I shouldn't trust my own senses. It was imperative I remain alert to trickery, no matter who it might come from.

Other than Brad and Sue Ann, there was no one in the room I fully trusted. I doubted the others trusted me, either. None of us came without baggage of some sort, without hopes of proving something.

I wanted to find out what happened to my husband and who killed Jerome.

Brad and Sue Ann did as well.

But the others?

There was no telling what Dolores wanted and Liz, who was unreadable, probably most wanted to be left alone. Yvonne and Fred wanted to prove he was innocent, whether or not he was. Mare remained a wildcard. Had she been in love with my husband? What did she hope to gain? I suspected Mrs. Mitchell was here simply for amusement, but I couldn't be certain, even of her.

Even Karen, the professional psychic medium, wanted something. I suspected Dolores paid the medium for her services, and perhaps that was enough motivation. I had no way of judging if she was legitimate or phony, but I felt certain she wanted to prove her authenticity.

Metal clinked upon metal once again, and all of us focused on the center of the table. The tambourine didn't move, yet there came another clink.

Seeking the direction of the noise resulted in no answers. Karen started the heavy breathing that portended a possible spirit visitation, and I could no longer hear anything above the wheezy, raspy sound she created.

In the back corner, I sensed more than saw the off-duty officer's excitement as he filmed the proceedings.

At last, Karen spoke. "Unhappy."

The timbre was low and sad.

"Is that you, Dan?" asked Dolores.

"Unhappy," replied Karen, with neither a confirmation nor denial. It didn't sound like the same voice as before when I'd been certain Dan's spirit had visited us.

"Tell these people that my husband had nothing to do with Jerome's murder," demanded Yvonne. "Tell them he didn't break into Amy's house."

"Of course he didn't," said Dolores calmly. "He wouldn't have had time, now, would he?"

Fred drew in an excited breath. "I was in our car in front of the Tavern the night before last. Did you see me? I've been looking for a witness."

"Of course I did," said Dolores. "You were waiting in the car while your wife went in. Isn't that right, Yvonne?"

Brad stiffened and whispered, "If stating he was in the car isn't feeding her information, I don't know what is."

Yvonne's voice trembled with relief. "Thank God. Yes. That's right. You heard her, Brad."

My mind could barely process the thought that Fred might be out of the woods. It didn't mean he was off the hook entirely, but it definitely threw a spanner into the works. If he wasn't the one who smashed my china, then how did his notes end up in the shards?

Sue Ann's theory that the killer had framed Fred gained credence. I shot a glance at her, but she wasn't paying attention. Her attention was focused on the head of the table.

Dolores was very suggestible. It was possible she'd merely agreed with Yvonne and hadn't been there at all. I didn't remember seeing Dolores that night, and no one had mentioned it.

"I'll need to take your statement on this in the morning," Brad told her.

"Absolutely," she reassured him. "But now, I'd like to find out if my son is present. Dan, are you with us?"

The medium had continued her odd breathing, but now she spoke. "Unhappy."

My thoughts were more caught up in wanting to learn if Dolores truly had seen Fred that night than in the séance. I inhaled, ready to ask her more questions, but Brad must have intuited what I was about to do, because he whispered in my ear, "Be patient."

Now I'm not one to get all girlish over small things. As a teenager, I had crushes on dead authors, not lead singers. But let me tell you, his soft, heated breath on the tender skin at the side of my face silenced me fast. I was too busy experiencing shivers and quivers and an unexpected hot core of lust springing up inside me like a boiling lava pit. It's a wonder I didn't swoon on the spot—or beg him to take me.

Nana once told me I was a late bloomer, and for the first time I suspected she was right. I'd never had a reaction to a man the way I reacted to Brad, now, here in the dark. But there were ten other people in the room, and it was a totally inappropriate moment to release my libido.

Karen spoke again, but this time in a high-pitched, girlish tone that washed right through me like an icy shower. I thought I might recognize the voice, but I wasn't certain. How could I be sure?

"Dolores, I told you," Karen whispered. "I told you not to cover it up."

Dolores gasped. "Nana? Frances, is that you?"

She recognized the voice, too. My grandmother, whose first name was Frances, but whom everyone generally called Nana because she preferred it, spoke in the same girlish tones as Karen did now. Chills climbed my spine. Was this truly my grandmother?

"Always said you were gullible, didn't I?"

"Nana, it is you?" asked Dolores. But rather than address the medium, she turned toward the caged skunk.

"Silly is as silly does," replied the medium. Her words trailed off, and the deep breathing returned.

"Don't go," pleaded Dolores, but the medium didn't respond, even after Dolores shook their united hands. "Please don't go."

Icy wind swept through the room, far too cool to have come from outside, sending the draperies billowing. Karen slumped headfirst to the table, then abruptly straightened.

This must be Dan, I hoped, since that had happened the last time he'd visited.

Karen's voice was loud and deep. "Check the books."

I didn't recognize the voice. It wasn't Dan's. It wasn't any voice or intonation I recognized. What did books have to do with Nana or Dan? For a second time, I wondered how much of Karen's performance was simply that—an act to make us believe she was in contact with the otherworld.

The command came again in the identical deep voice, "Check the books."

"You want me to go to the library?" Dolores sounded confused, but hers was as good a guess as any at the meaning of the statement.

But she was met with silence.

Again wind swept through the room, and Karen swayed but remained upright.

Surprisingly, the next person to speak was Mrs. Mitchell. "Nana, if that's you, I have a request."

No one said anything, but I thought I caught a faint clink of metal once more. Where was that noise coming from?

"You know that recipe for moisturizer—" She broke off at a louder metallic clang, but when it didn't continue, she said, "Well, the least you could have done was share it with your friends."

Karen continued swaying in her chair, but other than a low mumble, she didn't communicate.

The off-duty officer repositioned his camera to get a better angle on her. It was good thinking because it would at least be interesting viewing later, whether or not it proved anything.

Metal clanged again, more loudly than before, and at last I realized where the sound came from. The birdcage enclosing the skunk—but not anymore.

The intelligent animal escaped from the cage and skittered directly toward the off-duty officer. Judging by her hissing, I could only think she didn't like being caught on film.

Although it was difficult to see in the dim room, it looked as if the skunk pounded her front feet, then did a headstand and raised her tail at the officer.

The officer let out a yelp. Then chaos ensued as the smell of fresh skunk filled the room.

Brad leapt from his chair and darted to the light switch.

It took a second for my eyes to adjust to the bright light, but when they did, what I saw was priceless.

Karen had covered her face in her scarves. Dolores covered her own nose with a linen napkin. The off-duty officer had raised the camera tripod in an attempt to fend off the irate skunk, who had cornered him by the bay window. Fred and Yvonne fled the room with looks of horror on their faces. In her attempt to flee the area, Mrs. Mitchell jumped from her chair so quickly it toppled. I couldn't see Sue Ann's face because she was doubled over in laughter. And poor Liz just sat there, her eyes welling with tears as she shook her head sadly.

Nana the skunk wasn't through with the officer, however. She performed her headstand once again, knocking against the legs of the tripod.

Yvonne screamed, "Watch out!"

The tripod wobbled, then crashed directly onto the table, narrowly missing Karen, who'd ducked at Yvonne's outburst.

The video camera shattered against the heavy oak table, and pieces scattered around the room. The disc flew in one direction while the camera's arm flew in the other.

Within seconds, Mare was on her feet. She grabbed the skunk and deposited her back in the cage, then asked Liz to remove her from the room. Dolores ran to get a bottle of ketchup which she insisted would help remove the stench.

"Looks like this party's over." Brad pushed back his chair. "I'll talk with you later."

"I was afraid of that," I said, trying not to breathe.

Liz pulled back the curtains on the bay window and threw open the windows. There wasn't enough breeze to eliminate the odor.

Brad ran to help the officer pick up the damaged equipment. Then the two of them left as quickly as possible.

While Dolores was in the kitchen, most of the guests made a speedy getaway, and no one could blame them. A skunk's best defense is extremely pungent.

Me? Even though it sounds strange, I discovered I didn't mind the odor so much. I'd heard there were some people who like the smell, and I'm apparently in their number.

Go figure.

CHAPTER TWENTY-TWO

Mama's Secret

Although I offered to stay and help clean up after the skunk, Liz sent me on my way because Mrs. Mitchell made it widely known that she wanted to get out of there. As her driver, I had little choice but to take her home. Pronto.

Because she was concerned about the stench infusing her upholstery, we sat with large, black plastic trash bags spread out between us and the car seats.

It only took a few minutes to make the drive, and Sue Ann followed us in her SUV. However, I felt guilty about leaving Liz to deal with Dolores' mess. Once we arrived at my house, Sue Ann ran off to borrow my shower, and I called Liz.

"Are you sure you don't want me to come back and help?"

"Positive," was Liz's firm reply. "Mom's busy dousing the room with canned tomatoes, and she's happy as can be."

"I guess it's good to keep her occupied."

She hesitated, then said, "Yeah. I've been worried about her."

Suddenly the words of the medium came back to me. What had she told Dolores about not covering something up? Had she meant the murder? Or Dan's whereabouts?

"You don't think she—" I bit my tongue. There was no need to worry Liz any more, especially since my thoughts pointed to her mother as the guilty party. It had been a long day, it was late, and I was probably wrong.

"I don't think what?" Liz asked, her tone suddenly hard-edged.

"You don't think she needs our help tonight?" I quickly asked, trying to gloss over what I'd almost let slip.

"Definitely, no." She didn't call me on it.

Which was good, because the urge to talk my ideas over with Sue Ann compelled me to end the phone call right away. However, as soon as I hung up with Liz, another call rang through. Caller ID revealed it was Jerome's elderly aunt, who lived in a senior retirement complex in Texas. As his only living relative, most likely she was calling to tell me about funeral arrangements. Although we'd never met, when we'd spoken on the phone previously, I'd thought we'd hit it off.

"Hi, Patty."

"Hello, Amy. I'm calling to let you know about the arrangements I made with the coroner's office." Her tone was clipped and cold.

Maybe some people handle grief that way. I ventured, "I'm so very sorry, Patty, about Jerome. He was a wonderful man."

Rather than reply to my statement, she continued, "His body should be released day after tomorrow. I've signed a power of attorney, which will allow them to cremate his remains. I contacted the funeral home, and there will be a brief memorial service on the weekend."

No funeral, then. "A memorial service is a good solution. Jerome's friends and clients would like to remember him. Will you be coming up? We've never met, but—"

She cut me off. "The arrangements have all been made. No sense in my traveling that far."

Why was she being so unfriendly? We'd both lost someone we cared about, but she didn't seem willing to talk about him with me. She only wanted to give logistical details. I reminded myself that after the death of a loved one, some people concentrate on getting things done as a means of dealing with the loss.

"An obituary will appear in tomorrow's newspaper. Please notify anyone you think will wish to attend. Good-bye."

And that was it. She'd hung up.

While I'd been on the phone with Patty, Sue Ann had returned to the kitchen wearing a pair of my slacks and one of my T-shirts.

I turned to her. "That was Jerome's aunt. She called to tell me about the memorial service. She asked me to tell anyone who might want to attend. She hung up so fast, it was like she thought I was contagious."

"That's odd. But you know, some people get freaked out over death." She crinkled her nose. "Why don't you go grab a shower, too? Then you can tell me about the plans."

I did as she suggested. Hopefully the scented shampoo and soap I used would remove the worst of the skunk smell. Once I'd pulled on stink-free clothes, I returned to the kitchen.

"I made us some cocoa." Sue Ann placed the mugs on the table.

Taking a seat, I began filling her in on the plans for the memorial service.

"I wonder what Jerome would want?" she asked.

"I think if we were able to ask him, he'd want all of his friends to say a little something about him. Share stories. That kind of thing."

"That's a good idea. You should tell everyone about the time your foot got stuck in the dishwasher and he came over to rescue you."

Maybe it was the memory, or maybe it was simply that I'd finally had more time to think about losing Jerome—but I burst into tears.

Sue Ann grabbed a box of tissues from the counter and placed it in front of me. I grabbed a handful and dabbed at my face, but the tears wouldn't stop coming. At last I calmed down enough to speak. "It's just so wrong that someone would take his life that way. It makes me hurt, but it also makes me very angry. How can someone be so heartless?"

She reached over and hugged me, and for the second time, the two of us wept for our dear friend. When at last our tears subsided, I said, "I don't understand it. I'm not sure if I ever will."

Sue Ann grabbed a fresh tissue and blotted her eyes. "We're quite a pair, aren't we?"

"You said it." I blew my nose, then took a sip of the cocoa. It wasn't hot, but it was warm enough to thaw any ice remaining in my veins. "This is good. Thanks for making it."

"You're welcome. Now that we smell better, do we need to go back over to Dolores'? What did Liz say?"

"She doesn't need our help."

"It would be easier if she'd let me clean it up now, because otherwise I'll have to take care of it the next time I clean their house. It'll be much harder once the scent has set in."

"She said Dolores is taking care of it with canned tomatoes."

"Good heavens. That'll be a bitch to clean up."

"Liz said she was worried about Dolores. Remember when the medium told Dolores about covering something up?"

"That's right. She said, 'I told you not to cover it up.'"

"Do you think she meant Jerome's murder? I've always thought Dolores only had one foot in the sanity zone, but is she crazy enough to kill?"

"Hmm." Sue Ann sipped her cocoa while she thought it over. "I suppose it's possible, and it was funny how she jumped to give Fred an alibi. If she's his alibi, then he's hers."

"But why kill Jerome? And if she killed him, does that mean she also murdered her own son?" I ran over possible scenarios in my mind, trying to unscramble everything we knew about the killer. It seemed logical to presume that whoever blackmailed me also killed Jerome.

"Jerome was about to propose to you, yes?"

I grimaced. "Maybe. Probably."

"Do you think Dolores might have killed him so that you'd remain her daughter-in-law? Maybe she thought he'd steal you away from her."

"I don't think that's a strong enough reason for her to kill him." I shook my head. "And it doesn't explain the blackmail notes saying Dan was still alive."

"It might make sense if she'd heard you were about to have him declared dead, Amy, in an odd, Dolores kind of way. Once he's legally dead, then you're his widow rather than his wife."

I remained doubtful. "Then what do you think happened to Dan?"

"Maybe it was an accident. Then, when his body didn't turn up, she was able to pretend he was still around. Maybe that's what the spirit was referring to—her covering up Dan's accidental death."

"I don't think so." Sue Ann's new theory might be possible given Dolores' odd view of the world. I was sure, however, that Dolores and I were genuinely fond of each other and she had cared deeply about my grandmother. "Dolores wouldn't destroy Nana's china teacups. I can't believe she'd threaten me and break into my house."

"The manager at the Tavern saw Dolores talking with Jerome just before he was killed."

A lead weight sank into my stomach, and I thought I might be sick. I pushed the cocoa away from me. "There has to be some other explanation."

"I think we need to tell Brad about our suspicions."

"Let's sleep on it. It's too late to call him now, anyway."

Her expression turned mutinous. "I think he needs to know."

"He's a good detective. He's probably already considered Dolores. But if you want, we can go down and see him first thing in the morning. He's planning to take Dolores' statement then, and maybe we can watch."

She nodded, but I wasn't certain she was convinced, so I changed the subject. "Did I tell you about the story I'm working on? It's about a lady wrestler, and I've been working on my moves. They have all sorts of crazy names."

In the wee hours that night, the writing muse had me in its dreadful clutches. Sue Ann had long since headed home, and I was hard at work on my latest confessionary delight. Some writers refer to their muse as *the girls in the basement* or *the boys in the attic*. I, however, think of mine as *Jimar*. Jimar is from Jamaica and wears dreadlocks, natch. He demands that I sit for long hours in front of my computer and type. In short, he can be a true PITA.

On the upside, he's extremely entertaining and no one does reggae better.

That night he was no less entertaining. My fingers flew across the keyboard as I developed my latest story. I was deep in the writing zone when an unexpected sound gradually lifted my creative fog. It was a knock. At my front door.

Wondering who it could be, I clicked to save my file, then headed to the door. No one can say I haven't learned from experience. I didn't immediately answer the door. I looked through the window but didn't see a car parked in my driveway.

Was it Mrs. Mitchell or another of my neighbors? Or had the murderer come calling?

Without opening the door, I called, "Who is it?"

"It's Liz. Can I come in?"

I quickly slid back the safety lock and opened the door. Earlier I'd thought Liz looked worn-out. Now she looked half dead. Hair stood up on her head at an awkward angle, as if she'd just risen from bed. Her clothing was rumpled and had that slept-in look. Her purse was strapped over her shoulder like bizarre leather armor. "What's wrong?"

"I couldn't sleep. I'm so worried about Mom." She came inside, and I hesitated for a moment before leading her to the kitchen because she looked like she needed tea or even something stronger.

"I didn't see your car. You didn't walk, did you?"

"I thought walking would help clear my head."

"Let's sit down in the kitchen. I'm sorry about the mess in the den. Eh, I was moving furniture around." Well, I kinda had been. I just hadn't put it back yet. My stuffed bunny lay in a heap on the floor where I'd left him, looking lonely.

Within minutes, Liz took a seat at the table, then lowered her face in her hands. "Mom's just not herself."

"Want me to make some tea while you tell me about it?"

"That would be nice."

It didn't take long to set things up, and while the water heated, I joined her at the table. "Is Dolores ill?"

"Maybe." Liz straightened. "Maybe that's it. But she doesn't seem right—in her head."

"Worse than usual, huh?" There was no way I could share my fears about Dolores with Liz. Instead, I needed to be a sounding board and encourage Liz to get Dolores whatever help she might need.

"It's not just the skunk. She's been secretive, hiding things from me. Going out of the house without telling me where she's going or where she's been."

"Did you talk to her about it?"

"When I brought it up, she told me to mind my own business."

"That doesn't sound like her." The kettle boiled, so I went to take it off the burner and fix our tea. Since Liz was my guest, I gave her the teacup Brad had purchased for me, and I took the Pennzoil mug for myself.

When I brought the cups to the table and slid the teacup in front of her, she looked down at it oddly, as if surprised. She reached for the sugar bowl in the center of the table. "The burglar missed one, I see."

"Oh? The teacup? I guess everyone in town knows about Nana's cups being smashed. That's one Brad bought for me. Wasn't that sweet of him?"

She nodded. "Very thoughtful. Do you have any milk or cream for my tea?"

"Sure." I went to the refrigerator and pulled out a carton of milk, then reached into a cupboard for a cream pitcher.

"It's nice how everyone looks after you, Amy. Sue Ann, Dan, Jerome, and now Brad."

I frowned. They all are, or were, at the very least my friends, and friends do nice things for each other. While I had relied on them, I was learning to do more for myself. The new, more independent me looked forward to being able to do things for them rather than vice versa.

I poured the milk into the pitcher. It was an odd comment for Liz to make, but then, she wasn't herself. She was draped in anxiety. I brought the milk to the table. "I look after myself."

Liz narrowed her lips, but didn't reply. She added the milk to her tea, then tasted it. "This is nice."

"I'm glad you like it." Neither of us said anything for several moments, and I wondered what had driven her out of her house so late at night. There had to be something specific she wanted to discuss with me. Perhaps her thoughts had led her in the same direction as mine had led me and she was looking for confirmation or denial. "Do you want me to talk with Dolores?"

"Not really. It won't be of any use." She lifted the teacup and drank.

"I hate seeing you like this, Liz. So hopeless. You're the sister I never had, and I want you to be happy."

Liz had a mouth full of hot tea, and her cheeks billowed before a stream of the hot liquid spewed from her mouth as she laughed out loud. Tears rolled down her face, she was laughing so hard. Her hand slapped the table over and over again.

This was an extremely strange reaction to what I'd said. I pulled back in my chair and couldn't help wondering if caring for Dolores had sent Liz around the bend. Living with her would have done it to me years before.

Her laughter abruptly ended in shoulder-clenching sobs.

Feeling like a witness to some manic-depressive TV reality show,

I was stupefied.

"Liz? Are you all right?" I extended a hand to comfort her.

She swatted it away. "I just can't believe you would feed me that bull. That's all."

"Huh?" I shook my head back and forth, hoping my brain would start working again. Was this some kind of dream? Had I fallen asleep? "What bull are you talking about?"

"All that love-fest crap about being your sister. You and your friends have spent most of my life making it intolerable. Whispering, huddling in corners making fun of me."

I shoved my chair back from the table, wanting to shake some sense into her. But this was Liz. She was distraught. I needed to be gentle with her. She probably didn't know what she was saying. "I've never made fun of you, ever," I said. "And you know I love you."

"Ha," she spat out.

If this had been one of my confession stories, my editor might have suggested toning down the melodrama. But this wasn't a story. It was my life and I didn't know how to proceed. "If I have ever hurt you, Liz, I'm sorry. You probably misunderstood something."

"It doesn't matter." She reached in her handbag. "I'm bored with this."

"You're confusing me. I thought you wanted to talk about Dolores."

She shook her head sadly. "You're just too easy, Amy. You've taken all the sport out of the game."

Have I mentioned before that I'm kinda slow sometimes? While I was concerned about Liz, until that moment I didn't feel afraid. Now, suddenly, my writing-deadened brain kicked into action. And my writing muse, Jimar, yelled in my head, "Get outta there, girl."

I stood, and when I did, Liz pulled her hand out of her purse. But her hand wasn't empty. In it was a double-edged knife. I couldn't believe it. "You're not going to stab me."

"Not if you sit down and drink your tea like a good little sister," she taunted, shaking the blade at me like a mother might wag her finger at a naughty child.

I met her gaze, dread filling me. "You put something in it, didn't you?"

"Just something that'll help you sleep."

CHAPTER TWENTY-THREE

My Lover is Afraid of Me Because i'm a Lady Wrestler

You know how they say your life flashes before your eyes when you're drowning? It doesn't work that way when someone is trying to kill you.

Endorphins kicked in, along with a long-dormant prehistoric instinct to survive. Blood rushed to my brain. My muscles tensed, ready to spring, dart, or run. "I think I'll give the sleeping pills a pass."

Liz lunged at me with the knife as I sprinted toward the front door and my escape. But she was a trained runner, an athlete, and I led a sedentary life. She caught up with me in the den, slamming into me from behind and knocking me to the floor.

I fell straight forward on my right elbow, and pain splintered through me. But there was no time to deal with it now. Liz had a knife.

With a rolling motion, I managed to climb into a crouch, facing her.

"Just drink your tea, Amy. It won't hurt," she assured me. "I can guarantee this knife will. I sharpened the blade before coming tonight."

"If you're going to kill me, just do it."

"That wouldn't be very satisfactory, now, would it? The police wouldn't believe you stabbed yourself over self-guilt. Brad wouldn't buy it for a second."

Suicide. She wanted me to drink the tea so it would look like suicide. But she couldn't guarantee that unless . . . "What about a note?"

"It won't take long to fire up your computer. By the time you're asleep, I'll have composed your little missive." She jabbed the knife at me. "Get up."

If she was going to kill me, and I had little doubt she'd succeed, she was going to have to do it in a way that signaled murder. I didn't want Sue Ann or Brad or Dolores or even Mrs. Mitchell to think I was a cold-blooded killer. Like Liz. "Make me."

Again she jabbed toward me with the knife, but I knew she didn't really want to stab me. There would be no way to pass it off as a suicide. This gave me the upper hand. I glanced around, looking for a weapon of my own. With any luck, I could do some serious damage to her skull.

But the only things I saw within reach were the TV remote, a pile of books—and my stuffed bunny. I waited for Liz's next move. She slashed out at me, but my attempt to grab her wrist failed. The books on wrestling had said it was all about control. *Control the wrist, control the arm, control the opponent.*

She thrusted again, but this time I secured her wrist, then twisted it. She grunted.

I twisted her wrist more as I flung her arm up, sending the knife flying.

"Take this," I said, pivoting behind her and circling her neck with my arm. I hooked my leg around her left thigh and pulled back on her neck with my left arm, forcing her to fall forward. All the practice I'd done on poor Bunny was paying off. I had neatly executed the go-behind-takedown maneuver.

She squirmed beneath me, but I'd trained for this moment and now leveraged my weight against hers. My left forearm strangled her as I buried my knee in her back, and with my free hand I yanked her right foot upward. This was the dead man's cradle. I'd invented it during my research, and it worked. "And you said everyone takes care of me."

"Get off me, you bitch," she growled.

"Now, is that any way to talk to family?" I asked, shoving my knee into her back. The dead man's cradle delivered everything I hoped for. Liz was hopelessly pinned in place, like an insect pinned to a mounting board.

I held her face down to the ground, my right hand clinging tightly onto her ankle, my other arm around her neck, and my knee buried into her back. There was only one problem, and I hoped Liz didn't figure it out anytime soon.

While I had her pinned in place, for now, I couldn't actually do anything other than wait for help to arrive, and that likely wouldn't happen for hours. It was still three hours before dawn, and no telling how many hours before Sue Ann would show up.

If I moved before then, Liz would escape. I didn't dare risk it. Now that she knew my wrestling moves—and I only had the two—she'd be able to deflect them. However, if I got her talking, maybe she wouldn't have time to think about how to get away. "There's one thing I don't understand, Liz. What happened to Dan? Did you do something to him?"

"He was going to fire me. My own business, and he wanted to send me packing."

"That's not like Dan, but it wasn't *your* business. It belonged to both of you."

"I told him he didn't have to live with Mom, but he wouldn't listen. Just kept ranting about my skimming money from the business. It was *my* money. I'd worked my ass off licensing his inventions."

I didn't bother to point out that they were Dan's inventions and the two of them were supposed to share income. "Did you offer to give it back?"

"Of course I did. But he wouldn't hear me out. He started shouting at me for licensing your toilet without his permission. What's so special about you, anyway? Why do you deserve to keep an invention all to yourself? You're just a clingy little woman who can't do anything for herself, not even clean your own toilet bowl."

My self-cleaning toilet? This was about the toilet Dan had made for me? I couldn't believe it could be over something so mundane. Dan had specifically invented the self-cleaning toilet for me, but I hadn't realized he'd intended it to be exclusively mine. "I wouldn't have cared."

"I told him that, but he insisted our partnership was over. I told him he wasn't any good at selling his inventions and it's not like he would have been able to license anything without my help." She grunted, trying to yank her ankle out of my grasp.

I dug my knee into her back and pulled tightly on her neck, which enabled me to keep hold of her foot.

She stopped struggling.

"You're very good at the licensing end of the business." I wanted to keep her talking. While I could hold her in this position for a while longer, I didn't know at what point I would tire out. It was best to conserve my energy if possible. "He wouldn't listen to you?"

"I only needed the money so I could have a place of my own. But if he fired me, I'd never get another job. I'd be stuck with Mom forever."

"You have skills. You could have gotten another job."

"Not if he had me arrested for embezzlement."

So that was what this was all about. Liz had stolen money from the business, and Dan had threatened to have her arrested. Liz was completely insane. That much was clear. "What happened next?"

"I grabbed the damn toilet seat he was holding and hit him with it. I didn't mean to kill him. But the gears on the mouse thing were jagged." She bit back a sob. "It wasn't painful, Amy. I wouldn't have hurt him on purpose. Just like you won't feel any pain either."

With that, she contorted her entire body, along with mine, almost dislodging my hold.

Again, almost. But my cradle move held, and she remained under my control. "Stop that, Liz. You'll only get hurt because I'm not letting you go."

"I'm tired now. Please let go." She sounded completely normal, as if we weren't in a life-or-death struggle.

What was amazing was how normal Liz had seemed all these years. How at times she'd comforted me when I'd cried over Dan's disappearance. How I'd felt sorry for her having to live under the same roof with Dolores. Even now, she almost elicited my sympathy.

Almost.

She'd murdered her own brother. Poor Dan. He wouldn't have stood a chance against her. My gentle husband would never have expected her to lash out at him. My heart broke for him.

At long last, I had an idea of what had happened to him, of how Liz had pretended to grieve along with the rest of us. She'd calculatingly watched the people who loved Dan try to deal with his disappearance, try to pick up the broken threads of their lives, and she'd stood back and done nothing.

But even if Dan's death had been an accident as she claimed, and

I wasn't convinced deliberately hitting someone over the head could be called accidental, it stretched my credulity to believe Jerome's death was anything other than murder. Even now she was planning how to murder me as well. She had to be stopped. She had to be brought to justice, and I would see to it she was—even if I had to keep her in this position for the next week.

"What did you do with Dan's body?"

"Dumped it off the old Burns Street Bridge into the Verdigris, along with his stupid invention. Evidently the weight of it held him down. He didn't float up like Jerome."

She grew silent, and I guessed it was because she hadn't intended to bring up the fact she'd killed someone other than Dan. At last she said, "Look, Amy, you're the sister I always wanted, too. If you let me go, I promise to leave you alone. I've got just about enough cash to make a clean start somewhere. Maybe in the Caribbean. Somewhere without an extradition agreement. Just let me go, and I'll be out of your hair. I'll sip mai tais on a beach far, far away from Independence and from my mother. Just let me go."

Yeah, right. Like I'd believe anything she said ever again. "Why did you kill Jerome?"

She sighed. "His death was all your fault, you know."

"My fault? How?"

"If you hadn't filed with the probate court to have Dan declared legally dead, none of it would have been necessary. Everything was fine for the past seven years. Then you had to go and wreck it all."

"But, Liz, I was about to lose my house. I had to do something before the bank foreclosed on it."

"If you'd been patient, I would have left town and no one would have been the wiser about Dan. But with probate comes an audit, and I couldn't let Jerome look at the books. He'd have immediately seen I was holding money back. Plus, he knew about the toilet. Your toilet."

"He knew Dan didn't want you to license it?"

"Years ago Jerome witnessed an argument Dan and I had about it."

"That explains the photo in Jerome's cell phone."

"So that was the evidence Jerome mentioned. He said that while he was out of town he'd seen the toilet in one of his client's homes. Said he had evidence I'd stolen Dan's invention."

"Brad showed the photo to Sue Ann and me."

"Crap." She grew silent for a moment, then snickered. "Another good reason to make your death look like a suicide."

"It's not going to happen." Regretting having told her about the photo, I searched for something else to ask her. "When did you talk with Jerome?"

"He called me while he was out of town to ask about the toilet. I had to admit I licensed it, but I led him to believe I'd done so after Dan's disappearance. I tried throwing him off the track and told him about the blackmail note." She chuckled. "One little note had you hopping scared, didn't it? And Jerome was very unhappy to learn you hadn't mentioned it to him."

"I didn't want to worry him."

"I thought he believed me about the toilet, but when he questioned Mom at the Tavern that night, it was apparent he hadn't. When Mom told me about his questions, I realized it was simply a matter of time before he asked to see the books. So he had to go."

The thought that I'd been living in such proximity to someone so heartless, without ever having a clue, made my head pound. I'd taken Liz for granted, without truly learning who she was. As far as I'd been concerned, she was the person I wanted her to be. I never saw her—not truly—and I wondered how many other people I'd taken at face value without looking deeper. It was a side of myself I didn't like very much. "And you don't feel any remorse?"

"You don't have to live with Mom," she sputtered, as if that explained everything.

Dolores is crazy-making, but she isn't so impossible that it would drive someone to murder. Liz could have managed to leave home long before. She must have had a screw loose all along. Why hadn't I seen it before?

But I wasn't the only one. Not even someone as perceptive as Sue Ann had noticed the psychopath who lived at Liz's core. My muscles began to ache and scream, but I maintained my hold on her. She wouldn't bat an eye at sending me to join Dan and Jerome.

"You know," said Liz conversationally, as if we weren't at a standstill, as if nothing at all were wrong, "I think I let you stop me tonight because I'm so fond of you."

"Let me? You've tried everything to kill me. And the only thing standing between you having your way is the dead man's cradle."

"That what you call this move?"

"It sure is."

"I was thinking. You're trying to save your house from foreclosure, and I have a wad of money tucked away. I think there's enough for both of us. You can save your house and I can exit stage left. What do you say?"

When I didn't immediately reply (because what I truly wanted to do was smash her head against the floor), she must have thought I was considering her offer.

"Really, Amy. I'm only letting you hold me down because I don't want to kill you."

That did it. Now I was seriously pissed. "How could I trust anyone who'd murder her own brother?"

Again she fought against me, but I was prepared. I dug my knee deeper into her back, and she made a gratifying sound of pain. "Ow."

It looked like I was going to be in for a long night, but I had one advantage over Liz. I was used to odd hours and staying up late writing. It didn't matter how much athletic training she had—she was already tired from dealing with Dolores, the séance, and the skunk.

However, I'd been writing, and those familiar late-night endorphins were pumping in me. Sooner or later, Sue Ann would arrive and I'd deliver Liz into police custody.

Just then, the beams of headlights filtered through the window. Someone had pulled into my driveway. Yes!

Soon a knock sounded on my front door, and I screamed at the top of my lungs, "Help!"

"Miz Crosby? Is that you?"

It was Eck the mechanic! "Yes! It's me!"

Liz struggled harder than before, dislodging her foot from my grip. I slammed my knee deep into her back, but it didn't make her stop squirming. I dug it in again.

"Your car's ready," Eck said. "Promised I'd bring her to you."

Thank God. Eck's timing couldn't have been better. "Eck, I need help! Come fast."

The doorknob jiggled, but I realized he couldn't get in. Liz rocked her body, trying to get loose. Fighting for my life, I screamed, "The code is *hello*! Punch in *hello*!"

Within seconds, Eck entered the room. "What's going on?"

"She's trying to kill me," I cried.

He jumped to action, grabbing Liz's head and pushing it to the floor. Liz slumped, completely defeated. "That's your security code? Hello?"

"Yeah."

"There's no letters on your lock," she said.

"Will you hold her down while I call the police?" I asked Eck.

He grabbed Liz's arm and pulled it behind her back, then lowered his weight on her while I backed away and ran for the phone.

As I dialed 9-1-1, I heard Liz say, "I tried every combination I could think of on that damn lock."

Eck's tone was reasoned and calm as he replied, "This is Independence, home of the Neewollah Festival. We do everything backwards and upside down. Made sense to me."

Before I'd completed my phone call with the 9-1-1 operator, I heard Brad call my name.

"Amy! You okay?"

I looked around the corner and saw him and Sue Ann stop at the entrance to the den. They paused, each astounded by the sight before their eyes.

Sue Ann saw me first.

"We were right, Sue Ann, about *Cherchez la femme.*" I gestured toward Liz.

"I see. Thank heavens you're okay," Sue Ann said. "We were so worried. We just came from Dolores'. She told us she thought Liz was going to harm you."

I grinned—a huge Cheshire cat smile. "I'm fine. You don't have to worry about me. But you better make sure Eck doesn't lose his hold on Liz."

Brad frowned, but I knew it was because of concern over me. He stepped forward, pulled a pair of handcuffs from his back pocket, then neatly clicked them around Liz's wrists.

Eck stood, smiling, but looking somewhat awkward.

"You saved me again, Eck. You're my hero."

"That was nothing," he said modestly. "But I'm really gonna be your hero because I brought you your car as promised. She purrs like a kitten."

Brad pulled Liz to her feet. "Now what's going on here?"

"She tried to kill me," I said.

"That's not true," Liz cried. "Mom's crazy. Amy attacked me for no reason. Keep her away from me!"

Thankfully, Brad didn't buy her line of reasoning. "What were you doing here so late at night?"

"I was worried about my mother and came to talk it over with Amy. She pulled a knife on me." Liz nodded her head toward the double-edged knife. "Look. There it is."

"She's lying, Brad. She pulled the knife on me when I refused to drink the tea she laced with sleeping pills." The trauma of the night's events began to set in. My arms and legs ached as if I'd run a marathon. My head pounded relentlessly, and I was completely exhausted. Mentally I wasn't in much better shape, and I started to tremble. "She wanted to make it look like a suicide."

"Don't listen to that bitch," insisted Liz. "She was trying to kill me. If Eck hadn't come when he did, she'd have succeeded, too."

"I used the dead man's cradle to keep her immobilized until help—Eck—arrived," I argued. I sought Sue Ann's help. "You believe me, don't you?"

Sue Ann launched herself across the room and pulled me into her arms. "Of course we believe you. When Dolores realized Liz had left the house, she called and told me about Liz's crazy behavior."

"So Dolores knows?" I understood wanting to protect your child, but I couldn't understand being willing to allow your child to harm others.

"I called Brad and when we came over, Dolores confessed everything." Sue Ann gave me a gentle squeeze. "She wasn't certain, but she suspected—especially after she realized Dan was dead. Until the first séance, she'd been able to pretend to herself that he had simply started a new life somewhere else."

"Dolores has been covering up for Liz most of her life," Brad said, "ever since she killed a neighbor's pet when she was a kid. Dolores was trying to protect her. Tonight she realized she'd been wrong, and she was terrified Liz would hurt you."

And she would have, had it not been for my new skills as a lady wrestler, and the dead man's cradle.

The sun had long since risen before the police finished gathering evidence at my house. I watched as Brad helped an officer settle Liz into the backseat of a police vehicle. He silently joined me on my porch as we watched the vehicle drive away.

The emotional process of sorting through what Liz had tried to do to me was grueling. Knowledge of what she'd done and what she'd been hiding still hadn't quite sunk in. I couldn't completely wrap my mind around the idea that I could love someone who had no more regard for the people in her life than she would for an annoying fly she swatted away. It blew me away that she could have killed Dan, her own brother. Learning she'd thought of me so differently than I'd thought of her ultimately changed me, and I was only just beginning to see how that would play out.

Sue Ann was asleep on my bed, and I bit back a yawn. However, after Liz's attempt to put me to sleep permanently, I wasn't sure if I'd ever be able to sleep again.

It felt good to at last know what had happened to Dan and that he hadn't chosen to leave.

One of the officers had told me the police would dredge near the old bridge to search for Dan's body. I hoped they'd find him. There would be closure in recovering his body and holding a funeral for him. With that would come healing for both me and Dolores. This was going to be very hard on her. A sense of gratitude almost overwhelmed me. Even knowing she'd lose her daughter, she'd tried to protect me by coming clean about Liz.

I was alive.

I drew in a deep breath and slowly exhaled, experiencing the moment. It's amazing how beautiful life is when it's almost been stolen from you. My gorgeous redbud tree was in full bloom, its lovely purple flowers dancing in the morning light. My heart lifted.

I'd made good on my promise to see that Jerome's death was vindicated. Justice would be served.

And speaking of justice personified, he—Brad, that is—looked good with day-old stubble and wrinkled clothes. In fact, pretty darn good.

"Thanks for believing me," I said. "You could as easily have believed Liz."

"No. I believe in you." Brad looked deeply into my eyes, and I thought for a moment he'd say something romantic. Instead he said, "I still haven't forgiven you, though."

"For what?"

"For suspecting me of murder."

"I never said that," I quickly denied. The night at the Tavern seemed like eons ago.

His smile was tired as he said, "You didn't have to."

I raised my hand and brushed it against his almost-beard. "Come to think of it, I'm kind of glad I *almost* accused you of being fixated on me."

"So you admit it?"

"Only if you will. Because if I hadn't suspected you, I wouldn't have known something important. You never denied being fixated on me."

I've seen many people blush before, but Brad's blush beat them, hands down. His skin turned the brightest shade of crimson I'd ever seen on a person's face before.

I found it endearing. "So, you wanna go out sometime?"

EPILOGUE

Killed in a Fit of Rage

Two days following Liz's arrest, we had the memorial service for Jerome. The funeral parlor was crowded to overflowing, not only with his friends and business associates, but also with local and regional media and anyone in town curious enough to come.

Liz's arrest and the story of what she'd done made national headlines, and I'd been dodging reporters ever since.

The memorial was lovely, and I felt extremely proud that I'd had a hand in apprehending Jerome's killer. Perhaps his soul up in heaven knew what had happened. If that were so, I hoped he knew we loved and missed him.

But it was especially hard to say good-bye.

Sue Ann attended the service with me, and for once I'd driven. My Gremlin drove like a dream. Eck had done a wonderful job rebuilding her, and as he'd said, she purred like a kitten.

And speaking of cats, it was time to get mine back. I approached Mrs. Mitchell, who had found another victim—I mean, potential younger man. He was the new minister at the Baptist church and, considering his youth, I thought he might need rescuing. She'd cornered him near the altar, where he had presided.

"Mrs. Mitchell, I wonder if I might speak with you, please?" I asked.

"If you'll excuse me," said the minister as he made his retreat, "I have, um, sermons to write."

Poor man.

Brad's gaze met mine, and I could tell he had great empathy for the minister.

"You picked a fine time to interrupt." Mrs. Mitchell gave me a haughty glare.

"Sorry. I was just wondering," I said, "about my cat. I thought I might bring him home?"

"Oh, Chappy." She patted my hand. "You know, dear, he's so comfortable at my place. He's settled in, loves to snuggle up on my recliner with me. I think he would be happier if he extended his visit a little longer."

It was obvious she adored the cat and he her. "Are you saying you want to keep Chappy?"

"I would love to keep him." The happiness twinkling in her eyes told me she'd forgiven me for saving the minister. "As a favor to you, of course."

"How exactly is this a favor to me?"

"My dear, you're going to be so busy settling your husband's estate now that we know what happened, testifying at Liz's trial, and getting your affairs in order." She continued listing reasons why my bringing Chappy home would be a terrible idea.

I realized with a sinking heart that I was not going to get Chappy back, at least not without doing something drastic—like catnapping him. And anything I did was going to ruin my relationship with my neighbor, who had become my friend, painful as that was to admit.

Even though I'd become attached to the kitten and knew I'd be a great cat mom, Chappy was obviously crazy about Mrs. Mitchell, too. What could I do? "Mrs. Mitchell?" I interrupted. "Chappy will probably be happier with you. I can come see him whenever I want, can't I?"

"Of course, my dear. He would be sad if you didn't come over to play now and then."

It also occurred to me that according to rumor, Chappy had brothers and sisters I could rescue if I just went to hang out around the chapel. Or I could even talk to Mare about rescuing some other homeless kitten. My heart felt a little lighter.

And so it was that I left the funeral home, minus one boyfriend, one sister-in-law, and one cat. But on the upside, there had been a message on my voice mail from a media outlet asking if I'd like to write a short story for them about the dead man's cradle.

❧❧❧

After leaving the memorial service, I dropped Sue Ann off at her house, then headed home. As I pulled my Gremlin into my driveway, I noticed someone standing at my door.

It was Dolores. With a stack of suitcases. And a skunk in a birdcage.

"There you are, dear," she called as she waved enthusiastically. "I didn't want you to be lonely, so Nana and I are moving in."

DARK SECRETS

⌒ OF THE ⌒

OLD OAK TREE

DOLORES J. WILSON

Following the end of her fifteen-year marriage to a high-powered attorney, Evie Carson returns to her small, Georgia hometown to open a fashion boutique. From the protective covering of her father to the tarnished shield of her husband, Evie has always lived behind the armor of a man. But she sees this move as her first step toward the peaceful, happy life she wants.

Trying to recapture a few moments of her youth, Evie climbs to the ruins of her childhood tree house. While hidden by the massive branches of the old oak tree, Evie is stunned into deadly silence as she watches Jake—a mentally challenged community member—enter the clearing below her with a nude, lifeless body over his shoulder. Hovering above the macabre scene, Evie is forced to look on as a grave is dug. When the body is rolled into the hole, Evie realizes the dead woman is her childhood friend whom she hasn't seen in years.

The authorities are sure once Jake is arrested, the town's nightmare will be over. But when he turns up dead and Evie's home becomes the center of bizarre events, Evie and an investigating state trooper fear she may be the next victim. Wondering if she can trust him, or anyone, Evie alone must face the *Dark Secrets of the Old Oak Tree*.

ISBN# 978-160542106-3
Hardcover / Suspense
US $24.95 / CDN $27.95
MARCH 2010
www.doloresjwilson.com

HOT FLASH

Kathy Carmichael

On Jill Morgan Storm's fortieth birthday, she declares she is through with love. A conviction well justified, considering her first husband didn't leave her for another woman; he became one! More recently, her love affair came to a screeching halt when her lover dumped her for a young undergraduate. To make matters worse, the teeny-bopper stole Jill's "well-seasoned" frying pan, and when you're a sous chef, that's no small offense; it's a major felony.

When financial obligations threaten her son's dream of attending art school, Jill and her friends devise a foolproof plan to audition candidates for a new husband. The search for Mr. Right is on.

There is one problem, however. His name is Davin Wesley, an annoying third-grade schoolteacher, who relentlessly plagues her days, haunts her nights, and propels her libido into overdrive. She knows he is absolutely, undeniably wrong for her. So why, then, does Mr. Wrong take her breath away, curl her toes, and give her a hot flash every time she sees him? More importantly, what will she do if Mr. Wrong is actually Mr. Right?

ISBN# 978-193475503-7
Mass Market Paperback / Contemporary Romance
US $7.95 / CDN $8.95
AVAILABLE NOW
www.kathycarmichael.com

ANNA LOUISE LUCIA

In the fatal heat of the Sahara Desert, Alan Waring extracts a smart card from a laptop computer held in the hands of a baked corpse. This is his assignment. This is what he does best. The information this card holds changes the rest of his life. What was once just a job turns into a life-altering experience that brings him in touch with his inner spirit and a woman who reaches into his very soul. When she accidentally walks off with his bag and the precious data it contains, Alan must pursue this vulnerable woman into the dangerous clutches of the Algerian enemy to save his career and to protect the passion of his heart.

Mari Forster has always dreamed of visiting Morocco. Grieving over the death of her father, she visits a dilapidated home once owned by her grandfather. In the decayed, neglected courtyard of this abandoned residence, she encounters Alan. She doesn't anticipate meeting the man who will bring vigor and joy back into her life. Nor does she realize her chance interlude is with an undercover agent.

Alan senses Mari's loneliness and cannot focus on his assigned task. Under the scorching sun on treacherous arid terrain, he discovers that Mari fills a void inside that the thrill-seeking part of his character has never acknowledged. He must be her hero . . . or they both will die.

ISBN# 978-193475508-2
Mass Market Paperback / Romantic Suspense
US $7.95 / CDN $8.95
AVAILABLE NOW
annalouiselucia.com

The Rock & Roll Queen of Bedlam

Marilee Brothers

Leggy, karaoke-singing Allegra Thome spends her days teaching dysfunctional teens and her nights with wealthy new boyfriend, Michael. The rough patch following Allegra's divorce is over, and life is grand. But when Allegra lands in the middle of a drug bust and meets Sloan, a rough-around-the edges DEA agent and, later that day, a throwaway kid from her class disappears, things quickly head south. Sloan, who has the tact of a roadside bomb, is attracted to Allegra and alienates Michael. To make matters worse, nobody seems to care that Allegra's student, Sara Stepanek, is missing.

Add to the mix a rural Washington State town under the spell of a charismatic minister who doesn't hesitate to use secrets of the rich and powerful to keep them in line, even while withholding his own dark past, and Allegra's search for Sara becomes a race against time with dead bodies piling up and her own life in peril. Under the circumstances, it's not surprising things come to a head at the WWJD (What Would Jesus Drink) Winery.

ISBN# 978-193475546-4
Trade Paperback / Suspense
US $15.95 / CDN $17.95
AVAILABLE NOW
www.marileebrothers.com

Be in the know on the latest
Medallion Press news by becoming a
Medallion Press Insider!

<u>As an Insider you'll receive:</u>

• Our FREE expanded monthly newsletter,
giving you more insight into Medallion Press

• Advanced press releases and breaking news

• Greater access to all your favorite
Medallion authors

Joining is easy. Just visit our Web site at
<u>www.medallionpress.com</u> and click on the
Medallion Press Insider tab.

m e d a l l i o n p r e s s . c o m

DISCARD-10

F

Carmichael, Kathy
    Diary of a confessions
queen.